Spirit of the Trail

by E.H. Haines

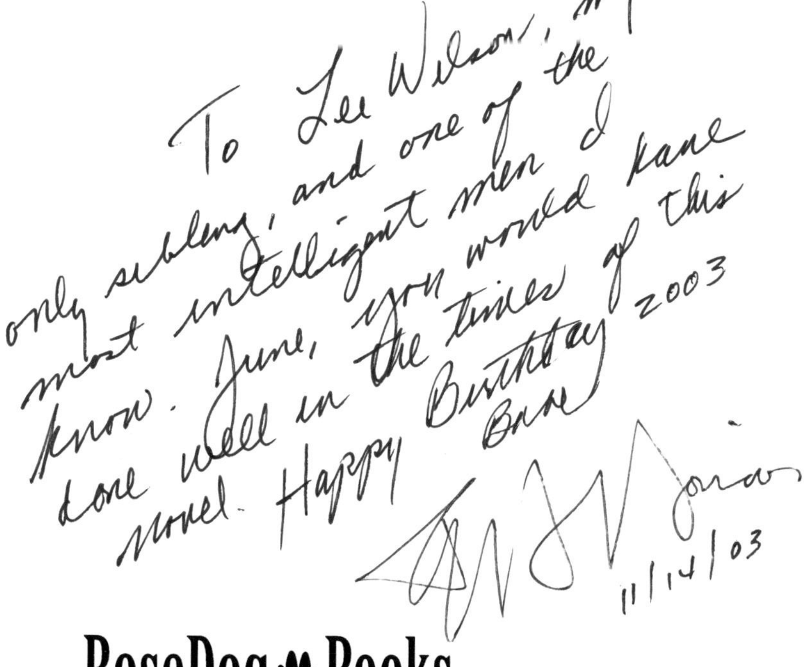

RoseDog Books

PITTSBURGH, PENNSYLVANIA 15222

ISBN # 0-8059-9283-9
Printed in the United States of America

First Printing

For information or to order additional books, please write:
RoseDog Books
701 Smithfield St.
Pittsburgh, PA 15222
U.S.A.
1-866-834-1803
Or visit our web site and
on-line bookstore at www..rosedogbookstore.com

To my wife Gloria ...
for her kind and loving patience

Prologue

Three hundred and twenty one miles beyond Santa Fe, where the dreadful heat radiated from the sun in its circuit, the small troop huddled. The Kiawas attack had been brutal, and Captain Aldridge struggled with the bloody memory so freshly ingrained in his mind. Four of his men were killed in the first five minutes. A fifth man died three days later, after a two day, vicious sandstorm and a festering wound from a Kiowa arrow. Only the Captain and two men remained alive.

Captain Aldridge leaned against his horse and watched the Catawba scout. His name was Iron Paso and he had worked the trail with the Captain for three years. They weren't beer drinking friends— the Captain was too West Point for that— but they respected each other and the code each man lived by.

The Captain, with his thin smile and worn uniform, brushed sand from his mustache, yearning for anything to wet his lips. He watched the scout retrieve several items from his riding sack. Paso turned and gave him a amicable but strange smile. The young Captain recalled telling his fiancée about it. The Indian's smile didn't turn up; it turned down.

Paso walked to the lone pack mule. Animals were always comfortable with the graying scout. He stroked the mule's nose in the early gray light of dawn. It's eyes remained shut, but it nodded its head. He stroked its ears several times, giving the right ear a tug.

The animal was almost asleep again.

Paso held a battered tin cup with his mouth, and he stretched out the animal's long right ear with his left hand. Cutting the main blood vessel of the ear with his razor- sharp trail knife, the mule bucked its head as if stung by a blow fly. Instantly, the blood pumped into the cup; Paso's head went back and forth with the movement of the mule. The Indian sheathed his knife and removed the full cup from his mouth. He then sealed the wound with tobacco from his chew and stroked the animal's nose.

"This will strengthen you," Paso said. He handed the cup to the parched Captain. "How does the arm feel?"

"It's okay. I'm just glad it was my left arm," Captain Aldridge said. The day of the attack an arrow had gone through his upper left arm and imbedded itself into his side holster. He took a small sip of the warm blood, forcing it down. He shook his head in disgust.

"Try and get the Sarge to take a swallow," Captain Aldridge said. Captain Daniel Aldridge, Scout Iron Paso, and Sergeant Charles Stockholm were all that remained of the eight-man unit that had started northeast along the Santa Fe Trail three weeks before. The Sergeant had taken an arrow in the lower back, and Paso and the Captain had to pull it out just below the navel.

The Captain watched the scout pour the liquid into the barrel-chest sergeant, but the man was unconscious. The brawler from Baltimore may never taste the beer and women of Santa Fe again, thought the young Captain Aldridge. As the heat of the day enveloped them, Aldridge watched his horse wearily swish its tail.

Valor, the Captain's mount, was the only horse alive. The animal had survived because it had been trained to lie down on command; his instructor had been Ann Sublette, the Captain's fiancee. Captain Aldridge kept the horse down during both the raid and the storm. Neither he nor Paso understood how the mule had survived.

"Valor and the mule will be dead in two days without water," said the Captain. He took a second swallow of the blood and choked it down, handing the cup back to Paso.

"If I can get Valor back to Middle Spring, we'll make it," said the Captain. "It can't be more than thirty miles. You stay with the Sarge. I'll fill the canteens and get back, and then we'll return to

Santa Fe and regroup."

"Ain't much to regroup," Paso said, "but you're right. Going back is best." Paso looked over at Stockholm. "We'd better bury the Sarge up to his neck; he won't lose as much moisture that way. I did it with two of Smith's men in '21 and it worked." The scout swallowed his third shot of mule's blood.

The Captain helped clear away the sand as Paso dug a hole for the sergeant. They dragged him slowly into the hole and covered him up to his neck. Finally, they placed a light cotton shirt over his head. The sun was now up and it was the start of another sweltering day in the flat, treeless jornada.

The sun separated from the horizon when the Captain started south. He knew he must maintain a bee-line march and that he must conserve Valor's strength. The Santa Fe Trail was not the well-marked road his friends back east thought it was; even Ann had asked him about the width of the "road." No, this wasn't Pennsylvania. The land was open and barren and went nowhere.

The attack had occurred on the most dreaded stretch of the trail. It was flat and dry, utterly featureless, and the more bewildering for the maze of buffalo trails that furrowed its surface. The country was parched by drought and no discernible trace marked the course of the wagons that had driven across this desert

The young Aldridge steered Valor well clear of the five shallow graves he had helped Iron Paso dig. A half a mile beyond, they passed the smelly, bloated remains of a dozen horses and mules in the early morning sun. This was where the attack had started. Most of the animals had been shot by his own men; their bodies provided cover from the circling Kiowas. Out here, bodies dried and blew away in the wind, and the sandstorm had helped to cover their remains. In this desolation there weren't even coyotes or turkey vultures to hasten nature's decomposition. Only a few burrowing kangaroo rats scurried across the plain, from time to time.

If there had been shade, he'd have rested Valor, but now there was nothing –no trees or boulders to break the packed white soil of the land. The young officer felt his tongue swell and fill his mouth like a dry rag. He had shared his last water with his horse. It hardly wet the poor animal's mouth, but Valor seemed to understand.

That was over two days ago. The horse plodded along heavily and Aldridge knew that he was suffering from severe dehydration. Hell, he was too. They all were.

With the sun now directly overhead, Aldridge dismounted and checked his compass. He'd walk a while. The only sound on the endless sandy plain was the rustle of five empty military canteens at Valor's side.

He thought of Ann. It had been ten weeks since last he'd seen her. Their last rendezvous before he left had been difficult, but they tried to focus on their future together. She would make the perfect wife for him. He, the rising West Pointer; she, a beautiful feather in his cap. Perhaps she was a bit too independent, but that's what made her so exciting in his mind. Automatically, he turned and stroked his horse's nose. Valor had played a big part in getting to know his bride to be.

The Captain watched a fringe-toed sand lizard dart back into his burrow. It was the first life he had seen today. He walked Valor along the dry creek bed and looked out into the early evening sky. He thought of the Middle Spring, so far off in the distance and he walked on in a daze, full of hunger and thirst. Eventually, he mounted and began to ride once again, pushing on as the sun began its slow descent.

Sometime in the night, Valor stopped and went down on his front knees. Startled by the fall, the Captain talked softly to the horse and stroked its bony nose. The animal struggled to its feet with the man's help. Aldridge knew if the horse lay down it would never get up again. They plodded on. An hour later, at dawn, the young officer saw the first scrub trees of the Middle Spring. Valor could smell it in the breeze.

During the spring months, the little stream fed the Cimarron River, fifteen miles to the south. But at this time of year, Middle Spring was nothing more than a narrow, stinking pool. It was covered by green scum.

Just as the sun peeked over the horizon, they reached the pool. The Captain stripped the animal and let it wade into the tepid, foul water. A handful of black vultures patrolled the area. The large birds showed little fear of the new arrivals, shaking their odd black heads. Moving about on their hairless slender legs, they hissed and grunted in annoyance. A drowned prairie dog floated along on the far edge of the pool.

The Captain walked twenty yards downstream from the south end of the pool and dug into the sand of the dried creek bed. He removed his left arm from its sling. It ached regardless of how he held it. About a foot down, water started to gather in the hole. Captain Aldridge lay by the hole for an hour and drank the water it accumulated. It was hot and bitter with the distinct flavor of lime. He had never tasted better.

Valor came out of the pool and started to eat the scant plants that grew along the shore. Far to the southwest the officer saw the Sangre de Cristo Mountains.

Aldridge knew that he must rest at Middle Spring. That way, he could fill the canteens with the better water, but most important it would give Valor much needed rest and food. They'd leave right at sunset and, with luck, reach Paso and Sarge the following morning. He still had a few rations, but enough food for the horse was a problem. While he waited for the water to accumulate in his small well, the Captain skinned the tender under bark off the four cottonwoods near the pool. He could feed this to Valor.

The day passed quietly as Aldridge laid under the shade of the small scrub bushes. He thought how this misadventure would fascinate his younger brother, Stan. For the past ten years the Captain had been like a father to the younger man. They shared a fascination with the West, and Aldridge felt a sense of responsibility for his younger brother who looked up to him.

The heat of the day began to pass. The ride back would not be so bad, since both Aldridge and Valor were now rested and full of water and food. He thought of Iron Paso and the Sarge. Would they be happy to see him! He rode northeast for over an hour when he suddenly saw men far off to his left in the haze of the setting sun. They must have trailed him, a mile or so off, for some time. The party of a dozen Comanches were cantering toward him. The man from the 'Point' knew they were Comanche by the way they sat on their ponies, and an icy chill ran through his hot blood. He knew the tribe and its fierce reputation. A brave front was his only chance, and he rode cautiously toward the red men. A brief parley followed, but neither understood the other, and the Indians paid no attention to the Captain's signs of peace.

The Comanches began to spread out as Aldridge tried to keep them in front of him. Valor danced nervously, and, with a piercing cry from a brave, the animal was startled into wheeling. One of three braves with a rifle fired at Aldridge's back, and the musket ball tore in near the right shoulder. A flood of crimson covered his dusty blue jacket, as he tried to stay on his horse. He turned Valor and leveled his Springfield at the gang's chief, knocking the leader from his horse. He dropped his rifle and reached for his pistol. The yelping group of savages were now upon him, they rushed him with their lances, thrusting and stabbing. The Captain fell from his horse; the minutes of his life flashed before his eyes.

In the distance, a red sun dropped out of sight.

1

It was that soft hour before dawn. Stan Aldridge had always been an early riser and during the summer he had come to appreciate this singular time in the mountains. A few brief moments to consider the direction in his life, Stan would wake before the others and greet the sun.

On this morning, the only sound in the Company tent was the measured breathing of Lew Morris. Stan had given Morris a cup of camp whiskey made by Spider earlier in the evening. Spider's barrel-size mix was made from equal parts of alcohol and river water, plus a pot of strong coffee for color.

There was Morris, the weary mail-rider, now slumped against a bail of beaver pelts. He was asleep five minutes after downing the whiskey. Stan sat down at the clerk's desk and studied the soft horsehide mail pouch. Did it contain a letter from Lynn? He knew it was best to forget Lynn, but he couldn't.

By the desk lamp, Stan worked the pouch open. It was bound with two straps and a wax seal. There was no letter from Lynn. It contained four letters for Stan's boss, Bill Sublette, and three for the Scottish sportsman Sir Warren Kent. One letter for Sir Warren, post marked from Boston, looked personal. It had an odd odor. He doubted it was from a woman.

It wasn't much for Morris to ride eight hundred eighty miles with, but Sublette had arranged this third and last delivery before they had left St. Louis three months before.

Through the open tent flap, far to the East, Stan saw the first fine line of light outline the Wind River Range. In two weeks he would be heading East, preparing for his final year of medical school. It had been a good summer, a good experience. In the distance, Stan heard a rider coming up from the Green River through the cottonwoods. Someone else was awake.

Stan was surprised to see Sir Warren Kent, not at all an early riser. Hunting and adventure had drawn Sir Warren Johnson Kent, Scottish Lord of Grandtully, to Wyoming Territory. Stan Aldridge wondered how it felt to have that kind of wealth and freedom?

"Good morning, Stan," Sir Warren said. He was handsome and trim for his age, always neat and well groomed.

"Morning. . . you're up early." Stan gathered the letters for Sir Warren. "I've got mail for you."

"Well, well."

Stan handed him the letters.

"I could not sleep thinking of George," Sir Warren said, taking a seat by the lamp at the main trading table. Sir Warren's clerk George Hollis had been bitten by a rabid wolf a week before and in his crazed ways, he had disappeared from camp. Jed Walker had offered to have his dog try and track the man, and Jed had asked Stan to go with them.

Stan went out to the small fire he had made earlier. All was quiet except for the crickets. The air was crisp and not wrought with the summer heat that would soon be upon them. As he put on the pot of coffee, Stan thought about the Scottish nobleman. At thirty-eight, Sir Warren was fifteen years his senior. The Baronet had spent the summer hunting with Walker and Sublette and sparking Indian squaws. Stan, a summer employee, had to spend his time manning the trading tent of the St. Louis Fur Company with Spider Reedstrom and his men. He carried the steaming pot into the tent.

Stan poured two cups of coffee and watched Sir Warren intently reading his letter postmarked from Boston. "My God," said Sir Warren, motioning Stan to take a seat at the table, "this letter is from my brother." Stan's mind flashed to thoughts of his own brother, Dan. He wondered, once more, what God could be to take a man like Dan, in the very prime of life. In his mind he had played a thousand scenarios on how Dan had died. They all ended with a similar painful and gruesome death.

Sir Warren handled the three hand-written pages carefully. Stan sipped his hot coffee and watched the Baronet's brow wrinkle and mouth twitch as he read.

"Leon has been shanghaied," Sir Warren said, in a low voice. He put his hand to his chin, and looked at Stan, bewildered.

"Shanghaied?"

Sir Warren nodded and reread the letter before putting it down. There was an unreal silence between them.

Stan pulled on his coffee. What could he say? Sir Warren seemed lost in the past.

"Leon is your age. . . he will be twenty-four in December," said Sir Warren. For the first time Sir Warren Kent looked old.

"He is being held on a Russian trawler," Sir Warren said, scanning the letter. "It slaughters sea otters. . . or whatever, for the China market." His Scottish accent sounded strange out here in the early morning air of the river valley.

"I wonder how he got the letter to the post office?" Stan asked.

"He has told the Captain who he is," Sir Warren said. "Listen to this: Captain Ivanov will release me for five thousand pounds in gold or silver. It must be in eagles, half eagles, or silver dollars. He will take nothing less.'"

Sir Warren put the letter down and knocked over his coffee.

"Sorry, Stan," Sir Warren said, snatching the letter up from the hot liquid.

Stan mopped up the coffee with an old rag and refilled the cup. He'd make more.

"They want a ransom?" Stan asked. Sir Warren removed his black bollinger, placed it on the table, and nodded.

"If you had the money, could you get him in Boston?" Stan asked. Stan knew Sir Warren had the money, for Spider had said he was a generous man and that money meant very little to him.

"The ship, the *Helenka*, will be in San Francisco Bay or Monterey in three or four months," said Sir Warren. He picked up the letter and turned to the last page. "Listen to this. . . 'My dear

Brother,'" he read, "'I regret the many difficulties I caused you and our father. However, if I had not told Captain Ivanov of my inheritance, I would be dead like poor Edsel. If they do not get the money, I will be keelhauled and left at sea."

Two sleepy trappers' entered the tent. Stan had work to do and he got to his feet.. What could he say to Sir Warren?

"Stan," Sir Warren placed his hand on Stan's arm. "Please keep this confidential. I need some time to sort it all out." Stan looked into the Scot's vacant and distant eyes and nodded.

Later, when the sun was reaching its apex, Stan rode out across the rugged basin with Sir Warren. Together with Jed Walker, they were tracking the rabid George Hollis, who hadn't been seen in days. Reaching a vantage point, they peered down the rugged hillside. Below, they heard the howling of Walker's dog.

"Think it has found George?" Sir Warren asked. He removed his bollinger and mopped his forehead with a large red bandana.

"Yep," Walker said. He eased down out of the saddle. "Let's climb down and have a look. But don't expect too much." It was mid July, and the back of Walker's shirt showed dark with sweat.

"Your dog will not attack will it?" Sir Warren asked.

"Not unless I tell him," Walker said. Stan smiled at this. He respected the rugged mountain man. In the scorching sun, the men clamored down the boulder-strewn hillside. With rifle in hand, they half-slid down the steep incline. After fifty yards, they reached a flat, sandy bench. Walker's huge, wolf-like dog, Ric, stopped howling when they approached. His silver-gray tail beat the sand when he spotted Walker.

From behind a large boulder came a thrashing sound – a strange, soft growl. The men froze and a chill rolled up Stan's spine.. The dog's black lips curled back over glistening teeth with a growl.

The men eased forward towards the boulder. Stan stayed behind, looking between Sir Warren and Walker. There, Dear God! he saw a naked man rolling violently in the sand and brush, drooling from the mouth. It was George Hollis and he was beyond reproach. Stan had never expected this.

Sir Warren called out "George! It's me, your employer, Sir Warren!"

"Jesus," Walker said, putting his hand on his dog to stop its deep, jugular growl.

The wild-eyed clerk came out on all fours. Stringy, blond hair covered his wild face, he did not recognize the men that surrounded him. Saliva dripped from his mouth as he bared his teeth. The right side of his face and ear, where the wolf had ripped him, was a hideous bright purple.

"George, it is Sir Warren. We have come to help you."

The rabid man leaped to his feet, pawing the air with his hands and growling like a wounded grizzly. His sun-burned skin was enflamed with dozens of scratches and welts. Sir Warren, holding out his hand, edged toward him.

"Get away!" the man screamed. His eyes were ember, searing with the heat of madness and the summer sun. He bolted off, with surprising speed, and disappeared among the rocks and boulders.

"Dear God! What can we do?" Sir Warren asked. His hand trembled as he adjusted the front of his shirt.

Walker stroked his mustache and the stubble on his chin.

"The best I reckon," Jed said, removing his battered military style wide-brim hat, "is to shoot him. . . Shit, he's full of rabies; he'll be dead in a day or two, anyway. Am I right, Stan?" Walker knew that Stan was in med school, but he considered Stan a full-fledged physician.

"True, it's too late to save him." Stan knew Walker was serious about shooting Hollis.

"No, we can not shoot him," Sir Warren said.

"Hell," said Jed. "There's nothin' we can do. Shit, he could bite you."

The three scrambled back up to their mounts.

The Scottish adventurer leaned on his horse and sighed.

"I have only known George a couple months," he said. "I hired him in St. Louis. He was a quiet man, and he would have been in the tent the night the wolf came if I had not been entertaining that little Shoshone squaw."

"Shit, Warren, you didn't know there was goin' to be a mad

wolf in camp," Jed said, climbing into the saddle. Stan had noticed that Walker and his partners Bill Sublette and Robert Campbell did not address the Scot with the 'Sir'.

The men turned their horses and rode back to camp without a word.

Stan sat at his desk figuring the night's receipts in the dying light of a camp lantern. Spider Reedstrom poured coffee into two battered tin cups and brought them to the table where Bill Sublette and Warren Kent sat in the Company tent. The sun had just peeked over the hills to the east.

"Sorry about George," Spider said. Outside, the low dusty hills near the Green River were taking shape.

"I will never forget that scene," Sir Warren said. "George snarled at us like a wild boar, Jed's wolf-dog ready to tear him apart. . . Damn. . . what a way for a man to go."

"Ain't no cure for rabies," said Spider. "We had a bull go mad over on the Wind River a few years back. Remember that one, Bill?"

"Yeah," Sublette said, "Lee and one of our other boys shot it, but not before it tore a drunken Flathead into two parts." Through the small tent opening, Stan and the other men watched the nearby hills slowly fade into a deep gold.

Stan's pen scratched at his table. He knew the man Sublette called Lee was Dr. Lee Larkin. He was now engaged to Sublette's sister Ann; the same Ann who was once engaged to Stan's brother, Dan. Stan had meet Dr. Larkin in St. Louis, and the physician had told him he should consider coming west to practice after his education. Larkin seemed like a fine man and had offered to help Stan get started if he returned to St. Louis.

met

Who knows, he might return to practice in St. Louis. The west was more open and free than the stodgy cities of the East. That's what his West Point brother had thought, and so far he agreed with Dan. It was well over a year since Captain Daniel Aldridge had been killed by Indians on the Santa Fe Trail, and it still hurt. Stan closed his eyes, a different hurt was Lynn Monroe. She had not returned his letters, at Columbia they had studied together and planned together, what had happened?

In the distance, Stan saw Joe Meeks approaching. A ripple of concern ran through Stan. He knew what Joe was up to.

"Listen up! All you whisky drinkin' beaver brains," shouted Joe, "I found me a coon who can beat Gray Cloud in the two-mile run." He got down from his horse and swaggered around the tent, where a dozen men drank and traded. They all knew Meeks, and they knew he was firing up another competition.

"For Christ sakes, Joe," Spider said, "the last Flathead you had finished near fifty yards back of Gray Cloud. I'm still chargin' whiskey to your tab. You'd better not lose again."

"Forget it, Meeks, I'll buy you a drink," Walker said. He got up and walked to the whiskey barrel and ladled out a cup for Meeks.

"What tribe is this one from?" Spider asked. Meeks took the drink and sat on a bail of beaver pelts. Stan moved his work to the main table, and his eyes met with Meeks. Meeks' gave him his broad bushy smile.

"He ain't no red nigger," Joe said. "He's white as you are." Several of the men nearby chuckled. Stan felt a quiver of heat flow up his neck. Maybe he shouldn't have let Joe talk him into the race.

"There ain't no white man gonna out run that red mother," said a red-bearded trapper named Henson.

Joe jumped to his feet and slammed his hand on the table. It sent Stan's coffee rippling over the edge of his cup.

"Hear this! I've got me a silver dollar for every man here! And it says my man can whip Gray Cloud's ass."

"Joe! Don't do this," said Spider. He grabbed Meeks' arm. "You'll be two years payin' off your tab." Joe gave Stan a wink, and went out in front of the tent to make his wagers. Sublette didn't like betting in the tent.

"Joe sure can liven up a dull morning," said Sublette, standing. "What's he into us for?"

Money was of no use at the trappers' rendezvous; the men kept a tab that the trappers paid off with beaver pelts.

"A hundred eighty-three bucks," Spider said.

"Shit, I like Joe," Jed said, with a laugh, "but I doubt he's got the pelts to cover that much. And, it looks like he's about to drop another twenty or more." A half dozen men had gathered around the stocky Meeks.

"Who knows? Maybe he found a winner," said an old trapper.

"The moon," said Spider, "is blue cheese, too."

Stan saw Sublette pour whiskey in his coffee. Must be getting old, he thought.

As he prepared the coffee, Stan wondered: What had he gotten himself into? The race was just one other event that fit into life. His brother, Dan, once had told him that risk and competition were part of everyman's life. Joe asked him to say nothing about the race, because Sonny Plotnik was going to run with Stan and they had devised a plot to tire and ultimately beat the Crow brave. Stan hadn't even told Spider about the race.

In the dry heat of the afternoon, a confused and boisterous mob of ninety white and red men milled near the starting line, fifty yards from the front of the Company tent

Stan bent down and dumped sand from one of his doe-skin moccasins. The knot of competition tightened his stomach as he laced his moccasins. He looked out over the course that disappeared north over a sandy bluff. He was eager to start.

"Now listen up, you trap rats!" shouted Joe. He stood in his stirrups and shook a heavy brass helmet, that he had borrowed from Sir Warren, above his head. "My man is Stan Aldridge. He's the tall one with the blond ponytail, from Sublette's company. Sonny is from Captain Bonneville's camp. Sonny practiced with Stan, they're friends, and he'll run with them."

"Aldridge needs a friend all right, 'cause he won't see much except the back side of that Crow," a trapper near Meeks yelled. The crowd scoffed as Joe dismounted like an ancient cavalry captain, and he marched toward the starting line slowly and deliberately. He swung his brass helmet high above his head.

Stan looked at Sonny Plotnik; Sonny, like Stan, wore only a loin cloth and moccasins. Stan knew his own skin looked milky-white like Sonny's in the bright sun. Both young men were muscular and well built, but Stan was a head taller than his black, curly-hair companion.

Stan smiled as he watched Meeks push his way through the crowd. Joe looked ridiculous in Sir Warren's armor, breastplate and tall brass helmet. The man is a showman, but you had too like him.

"Where's Gray Cloud?" Sonny asked.

"He's back by the tent; he likes to come to the line last," said the armored Joe Meeks. He motioned Stan and Sonny to confer privately with him. Beads of sweat glistened in the veteran trapper's sideburns and beard.

"Now, boys, remember our plan." Meek smiled. "Sonny, you run as fast and as far as your ass will carry you. If I'm right, Gray Cloud will want to lead the entire race. He can't stand anyone else in the lead. Stan, just run your best race, and save somethin' for the end. You'll whip him for sure."

"What if he don't take the bait?" Stan asked. Over Meeks' shoulder, he saw Gray Cloud and several of his Crow friends make their way through the crowd.

Meeks mopped his forehead with his lower sleeve. A wily smile crossed his broad face.

"It'll work," he said, "just run your race. You can beat that red nigger. That scrawny Flathead damn near took him in the last race."

The crowd trickled down the path to view the start of the run.

Gray Cloud stood upright at the starting line, taking off his blanket robe.

Stan studied his opponent. At six feet, Gray Cloud was one of the tallest Indians at the summer rendezvous. A yellow headband held back his deep-black, shoulder-long hair, which framed his broad face and bulging nose. Stan had figured him to be about twenty-five.

Stan's palms were moist, he never liked this period before the start of a race. He'd felt the same before his races in college. The three men lined up. Sonny flexed his muscles, while Stan stared at the expressionless Gray Cloud. The Crow's face showed nothing as he stared off into the blazing sun..

"Are you boys ready?" Jed Walker, the official race starter, asked.

"Okay," said Walker, "you all know the trail. Good luck."

"Get ready," Walker raised his pistol into the air. Stan stood ready with his hands on his thighs. The crowd grew silent. "Get set…" Boom! The pistol shot rang clear in the hot mid-day air, and the race was underway.

The three men ran quickly down the trail and were soon out of sight. After the first half mile, near the flat bench where the Bonneville Company managed its trading tent, Stan began to pace himself with long even strides. Ahead he saw Sonny and the Crow jockeying for the lead.

Soon the two disappear over the bluff. Stan trailed a good eighty yards behind the two. He soon picked up his pace. Beyond the bluff, the trail turned west, then looped back along the river to the starting line. From the bluff, Stan could see, far to the north, the shaded purple of the Wind River Range.

At the bottom of the bluff, a mile from the start, Stan came across Sonny bent over with his hands on his hips.

"He's blowin' hard," gasped Sonny, continuing to run a short distance with Stan, "but he's tough. Better pick it up." Stan saw Gray Cloud disappear into the cottonwoods along the river; he was still forty yards ahead.

Stan picked up the pace, and in the next quarter mile closed the gap to ten yards. They now were running over pine needles through the cool cottonwoods when Stan heard the labored breathing of his opponent. Sonny had done his job and Stan was thankful for that. Gray Cloud turned his head to see Stan, and suddenly Stan closed the gap to five yards. The trail now turned away from the river and the last stretch lay in front of them. The sun hung low and apprehensive in the thin mountain air. Stan could win; he had the energy, although his breathing came short and his legs felt heavy.

Running head to head with the brave, Stan gasped for air, his heart pounding his chest, but his legs held strong and in the final minutes of the race, he surged ahead of the fading Crow, and won by ten yards.

Stan looked for a space to sprawl out in the grass, but Meeks and the others wouldn't have it. They jumped and shouted around him. He stood for a few minutes with his hands on his hips.

"Stan," Jed Walker said, "come to the tent and get out of the sun. Meeks will be dancin' and singin' until midnight."

“Thanks,” said Stan, picking up his clothes. Spider wrapped a towel around him, and the three pushed their way through the crowd. Stan shook hands with several men and felt their slaps on his back.

Spider’s men roped off the tent for the remainder of the day, and they had set a barrel of whiskey in a small wagon nearby. Whiskey was sold and the men gathered greedily at the wagon. Stan followowed Walker into the tent where it was much cooler. Bill Sublette and Sir Warren were the only two inside; they were seated at the main table. Most of the tent was lined with boxes and bales of pelts.

“That was a good race, Stan,” said Sublette, circling the table to shake Stan’s hand. Bill’s huge hand felt like a small ham.

A bugle sounded out near the whiskey wagon, and Stan could see Joe Meeks on horseback, carrying a large American flag. He was accompanied by a young man blasting away on the bugle.

“Sir Warren,” said Spider, entering the tent, “you’d better get that crazy armor and hat away from Joe before he gets drunk and sells ‘em to an Indian.”

“Good thinking,” Sir Warren said. “I had better do just that. Joe has had his fun.”

The handsome Scot walked over and extended his hand to Stan.

“Excellent race, young man.”

Stan stood and thanked him. The man’s hand was firm and his smile genuine. The Baronet wore well-trimmed black sideburns and a pencil thin mustache. He had not talked to Stan further about his shanghaied brother, Leon.

Spider and Sir Warren walked out of the tent, towards the whiskey wagon.

“I’ll have to be going,” said Stan, standing.

He felt rested walking out toward the mass of people gathered near the wagon. As he made his way toward Sonny, a grisly trapper pounded him on the back and handed him a large cup of whiskey. They might even need to mix another barrel before this party ended.

The sun slipped below the bluff to the west while Stan and Captain Benjamin Bonneville talked over a cup of whiskey. The race was over now and many of the men were gone off in a drunken stupor. Captain Bonneville had helped Stan arrange his trip west and Stan respected his advice.

"You and the Scot," said the Captain, looking at Stan, "seem to have hit it off."

"Yes," said Stan, with a smile, "we talk mostly about books. His middle name is Johnson, after Samuel Johnson, who, I gather, was a friend of his granddad. I just know Samuel Johnson was an English writer. Anyway, Sir Warren isn't what you expect to find here in Wyoming. . . I'm going to talk to him tomorrow about a job. He needs a clerk for a trip to Santa Fe. . . I'd like to go there before going back East."

"I don't think it would be too wise," said the Captain. Stan could feel that Captain Bonneville didn't care for the Scottish big game hunter. Although born in Paris, to wealthy parents, the Captain was a disciplined man.

"Why do you say that, Captain?"

Stan regretted asking the question.

"In the past year," the Captain said, "the three companies here at the rendezvous have lost thirty-eight men. As far as I know, none drowned. They died with an arrow in the back or a hatchet in the head. This is a wild land. It isn't chasing a fox over the hills of merry old Scotland."

"We'd go with Jed Walker's group, then I'd go back to St. Louis with a caravan. It may be my only chance to get to Santa Fe. Dan wrote about it often."

"Walker's a good man," said the Captain, "but this isn't a country for afternoon tea or wine and cheese."

It was mid-afternoon the following day when Stan rode south along the Green River. He rode with ease on his black gelding, and he was glad that he didn't have more drinks with Joe and his friends. The party became long, loud, and wild.

From a distance, Stan had seen Sir Warren's tent many times in the past month. It was difficult not to see the blue and white striped, marquee-style tent, but he had not visited before.

In the shade of an awning made by one side of the large tent, an enormous black woman was shaving Sir Warren. Stan dismounted and walked into the shade. Sir Warren opened one eye and glanced at him.

"Ah, Mr. Aldridge," Sir Warren said, turning his head, "thank you for coming. Please have a seat while Diamond finishes. Yesterday was fun. . . tell me more about the race. Did you think you could beat the Crow?" The woman, wearing a brown bowler hat, eyed Stan while she sharpened the razor on a strap tied to her waist. She continued her work, and Stan took a seat nearby. There was a slight breeze up from the river.

"I don't think I could've beaten him without Sonny," Stan said. "It was Joe's plan. He thought Gray Cloud was obsessed with not letting anyone have the lead. He was right. Gray Cloud made the mistake of running with Sonny. Sonny is a darned good runner, too. Gray Cloud never recovered."

The shave completed, Sir Warren sat up. He wiped his face with a white linen towel. Diamond handed him a bottle of lotion, which he patted on his face. Sir Warren introduced his six foot, two-hundred-twenty pound maid to Stan. The hand Stan shook was strong, like a working man's. The woman spoke to Sir Warren in a foreign tongue, and lit up a long, black cheroot. Sir Warren chuckled.

"Diamond has been with me five years," Sir Warren said. "I hired her in northern Africa. She was in the slave running business and wanted out. She can out work and out fight most men. She understands English, but doesn't speak it. She just told me, if she were young again, she might lead you to the bush." Sir Warren smiled. "That is a compliment I have never heard before. She likes you. And believe me, you do not want her for an enemy. Let us take a walk down to the river."

Stan was two inches taller than the Scottish Lord, but he admired the fine physical condition of the older man. He heard many stories about the wealthy sport hunter, but Bill Sublette told him the Baronet, despite his lifestyle, was a fine and generous man. Stan respected Bill, who had been a close friend of Dan's. Stan followed Sir Warren through a pair of gnarled, old cottonwoods and sat on a bench built by Sir Warren at the river's edge. Stan had heard that Sir Warren often read here.

"I believe yesterday you said you attended Dartmouth College," Sir Warren said. "It was hard for me to hear with that bugle blasting in our ears."

"When Eddie gets on that horn, it's hard to shut him up," said Stan. "I was graduated from Dartmouth two years ago, and I have one more year of medicine at Columbia College." Sir Warren studied the river and stroked his mustache. Stan wondered what Sir Warren's education had been like.

"Why did you come to St. Louis and on out here?" asked Sir Warren. Several people had asked Stan that.

"Perhaps, like you, I wanted to see the West," said Stan. "Besides, my brother loved it out here."

"Bill told me about your brother; I'm sorry."

"He was engaged to Bill's sister when he was killed." Stan recalled it had been weeks after Dan's death before he could talk about it.

"That is what I understand." The two men watched as a pair of red-winged black birds battled for territory.

"I met Sublette my senior year at Dartmouth, and I later heard he was planning this trip. So here I am."

"You said you were interested in going to Santa Fe," Sir Warren said.

"Yes. Dan was killed on the Santa Fe Trail, and he had written often about the town."

"Comanches?"

"That's what the Army told us."

"Do you doubt them?" Sir Warren asked.

"Oh, no. We got a letter from an army scout. He was the only survivor. It was the Comanches." The men watched a group of six Sioux lead their pack animals, loaded with pelts, along the far shore of the river.

"Was he your only brother?" Sir Warren asked.

"Yes."

"As I mentioned to you my only brother, Leon, is about your age," said Sir Warren. "I regret that we have never been as close as I would like."

"Dan and I were very close," Stan said. He recalled his mother saying that she thought he idolized Dan too much.

Sir Warren tossed a stick into the river and they watched it float off.

"Sad," Sir Warren said. "Anyway, I need to replace George. He kept my trip notes, and did other odd jobs. I have arranged to go to Santa Fe with Jed Walker and his trappers. I would like you to go with me, as my clerk. You could go back to St. Louis with a regular caravan. I'm going to see if I can get to California. . .according to Spider, there is a trail west out of Santa Fe, but no one here knows much about it. I'll find out. It may not be too late for me and my brother."

Stan stood up and looked into Sir Warren's troubled hazel eyes; he knew that his own eyes, a slightly darker brown, reflected his sympathy for the Baronet.

"I've thought it over. I'd be pleased to go with you," Stan said. He extended his hand, and Sir Warren got to his feet.

Stan shook Sir Warren's hand; the Scot pumped his arm with enthusiasm.

"Good. You won't regret this."

2

The caravan slowly disappeared into the glare of a morning sun. Comprised of Bill Sublette, his men and his pelts, the caravan headed for St. Louis, eight hundred and eighty miles to the east. Mules and horses carried one hundred seventy packs of beaver weighing fourteen hundred pounds, two hundred fifty pounds of beaver castor, plus muskrat and otter pelts. Sublette hoped to sell the goods in St. Louis or perhaps further east, while his two partners would lead trapping expeditions in other directions: Robert Campbell to the northwest, Jed Walker to the southwest. Since the quantity of beaver had dwindled, and the Company was forced to range further and further for its product.

Right after breakfast, the rendezvous broke up and the trappers parted ways. Stan Aldridge and Sir Warren rode with Jed Walker's expedition southwest, where they hoped to find a better crop of pelts. The hazy morning sky began to lift and the heat of the day was already upon them.

"We will see new terrain today," Sir Warren said. He rode up beside Stan. "It is always a thrill for me, exploring a land I have never seen."

"Do you know any of these trappers with Jed'?" Stan asked.

"I have seen most of them at the rendezvous, but of the seven, I only know Joe Lapoint. He was with us last year in Yellowstone country."

"I know John Relle, he's a Canadian," said Stan. "One of Captain Bonneville's men. He had heard stories about the women in Santa Fe and was anxious to come."

"'When pleasure can be had, it is fit to catch it." Sir Warren smiled. "Spanish women have always been fascinating, but I would not care to slight those young squaws back on the Green."

For a week the party of twelve rode south. The weather had been decent but hot, and the men began to fear the dark clouds that always lingered in the distance, with the Front Range of the Rockies ominously looming to the west. Stan quickly adapted to the routines of trail life with Sir Warren's group. He was hired on as Sir Warren's clerk, and part of his job entailed writing the daily log. Two others, the black woman, Diamond Field and Pepe Ortago were responsible for food and supplies. An older man, Pepe Ortago, often called on Stan for assistance with horses and Stan was made responsible for the morning and evening fires.

It was a quiet evening on the plain when Sir Warren and Jed Walker asked Stan to join them in a drink of wine. As usual, they were seated at the small table that sat right outside of Sir Warren's tent. Stan was pleased, for it was the first time he was asked to join the two older men.

"Quite a dog," said Stan, rubbing the animal's massive head with both hands. The dog was always with Walker. Now he sat quietly watching Pepe and Diamond prepare dinner by the fire. The dog, called Ric, had a black coat, with a pale gray tail and a face full of piercing eyes- silver with dark green pupils. It was one of the largest dogs Stan had seen.

"His mother was a husky," Walker said proudly. "I won him, as a pup, in a game of bones with an old Piegan at Fort Henry. Accordin' to the boys at the Fort, Ric's father was a friendly three-legged wolf that lived in the area."

"I wouldn't tangle with him," Sir Warren said, sipping his wine.

"I had Spider weighed him a week ago, " said Jed. "What do you think he weighs?" The wind shifted to the north and Stan could smell the steaks cooking.

"Hundred twenty," Sir Warren said.

"I'd say one forty," said Stan.

" Try one fifty-two." Diamond placed two large pewter plates each with a huge steak, chalk lima beans, and hot biscuits in front of the men at the table. The smell of the biscuits reminded Stan of his mother's kitchen. Pepe placed a large white napkin containing a knife and fork beside each platter.

"Can I bring you anything, Mr. Jed?" asked Pepe.

"Two fingers of wine," Walker said. Sir Warren spread a pepper sauce onto his buffalo steak.

"Anything for you Master Stan?" Pepe asked, placing his friendly hand on Stan's shoulder.

"No thanks, amigo." Stan gave Pepe a wink.

"I'll bet you didn't eat like this on the way out with Bonneville," said Jed, watching Sir Warren tear into his steak. "I've found those military types eat fancy at home, but they're tight on the trail."

"True enough. The Captain's cook. . . a nice old fellow. . . but the poor man couldn't make a decent pot of coffee. I tell you, Diamond and Pepe could cook for Beacon Hill's best families."

Walker turned to Stan. "Tell me about the independent trappers. Have Isaac and Cotton been botherin' you?" Walker asked. The two men gathered the wood and buffalo chips for his group. Stan knew them, and he didn't like either.

"We've had a few discussions," Stan said, "on where I should gather firewood and such. They're alright," Stan lied.

"Cotton Crevier is okay," said Jed, "but watch Isaac. Isaac Labrosa is a bull, and, when he has drink, he gets mean,"

"Perhaps I should give you a hand with the wood for a few days and see about these two ruffians," Sir Warren suggested. He normally hunted game, and Stan thought it absurd for him to help in such menial tasks.

"Oh no, but thanks," said Stan, with a smile. "I'll work it out."

"Be careful. He can be a bastard," said Jed, finishing his wine.

"How many more days to Bent's Fort?" Stan asked, changing the subject.

"Four or five days, if we're lucky. The Fort's been built since I was down this way last, but Touisaint tells me it's quite a place. Old Frenchy don't talk much but he knows this area."

Three days passed and the rains stayed away. One afternoon, Stan found a bundle of dried logs and sticks along a dry stream bed that fed into a stagnant pond. He filled the buffalo hide sling that hung from his horse, Midnight. Stan hoped that Jed was right and that the party would reach Bent's Fort the next afternoon.

It was strange that Sir Warren had not mentioned his brother Leon since they separated from the caravan. Stan wasn't sure if he had even talked to Walker about his brother. He knew that Leon was on Sir Warren's mind but there was nothing he could do until they reached Santa Fe. Stan would not bring up the subject.

A light breeze fell over him and he thought of Lynn. Her hair lightly brushed against his face and he heard the sound of birds cawing in the distance. Leading Midnight out of the creek bed, he saw Isaac and Cotton gathering wood and buffalo chips in the distance. Cautiously, he led Midnight toward them.

Isaac Labrosa was sweaty and mean in the hot desert sun. He eyed Stan from below thick, bushy eye-brows and grunted something inaudible. Labrosa was five feet, ten inches tall and weighed two hundred seventy pounds. For a short time he had been a Cossack, but, after murdering an officer, over a woman, he escaped Russia for New Orleans.

"Told you to stay out of our way," said Isaac, walking towards Stan.

"There's plenty of wood in the creek bed," Stan pointed. He continued toward camp with Midnight. Isaac stepped up and grabbed the reins from him.

"You'd better go hide behind that black mammy," Isaac said. "Might just mess up that pretty mug of yours. I feel like crunchin' me some bone." Midnight shook his head up and down and snorted.

"Jed told us not to make trouble for the Scot's group," Cotton called out. He was a small, wrinkled man with a coonskin cap. "'Sides, we got enough chips for tonight."

"Shit, Cotton, I don't give a fart what Walker says. I don't bow to nobody, not that Scot or this fancy pants Easterner," he grunted. The blood surged through Stan's body, and he took a step toward the man with the ugly face. He'd like to smash in that face. Stan jerked the reins back from him.

"Okay, dirt face. See me at the Fort, if you want," Stan said, smelling the man's foul body. He walked towards camp.

"Bring that nigger bitch to tote your ass home," shouted Isaac.

By the end of the first week, Stan had become a regular member of Sir Warren's supper table. He enjoyed time with the two older men, and the food and wine were excellent. Most of all, he enjoyed listening to the events of the day, the stories of the past, and plans for the future.

Stan felt good. He had taken a swim in the pond before dinner and he tried to push the encounter with Labrosa out of his mind. The last two days had been enjoyable, as the parties traveled in a more easterly direction. Many of the mountains faded away to the west. Out here, the grass was good and the game remained plentiful.

"I'm surprised we haven't seen any Cheyenne or Comanche," Jed said. "Those buggers usually show up and try to put the squeeze on you for crossin' their land."

"It is hard for me to understand why anyone would build a fort out here," Sir Warren said with a forkful of steak in his hand. The men looked out across an unending sea of rolling dried grass. The last traces of sunlight lingered in the evening sky.

"I've heard the Fort is doin' well," Jed said. "The Santa Fe Trail is busy these days, and most caravans aren't using the Cutoff. It's too risky." As soon as he had spoken, Jed realized that the Cutoff was a sensitive subject for Stan. His brother Dan had been killed there, and Jed was not sure how painful those memories were for Stan. "That sends 'em right by Bent's Fort. The Fort gets the Indians and Spaniards trade, too."

"How far are we from Mexico?" Stan asked, sipping water.

"It ain't Mexico," Jed said, "but it's their territory. . . I think. Taos is a hundred sixty miles southwest of the Fort, and Santa Fe is four days further south."

The three men sat for a time, and Sir Warren and Stan finished their meals. Stan could do without the hot, dry August air, but thankfully there was a steady breeze flapping the tent awning.

"Isaac is tellin' the boys," Jed said, looking at Stan, "you and he are goin' to have a fight." Stan was hoping the subject wouldn't come up.

"Forget it," said Sir Warren, banging down his wine cup. Some of the wine spilled. "I will talk to the grimy bastard. What gave him that idea?"

"I'll be okay; I was bare-knuckles champ at college." Stan wiped up the wine.

"Shit," Walker said, giving both Stan and Sir Warren a helpless look, "Labrosa won't fight school yard rules. Those boys fight to cripple." Stan felt flushed.

" Jed is right," said Sir Warren. "I will give the asshole a bottle of wine; he will forget it."

"No you won't," Stan said. He got to his feet and put both hands on the table. "I'll handle it. Please stay out," he said bitterly, looking into Sir Warren's large and concerned eyes. "The man pushed me once too often."

Sir Warren pulled his chair closer to the table and looked at Walker. Jed raised his eyebrows and smiled.

"He's got guts," said Walker.

Stan walked off to move the horses to new grass, but he heard Sir Warren quote: "'Towering in the confidence of twenty-one.'" Stan felt his neck radiating with heat, but he knew he had to fight Labrosa. He would whip the bastard.

Two miles out, Stan saw the northwest bastion of Bent's Fort. Ten-foot adobe cylinders rose up thirty feet above the top of the thick adobe walls. The walls stood twice Stan's height. For one hundred fifty feet in length, the northern and southern walls enclosed the Fort with slightly shorter walls on the east and west sides. There was a second musketry tower at the southeast corner of the Fort. Stan figured that even British artillery would have trouble blasting into this fortress.

The day was cloudy and sultry, and thunder rumbled far to the west. Walker waved to a ragged looking man in the musketry tower and then led the party of twelve, with their thirty horses, around to the far side of the fort. There, on the eastern side, were two iron-sheathed plank entrance doors that swelled with heat and dust.

Walker halted the group in front of the massive doors and dismounted. Stan looked to his left and looked down the three hundred yards of grassy grade which ran seamlessly into the Arkansas River. Stan turned back to the fort upon hearing voices.

Two men with rifles spoke together in an enclosed watchtower as an older man wearing a white shirt and black vest joined the two.

Jed led his horse forward. He stopped near the doors and looked up.

"Mr. Bent, I'm Jed Walker. We met in St. Louis a couple years back, remember? I'm a partner with Sublette and Campbell."

One of the rifle men whispered into William Bent's ear.

"Sorry, Walker, but I ain't hearin' too well these days," Bent said. He turned and shouted back down into the fort.

"If you're with Bill Sublette, that's all I need to know. I've told the boys to pull the doors. You come in and get settled. We'll talk later."

Stan and Sir Warren rode side by side through the doors, as four men dragged them open.

"I didn't expect this," Stan said. He was surprised by the large courtyard with two-story buildings to the right and left and a single-story structure ahead. All were adobe or made of large stone. In the center was the stone well house. A number of Indians gathered near the trading store, ahead, and across the courtyard. Nearby was a tall pole flying the American flag.

"Nor I," said Sir Warren. "We will see what Jed wants us to do. We may have to camp outside." They waited while two of the fort's men talked to Walker. Stan noted that there were large corrals between the fort's outer walls and the rear of the buildings to the left and ahead. The sound of a blacksmith's hammer rang across the courtyard, and there was the faint smell of cooking meat. It could be pork. Stan hoped it was, for he hadn't had pork in months.

Walker gave orders to his men and they dismounted, walking their animals toward the two-story building to the left.

"Warren," said Jed, walking back to Sir Warren, "your folks can stay in a couple empty rooms near the store. We'll only be here one night. If you need things, get them before ten tomorrow. That's when we pull out."

Diamond swept out the musty, windowless, pelt storage rooms. Stan and Pepe unloaded and unsaddled their fourteen animals. Sir Warren headed for the trading room to purchase supplies.

Stan knew the word had spread that the Scottish Lord had arrived. Small groups of white and red men gathered. Three followed Sir Warren into the trading room. Stan led the animals by pairs into the corral and made arrangements with an old Indian to feed them; then, he headed across the courtyard to join Sir Warren in the trade goods store.

"Son," said an old trapper waving Stan down, "be that a slave nigger?" He motioned toward Diamond who was setting up a table in front of the two rooms. She was smoking her cheroot.

"No, no," Stan said in a soft voice, "she's no slave. She's a powerful Zulu warrior who served as Sir Warren's guide lion hunting in Africa. He told me once, when his gun misfired, she strangled the three-hundred-pound cat with her bare hands."

"Waugh! I ain't a gettin' in a huggin' match with that one," he said. He hustled back to his two friends.

A balding young man, wearing a gray vest and wire-rim glasses, approached Stan near the trading room.

"Sir Warren J. Kent, I presume," said the small man, squinting up into Stan's eyes.

"No. I'm Sir Warren's clerk," said Stan, with a smile.

"Ah, ha," said the man, with a broad grin, "then we're of the same flock. I'm the clerk for Mr. Bent." The men shook hands.

"Tell Mr. Kent, you and he are invited to dinner with Mr. Bent. Eight o'clock sharp." Stan watched the man turn and scamper back into his small office next to the store.

Stan turned to enter the store, and Sir Warren came out carrying a bushel basket full of purchased items. A young boy followed, carrying a second basket. Stan took the basket and set it on the table Diamond had erected.

"I was lucky. A mule train came by a week ago from St. Louis and left quite a few supplies," said Sir Warren. Diamond and Pepe took the two baskets into their room to sort and store. Most were various foods items and spices.

Stan and Sir Warren entered the dining room of William Bent. A large oak table and six heavy chairs stood solid on the pounded clay floor. The two large windows looked out on the fort's courtyard. Cheyenne Indian relics covered the wall opposite the windows. At the ends of the table, Bent and his partner, Ceran St.Vrain, were seated. Stan and Sir Warren sat with their backs to the windows; across the table sat Jed and an army captain named Osborne. The Captain worn a short jacket with nine gold buttons, and Stan could see his forage cap with gold embroider hanging on his chair. Dan had worn a similar jacket and cap on his last leave in the East.

"Is this your first trip to America?" asked St.Vrain. Two young women served each man a huge platter with shredded pork, red beans, and corn bread.

"No," said Sir Warren, "it is my third trip. Last year, I came west and went into the Yellowstone with Jed."

"He's never been to Santa Fe," Jed said. He poured himself more port wine from a large decanter. One of the women serving was quite attractive, and Sir Warren elbowed Stan, raising his eyebrows appreciatively.

"I'll write a note to the Governor for you," Bent said. "They change often, but, as far as we know, it's still Manuel Armijo. Like most greasers, long as he gets a cut, he's friendly. Just remember, down there, you ain't in the U.S. of A."

"Officials in Mexico City are nervous," said St. Vrain. "They're having trouble in California and Texas, and there's a ton of pressure on men like Armijo to keep control."

"Several traders and trappers have been jailed in Santa Fe this year," added the Captain. "Some for months, while the local officials screw around with Mexico City. When you get there, I'd report to the officials. As far as we know, they still authorize trading and trapping, but there will be a fee. They want to make sure everyone knows the town belongs to the Republic of Mexico."

Stan concentrated on his food, as did the others. He found the pit-cooked pork a delightful change from fire-cooked game. He and Lynn had had a great pork loin dinner at a little restaurant on Hudson Street near Varick in New York City, but he couldn't think of its name.

"This is the first pork I have tasted since St. Louis," Warren said. "It's good."

"We keep a few hogs at the fort," said St. Vrain. "Try that pepper sauce. Bill thinks I've gone Mex, and I do like their hot sauce."

Stan, too, enjoyed the sauce, and the port was excellent. During much of the meal, the Captain, a slight, bald man with a paralyzed left hand, told of his experiences in the Black Hawk War.

Candles lighted the table and shadows moved among the Indian relics on the wall across from Stan. The men finished their bread pudding and nursed the heavy black coffee. Stan could hear a commotion in the courtyard, and soon a rap came at the outer door.

"Come in," shouted Bent. A heavy bearded man stuck his head in the door His hat was in his hand.

"What's up, Sid?" Bent asked. Sid answered in a loud voice.

"One of the trappers that came today insisted you tell Aldridge that he's ready for the fight."

"Okay, Sid, I'll pass it on." The man withdrew. The door slammed shut.

"What's this all about?" Bent asked.

Jed gave the others a brief sketch of the problem between Labrosa and Stan. Stan felt his heart beat increase, as all eyes turned toward him.

"Labrosa has been drinking," Sir Warren said. "I did not hire Stan to handle a mess like this. He will forget it tomorrow. . . Jed and I will talk to the men." There was a heavy silence, and the attractive Spanish woman was clearing the table.

"Thanks," Stan said, with a slight smile, "but I have to see this through." He put his coffee cup on his plate, and he placed his hands on the edge of the table. He recalled that Dan had told him there'd be times like this, and he had helped prepare him. Besides, he thought, most of Jed's men are pretty decent. They're out there wondering if I'm an educated Easterner, who runs fast, or their kind of man. Stan felt his face grow warm.

William Bent lit his pipe, spreading tobacco down over his vest. His partner, St. Vrain, spoke.

"Don't worry, Aldridge. There'll be plenty of opportunities out here to prove yourself. Pick the right one. A man just gets dirty wrestlin' with a pig."

"Right," said Walker. "The problem is, Isaac ain't going to stay with Stan's college bare-knuckle game."

"Thank you all," Stan said, getting up from the table, "but I'm going to change my pants, and give it a try. This is my only pair left without a hole," Bent and Walker chuckled. "Mr. Bent, it was an excellent meal. Thanks for having me."

"Good luck, son," said Bent, standing and shaking Stan's hand. Stan's mouth was dry.

"I'll come with you, Aldridge," Captain Osborne said, standing. "I've handled matches before. We'll see if we can keep control." He and Stan made their way toward the door.

"Shit, Warren," Walker said, pushing back from the table, "you can't afford to lose another clerk."

It was dusk outside. Stan and the Captain walked along the building that housed Bent's dining room and the room Stan shared with Sir Warren. They could hear the laughter and commotion near the center of the courtyard as several torches danced about. Stan felt confident, relieved even to get on with it. He had an opportunity to show Sir Warren, Jed and the others he could take care of himself.

"I take it," said Captain Osborne, hustling to keep up with Stan's long strides, "you've fought bare-knuckle before."

"At St. Peter's, near Boston, and Dartmouth."

Diamond and Pepe sat at the table in front of the two rooms. When Stan passed, he smiled at them, and rapped the table with his knuckles.

"What's going on, sir?" Pepe asked the Captain. Stan stepped into the darkened room to change.

"Mr. Aldridge is going to fight some fellow who works for Jed Walker," the Captain said.

Pepe got up and entered the room. Stan was pulling on an old pair of buckskin pants.

"Who are you fighting, Master Stan?"

Stan liked the crusty old Spaniard. In Africa, Sir Warren had a set of ivory teeth carved for the man. He still wore them to this day.

"Isaac Labrosa," Stan said, tightening his moccasins.

Stan, bare-chested, stood and put on his green bandana. In the dim light he could not see Pepe's face, but he saw him remove his upper plate.

"I know of him. He is an evil man."

"I can take him, Pepe."

Stan gave Pepe a pat on the shoulder and left the room.

Diamond stood by the table with the Captain, and to one side stood Walker and Sir Warren.

"Diamond insists on blessing you," Sir Warren said. Sir Warren turned and spoke to her. Diamond stepped forward, setting her bowler on the table.

She placed her two hands over Stan's breasts. He felt her fingers working into the hair and muscles. With her eyes closed, speaking in her native tongue, she sang five words three times. A pale moon allowed Stan to see the concentration on her large black face. She was a true friend. Diamond removed her hands and opened her eyes as Stan leaned forward and gave her a hug.

"Let's go," said Stan. Without a word, the group headed for the blustering, torch-carrying mob.

3

Stan felt the pulsing rhythm of his heart as he led Captain Osborne and the others toward the milling throng of red and white men. He walked with long confident strides. He knew everyone at the Fort would be gathered for the fight. He was determined. . .he would win this fight for Dan.

Cotton Crevier fell into step with Stan and grabbed his arm as they neared the center of the courtyard. "Don't let him get a hold on you," Cotton said, "and watch his headbutts. Good luck."

"Thanks," Stan said. The withered old trapper disappeared into the crowd.

"Keep your chin down, and move your feet," the words of Dan and Lieutenant Ito ran through Stan's mind. I can do it, he repeated, I can do it.

The eager crowd seemed like a wild beast to Stan, as he and Captain Osborne pushed their way into the crude ring drawn in the courtyard sand. Stan saw Isaac in the center of the ring; his broad face looked brutal and inebriated in the flickering yellow torch light.

"Quiet!" shouted the Captain. The officer had a powerful voice for a small man. The noise subsided. "Quiet!"

Osborne's uniform helps, thought Stan. He watched Labrosa strip off his red cotton shirt and toss it into the crowd. He was a hairy man, oily, black curls of hair covered his arms, chest, and shoulders.

"This is a bare-knuckle match," said the Captain, in a resounding voice. "A round will end when a man goes down. He will be given two minutes to get to his feet or declare the match over. There will be no headbutts, or blows below the belt. Do you both understand the rules?"

"Yes," Stan nodded.

"Piss on your rules," Labrosa said. He shoved the Captain aside, and took a wild swing at Stan. Stan ducked the blow.

"You'll do," said the Captain, stepping between the two men and pounding his finger into Isaac's chest, "as I say."

"To hell," shouted Labrosa. He hooked the Captain's neck with his left arm and yanked him to his chest. He gave the officer a short, powerful rabbit punch to the side of the head. Captain Osborne slipped to his knees in the sand.

Isaac charged Stan, swinging a wild right. Stan dodged back, and delivered two solid jabs to Labrosa's face. Isaac's eyes widened, surprised at the power of the blows.

"Hold it!" Jed Walker shouted, shouldering his way into the ring followed by Ric. Labrosa feared and hated the dog. "Isaac, you should be horse-whipped. We'll have a fair fight or no fight." Ric growled at his master's side.

"Let 'em fight!" shouted several men. Stan helped the Captain to his feet, and Pepe and Diamond led the dazed officer back to the edge of the ring.

"This has gone far enough," Sir Warren said. He had followed Walker into the ring. The crowd chanted, "Fight! Fight!"

"I'm ready, Jed," said Stan. "I can beat him." He wasn't going to stop now. He felt he could smash the slow-footed Labrosa.

"All right!" Jed said. "Isaac, you fight bare-knuckle or I'll have Ric tear your balls out."

"I'll smash that Eastern piss head anyway you want," Labrosa said. The two men again squared off.

The fight developed into wild charges by Labrosa and Stan's sharp counter jabs. He battered Isaac's face. Minutes passed and the crowd grew more restless. Stan now understood that this kind of fight would not satisfy these men.

He raised his hands and signaled Walker to stop the match.

Labrosa's face was a bloody mess.

"Are your knuckles sore?" Jed asked, with a smile.

"A bit," grinned Stan. "This is crazy." The crowed booed; several men yelled, "Let's have a man's fight."

"Isaac, let's call it a draw," said Stan. He walked toward his foe and extended his hand. He saw a strange savage look in Labrosa's eyes as they peered from his battered face.

Labrosa grabbed Stan's arm and yanked him forward, and he headbutted Stan viciously, under the chin.

Jagged points of light flashed and ran about in the depth of Stan's mind. He sank to his knees. Jed, Sir Warren, Cotton Crevier, and others struggled to subdue the blood-wild Labrosa.

Stan smelled something strange and biting; it cleared his mind. He got to his feet, helped by Diamond, Pepe, and Captain Osborne.

"Thanks," said Stan, shaking his head and rubbing his chin. He took a few deep breaths. Several men in the crowd shouted, "Let 'em fight." Stan knew he must go on, and he was eager get at Labrosa, to win, to bash the brute.

Captain Osborne moved into the center of the ring. "The fight is over," he shouted between cupped hands.

Many in the crowd booed and shouted, "Let 'em fight." Someone threw a torch into the ring.

"This ain't no Army post!" someone shouted. The men clapped and cheered.

"I'd kill the fancy puke in a man's fight," Isaac yelled. Labrosa was guarded by Ric.

Stan felt blood surging through his face, neck and arms. He wanted to smash Isaac's face, and he now understood, to the men, the only way to fight was all-out. A bare-knuckle match was a game for officers and gentlemen in silk shirts.

"Tell them to clear the ring," Stan said. He placed his hand on the Captain's arm. "I'll fight Labrosa's fight." The Captain turned to Stan with troubled eyes.

"No! Stan, no!" Sir Warren said, gripping Stan's arm.

"I've got to do this," said Stan. He shook off Sir Warren's hand. In the dim light, Sir Warren's eyes were pale and large. Stan slapped him hard on the shoulder and grinned.

"Boss, Boss, I can handle it. It won't take long," Stan said. "Just keep the ring clear."

Cotton and several of Jed's men helped clear the ring, and the Captain again moved to the center. At one side, Walker was controlling Labrosa with his dog. Stan and Sir Warren stood across the ring.

"Quiet!" shouted the Captain, "The fight will continue." The men shouted their approval. "It will be no holds barred." The crowd roared; torches danced up and down. "It will continue until one man is unconscious or signals he's given up."

In the flickering light, Stan could see an eager leer on Isaac's face. The man wanted to kill him. Stan was happy now that Dan had insisted he practice all one summer with Lieutenant Ito.

"Let the fight begin."

Labrosa charged across the ring. Stan side-stepped; he gave him a solid blow to the back of neck, using the edge of his hand. Cautiously, Isaac circled, searching for a way to get a grip on his tall, young opponent. The crowd soon grew restless.

Stan whirled on his left foot; his right foot crashed into Labrosa's left ear. The larger man went down on his right knee; his face livid, he sprang up, charging at Stan. Stan sidestepped the bull-like charge, and again the men circled, looking for an opportunity. Stan saw blood seeping from Isaac's ear.

The frustrated Labrosa stopped circling.

"Fight like a man, you bastard," he said, motioning with his hands for Stan to come to him. The crowd started to chant, "Fight! Fight!" The two men stood facing each other. Both men glistened with sweat.

This is the time. Do it.

Stan took one quick step forward and left the ground. Isaac, shocked, never started a move. The heal of Stan's right foot plowed into his nose and jaw. Stan felt bones collapse in. The vicious blow flung the large man back, he landed on his head and shoulders with a resounding thud. Blood spewed from his unconscious, battered face. Stan was astonished by the effect of the kick-maneuver; until then he had only practiced on Ito's dummy.

The crowd went deadly silent. Stan could hear a nearby torch crackling. No one moved. A man in the rear shouted, "What's happened?"

"The kid just flattened the big trapper fella," came the answer. There was a smell of burning oil and sweat in the still night air.

Diamond stepped forward and placed one of Sir Warren's robes around Stan. The shocked crowd parted, as Captain Osborne led Sir Warren's group back toward their quarters. Not a word was spoken, his own friends dismayed by the fights sudden and violent end. All Stan could hear was his own heavy breathing and the crunch of the sand. He hoped he hadn't killed Isaac. He knew Lynn wouldn't have liked this night. He recalled that she had been upset when he told her he had studied the martial arts. If they were going to be doctors they were supposed to save life not destroy it.

Later, Pepe came as Stan lay in his bunk and told him that Jed's men had carried Isaac to the well, where Jed and Cotton had treated him. He would soon recover. Only his nose was broken. Pepe also reported that Sir Warren and Captain Osborne had been invited to William Bent's, with Jed, for a victory drink. Stan smiled when Pepe gripped his shoulder and laughed. Dan would have been proud.

The two large male elk were equals; both weighed close to eight hundred pounds. They had engaged in a mild territorial competition, not the violent attacks of the rutting season. However, their horns became locked. The two had their rumps up in the air to the full length of their hind legs The elks were on their front knees and unable to move their heads. Both animals' bloodshot eyes dilated with fright and struggled to look toward a large grove of quaking aspen. Both animals smelled the approach of a mountain lion.

The old, tawny cat moved out of the aspen through the dry grass of the meadow. The animal stayed low; it seldom hunted in daylight. But the lion was hungry, and it was lame. It had lost speed, and it could no longer run down healthy deer or elk. The two hundred pound beast fed on squirrels and raccoons. It crept down from its lair and into the deep grass of the meadow, pulled by the compelling smell of an elk feast.

Stan enjoyed the cool breeze in his face; he followed Sir Warren down through the fur and scrub oak of the mountain side. It had been a long but pleasant day. The two men were elk hunting, and Stan led a pack animal with the prime cuts of the cow elk Sir Warren had shot three hours before. In an hour, they would be back on the Purgatoire River, and Stan knew Diamond and Pepe would be pleased to replace the antelope steaks with elk for supper. A person chewed on antelope for a long time.

Jed Walker's men were trapping a stretch of the Purgatoire, just north of Fishers Peak. In two days, they would go over Raton Pass and head on south toward Santa Fe.

In the week since they left Bent's Fort, all of Jed Walker's men made an effort to meet and talk with Stan. Only Labrosa avoided him. Stan knew the man's pride hurt, and his face was a mess.

Stan and Sir Warren entered a large grove of aspen; leaves flicked silver in the afternoon breeze. Many of the leaves already showed yellow. Fall and the return to medical school was approaching for Stan. Since resolving his problem with Isaac, Stan felt pleased with his decision to sign on with Sir Warren, but he still planned to return to school.

The aspens thinned ahead, and Stan saw ahead of Sir Warren the long, yellow-green grass of an alpine meadow. Sir Warren turned in his saddle, holding a finger to his lips. Stan sat for a long minute. He could not see what Sir Warren saw. The wind fluttered the leaves of the aspen. Sir Warren motioned him forward. He moved up beside the Baronet, and he felt Midnight tense. Sir Warren pointed to the right, and Stan saw, across the meadow, the rear legs and rumps of two elk.

"Looks like a horn lock," whispered Sir Warren. "I have seen it once before in the Black Forest. Let us tie the horses and have a look."

Stan and Sir Warren walked side by side out through the knee high grass. Each carried his rifle. Stan carried a T. Gibbon, 54-caliber percussion piece. His father had given him the rifle. He was good with it, but he was not a rifleman equal to his Scottish employer.

Stan watched the two elk. They had stood quietly, but now

struggled to free themselves. He heard the snorts of their helpless torment. He speculated on how they could free the animals.

Suddenly, from the corner of his eye, Stan saw movement in the grass to the right of Sir Warren. "Watch . . ."

The large cat left the grass and in two long-bounding leaps crashed into Sir Warren. Stan saw the lion's nose and mouth glistening red. The veteran hunter was able to get his rifle up to shield off the charge. Both Sir Warren and the gray snarling beast rolled into the grass. The Scottish baronet struggled to his knees, but the powerful predator was already on its hind legs. The animal's front claws extended, its lips rolled back over huge teeth. It was flying toward the Scot's neck. In a fraction of a second its jaws would deliver a death clasp.

But it was the last leap for the aging beast. The six inch blade of Stan's Swiss stiletto tore into the animal's chest. The razor sharp double edge, with its pronounced medium rib, ripped through the beast's flesh to the hilt.

The animal gave a muffled gasp and fell limp and helpless onto Sir Warren, sprawling him flat into the grass. For several seconds, all Stan saw was the large tawny body of the mountain cat.

"Are you all right?" Stan asked. He seized one of the cat's front legs and pulled the animal off Sir Warren. The bewildered Scot struggled to his hands and knees. He sat on the ground and studied the dead animal.

"Well. . .God in heaven above. . .I did not hear a shot. . . what has happened?"

Stan rolled the lion over, exposing its bloody chest and the polished bone handle of his throwing knife. There was a faint smell of blood-wet fur.

Sir Warren got to his feet, beating his hat on his leg to remove the dust.

"Walker and I thought that toad-stabber of yours was just to look at," Sir Warren said. "I believe. . . I owe you one, a big one, young man." Sir Warren walked to Stan and extended his hand. Stan gave a broad smile, and the men shook hands. He picked up his own pale gray bollinger, dusted it off and placed it on his head.

"I was lucky. I haven't practiced in a while," Stan said. "But,

Lieutenant Ito said I was one of the best he had seen with a six-inch blade. He's the one who told me to carry it horizontally on the back of my belt."

"I would like to meet the Lieutenant someday," said Sir Warren. He studied Stan for a long moment. "I only hope that someday Leon will become a man like you. . . 'few things are impossible to diligence and skill.'"

Over the past weeks, Stan learned that Sir Warren often quoted, Dr. Samuel Johnson, the source of his middle name.

"Now, let us see if we can free those elk. Then, if you do not mind, I want to skin the puma. I will take it to the halls of Murthly Castle, and I will tell everyone about the young Yank who once saved my life."

"Fine," Stan said, laughing. "I'll make sure it's all in the log."

The two men walked through the grass to the exhausted elk. The animals stood helpless, without motion. Only their yellowed eyes moved as Sir Warren got on hands and knees to study the lock.

"You could not get those horns locked like this," Sir Warren said, "if you had a month to try. Go bring the butcher's-saw."

The men sawed the horns in two places to free the elk. When freed, the large animals stood as if drugged before finally staggering off.

"They're a lot bigger than the cow you shot," Stan said. He watched the stunned males trot off into the aspen.

"True, but not as good on the table."

Stan leaned forward and rested on the neck of Midnight. He had bought the large horse from a friend of Captain Bonneville's in New York. The single-file caravan had halted. Stan dismounted to relieve himself. They must be up between seven and eight thousand feet. He was the last man of the groups led by Jed Walker, but ahead he could see only three pack animals and Pepe; the huge rocks of the pass prevented him from seeing further up the trail to the cause of the delay.

He walked up to Pepe. "What's going on?" Stan asked. From Pepe's position Stan saw Sir Warren and the last man of Walker's group.

"Don't know," Pepe said. They heard shouts from on up the trail. A billowy cloud covered the sun, and there was a chill in the mid-day air. Stan walked on up the trail, giving Diamond a rap on her boot as he passed. She gave him a wink; an unlit cheroot hung from her lips. When he reached Sir Warren, Walker's man, Boatswain Brown, turned back and yelled to them.

"Nick Ryan and his boys got a hundred mules ahead. They've been all day and night clearin' a rock slide. Just got her cleared out."

"Jed must have rubbed Buddha's belly," Sir Warren said. "I will dig out my brandy tonight. We all could have been moving rocks for the next week."

A mile up the trail, near the summit, Stan passed through the newly cleared area. Looking up, he saw where a section of the precipice had crumbled and slid down, covering the trail. Sir Warren was right; they were lucky in a number of ways. If the boulders above let go, there would be no chance of escape for those below.

For three days the men continued to pick their way along the dry, rocky slopes of the Sangre de Cristo Mountains. Stan knew the name meant Blood of Christ, crossing the mountains must be some form of penitence. The country opened into high sloping plains as they rode southwest. Jed decided to follow the larger mule train; he figured they would have less trouble with the Mexican authorities in Santa Fe. But the travel was slow and there was no game.

"This is my last bottle of wine," Sir Warren said. He poured a glass for Jed and Stan.

"You timed it right," Jed said, "Ryan plans to enter Santa Fe at noon the day after tomorrow. Tomorrow night we'll be about five miles out of town."

"Why don't we just go right on in?" Stan asked.

"It gives the men a chance to clean up," said Jed, "and put on new clothes. Hell, Nick won't see those muleskinners for days once they get a belly full of wine and meet one of those brown chili peppers." Pepe served Stan and Sir Warren sizzling steaks and biscuits.

"Shit, Warren, where'd you get those steaks?" Walker asked. He and his men had eaten jerky.

"Pepe found some prime cuts this morning," Sir Warren said with a big grin. "Dig in Stan." Stan cut his portion, it smelled good.

"Not bad," Stan said. It was a bit tough, but the flavor was fine.

"Pepe, good job!" said Sir Warren, beaming. "Bring Jed a piece."

Pepe brought a steak for Walker.

"Tell Jed how you got the meat." Pepe had a broad grin on his craggy face.

"This morning, one of the mule-men can't get his mule to go," Pepe said, wiping his hands on his apron. "So I help him, but nothing work. Everyone else go; maybe half hour, now. So he unloads the mule. He puts the goods on his horse. Then he goes and shoots that mule right between the eyes. Bang! I've ate mule before; it's same. . . same as horse." Pepe stood back and squared his shoulders, and Walker chuckled.

"Pepe, it's real good," Stan said. "It sure beats the jerky we've been living on. You got anymore?"

"Sure, Master Stan."

An hour past sunrise, the party turned to the northwest and, after another hour, came to a halt on a stream that fed the Pecos River. Miles ahead in the foothills, Stan saw the outlines of the first low adobe buildings of Santa Fe. He washed and shaved at the creek. Pepe lent him a small brush and he brushed his gray hat and buckskin pants. He replaced his buckskin shirt with a red calico one and a pale doeskin vest. There was no reason to save his clothes any longer, he figured. After Diamond finished shaving Sir Warren, she trimmed Stan's hair. He preferred to keep his ponytail no more than four inches long. Sir Warren told him that with Pepe's tricorn hat, Stan reminded him of an early painting of the young surveyor, George Washington.

Jed kept his men a mile behind the mule-drivers. Stan heard shots from the men who anticipated the pleasures ahead. It had been ten weeks since Ryan's caravan rode out of Independence.

Two hours dragged by, and Walker's men sprawled in the dried grass waiting to advance. An early mist cleared, and Stan saw the dark, blue-green mountains to the north and east of the city. It reminded him of New England, and his thoughts turned to Lynn, Lynn Alice Monroe. Perhaps their plans had been too good to come true. Her father owned and captained a ship which brought hides from California to the Boston shoe market. Her mother was Spanish, and they lived in California. But her father had brought her east to be educated. Captain Monroe was still a Yankee at heart. Lynn would return to Columbia and study medicine with Stan. They would write each other and it would all work out. But somehow it. . .

"Well here comes our greaser escort," Walker said. He got to his feet. "Just smile and be friendly. This is Mexico, and these buggers want to make sure we know. They'll be real friendly while they figure out how much they can skin us for." Jed mounted and rode out to meet the Mexican authorities.

"They look official," Stan said. He and Sir Warren watched Jed converse with the four guards. Three wore blue military coats and shakos with brass plate and plume. They carried British Baker rifles with sword bayonets. The fourth wore a black coat with gold buttons and shoulder-boards and a tall black stove-pipe hat. He carried a long sword at his waist.

"I do not see how they can tax Jed," said Sir Warren, "until they see what he traps." They heard shouts and rifle shots as Ryan's men headed for town. The Mexican officials rode off and Walker returned.

"I meet with the Governor tomorrow at noon," said Jed, riding up to Sir Warren and Stan. "You'd better come, for you won't be leaving town with me. I've told my boys we're leaving in four days. Let's meet for dinner tonight and talk. The boys are champin' at the bit; meet me at eight at the La Fonda Inn." Jed rode off toward his mounted and eager men.

Stan brought up the rear. The group made its way single file along the dusty road snaking its way to the city. Stan passed low adobe houses with walled-off gardens and flat, grass-covered roofs. These became more numerous and soon the road became a street, walled on both sides. The street led to the main plaza. Narrow closed doors and windows were cut into the twelve-foot high walls. A few blanket-wrapped old men stood and sat along the dusty adobe walls; for them it was siesta. When they crossed San Francisco Street, Stan saw, to the north, the shady portals of the city's main cathedral. It reminded him of a church in his home of Morristown, New Jersey, where as a young boy he and Dan had attended a servicc for their father.

The plaza was a huge square with opposing groves of gnarled cottonwood trees in its two diagonal corners. Its size surprised Stan. It wasn't New York's City Hall area where shops now stretched down past St. Paul's to Trinity Church, but it was more than he'd expected. He thought for a moment of the Easter mass he and Lynn had attended at Trinity just this past March. It had been only days before she sailed home with her father. What had happened to her, and their plans?

Along each side of the plaza were crowded shops and offices. It seemed strange to Stan, the people, the noise, the smells. The novelty of it sent a tingle through him. The arrival of Ryan's caravan had caused a flurry of activity, like a stick in an anthill. The natives here were isolated by lack of proper roads and navigable rivers, and they hungered for Anglo supplies. The square was vibrant with noise- the tinkle and clang of bells, the braying of burros, the clatter of wagons. Ryan's men whooped their arrival, peddlers hawked goods, and traders argued.

On one side of the square was the Governor's headquarters. Here, from a high pole, flew the tricolor flag with its eagle and serpent. These mortal enemies made a strange pair, but perhaps it fit somehow, the eagle feeding on the serpent. After all, it was a culture of wealth and poverty.

At another side of the square, opposite the customhouse, Ryan's men unloaded their mules and led them out of town to pasture while Ryan haggled with customs officials.

"I've never seen a square this large," Stan said. He rode up to Sir Warren. An old Mexican pushed between them leading three burros loaded with pinon wood.

"This is a sight, all right," said Sir Warren, with a broad grin. Two lavishly dressed caballeros brushed past, riding well-curried mounts. "We had better find rooms. Then you and I will take a walk." Everywhere they looked vendors hawked their goods.

Two blocks off the plaza to the west they found the sprawling two-story La Fonda Hotel. The small lobby was quiet; an old man slept in a rocking chair. There was no one behind the desk. Stan found the room hot and stuffy. Sir Warren picked up a small bell and rang it. The old man in the chair never moved, but a short younger man emerged from behind a green curtain.

"Governor okay?" the man asked. He eyed Sir Warren and Stan and saw Diamond, Pepe and the horses through the open door.

"See manyana," said Sir Warren. "We need room for four. . . cuatro." He and Stan both held up four fingers. Stan would have brought Pepe in to interpret, but he knew Sir Warren prided himself on speaking several languages. Stan wasn't too sure about the Baronet's Spanish. The clerk pulled a book from under the desk, and studied it.

"No have; manyana, maybe," said the clerk. He shut the book.

Sir Warren was ready. He placed a silver half-dollar on the closed book.

The man picked it up and studied it. He put it in his mouth and bit on it with his eye teeth.

"Okay." The man broke into a big smile. He put the coin in his pocket, and he signaled them to follow him down a small alley to the rear of the hotel. There he showed Stan and Sir Warren a large, unfurnished second-story room, with a balcony and two windows; the windows were covered with sheets of mica. Stan was pleased for the room looked off toward the distant Rio Grande valley.

"We had better take this," said Sir Warren. "If we are here long, maybe we can find better." They unloaded, and Pepe and Stan led the animals to the Inn's stable and feed lot, a quarter mile to the west.

The plaza was a buzz of activity when Stan and Sir Warren returned. They brought Diamond and Pepe with them, for there were many foods on sale. Everywhere were displays, under the trees on coarse woolen carpets called jergaes or in the shade of the wide arcades that fronted the buildings of the square. There were loaves of bread, sacks of cornmeal and apples, corn, apricots, melons, grapes, peaches, tomatoes, and chilies. Butchers sold mutton hung from tree limbs, for small sheep grazed in large numbers on nearby plateaus.

Stan smiled to himself as he watched Diamond and Pepe haggle with a vendor over two live chickens. Pepe knew the language, but Diamond, standing tall and commanding, intimidated the old chicken vendor. Several other vendors found difficulty coping with Sir Warren's bargaining duo.

When the shopping was completed, Sir Warren took them into a small bakery where they had a fresh baked roll with honey. The delightful smell reminded Stan of his Aunt Sally's kitchen in Morristown. Finally, with Stan and Sir Warren helping, they carried the supplies to their quarters.

"You two fix what you want for dinner," Sir Warren said. "Stan and I will be eating at the hotel later with Master Jed." Stan knew that Diamond and Pepe normally ate what they wanted, but it was nice of Sir Warren to let them know it was all right.

"Master Stan, you watch those little bean-bunnies," said Pepe, with a broad smile. "They have a way of gettin' a young fellow's pecker stiff."

"Maybe you should come with us," said Stan.

"No. . . I don't steam up," Pepe said, "like in the old girling days. Once you get hair in your ears, it don't come up every time you see that wee mound of hair."

Stan and Sir Warren watched Nick Ryan and four of his men market their wares. Stan had met the small pleasant business man twice during the past weeks. He was a leather merchant from St. Louis, but, he found, there was much faster and bigger money in bringing goods to Santa Fe. This was his third trip with a mule train.

"I thought you boys," Ryan said, walking up to Stan and Sir Warren, "would be on your second jug. I'm sure my skinners are feelin' loose by now."

"We found a room and picked up supplies," Sir Warren said. "We are going to have dinner with Walker. Want to join us?"

"Thanks," Ryan said, "but my regulars and I eat and sleep right here the first four or five days. After we sell out, we take several days before we head back. I like this town, just don't cross the

Governor's boys or the padres." One of his men called, and Ryan returned to his goods.

Stan and Sir Warren stood for a time and watched Ryan and his men sell bolts of calico cloth, felt hats, and spices. Stan saw barrels of tacks, brass nails, and knives. There were rifles, buttons, needles, spoons and scissors. In several places there were lines of waiting Mexicans.

Stan and Sir Warren continued their stroll around the plaza. On the side near the Governor's quarters ran a two-foot wide open ditch. It provided the town its only water for drinking and washing. It was slow moving and had a slight swampy smell.

Under the cottonwood trees Stan watched four small boys play pitarrilla, a type of checkers. As boys he and Dan had play checkers during the long New Jersey winters. An old man leading a white burro and ringing a bell came to Stan's side. He removed his sombrero with a flare. Smiling, he handed Stan a large white placard. It read "Hot mineral spring bath." Stan walked to Sir Warren, who was studying one of the four cannons mounted in each corner of the plaza.

"How about a bath?" he asked Sir Warren, handing him the placard. A bath sounded good to Stan.

"Good idea," Sir Warren said. Sir Warren tried to determine the cost of the bath and distance to the spring. It seemed hopeless. "I believe it is a half mile," said Sir Warren. "Let's go." It was two miles into the mountains, but, a block off the square, the man provided a small, horse-driven carriage.

On three sides, vine-covered walls protected the steaming, rocky pool. In back, on the mountain side, was a solid rock wall. Stan and Sir Warren followed the man into a low whitewashed room where four older women directed them to strip off their clothes. Stan left his shorts on and felt embarrassed when one of the women came and pulled them off. His body looked bone-white in the pale light of the room. All the while the women talked among themselves and giggled.

"They want us to wash," Sir Warren said, "before we get in the spring." The women dumped two buckets of hot water over each man and scrubbed them down with a rag and a rough bar of soap.

Stan, nude and uncomfortable, wanted to do the soaping, but one of the toothless women insisted on washing him. One sang, and she gave Stan a big smile when he stopped her from a too vigorous scrubbing of his loins.

Stan was relieved when the ordeal ended. He squatted so his bathers could rinse him with two buckets of water. The women were still rinsing Sir Warren when Stan entered the hot spring area. It was a beautiful, eighty-foot wide pool with clear, green steaming water. Across the pool, through the steam, Stan believed there were five or six other bathers.

Stan, nude, was anxious to get into the water, but the water was stinging hot. Sir Warren arrived, and it took them ten minutes to get in to their necks. Stan was never in water this hot. At first it was a torture, but, then gradually, it melted into a mellow intoxication. He never felt like this before, drifting free in space and time. He and Sir Warren basked in the unaccustomed pleasure for an hour.

With a slow breast stroke, a man from across the spring swam, through the steam, toward them. Stan saw it was Jed Walker's guide Touisaint de Talon. He was the only man in Walker's group Jed relied on for travel directions. Touisaint was a private man. He was a stocky, gray-haired native of Montreal.

"Ah, yes," de Talon said, "I told my niece I thought it was the young man who fights with his feet and the Scottish hunter." Stan talked with the Frenchman three days after his fight with Labrosa. It was obvious Touisaint, like most of Walker's men, disliked Isaac.

"We're enjoying this," Stan said. "How did you find it?"

"It is owned by the Spanish family my niece works for. I have her bring me here when I come to town. It's a good place to get rid of the nits; you just hold your breath and go under and those little bastards are gone in no time."

"Uncle. Uncle. It is time," called a woman.

"Well, you boys enjoy, Evita has to leave," said Touisaint. He swam back toward his niece. Soon, Stan watched, through the steam, Evita leave the mineral bath. The woman was tall and beautiful. He and Sir Warren watched her every graceful move as she walked nude and disappeared into the rinse room.

"Oh, dear God," sighed Sir Warren. "There, young man, was a

near perfect woman. What breasts, and those buttocks."

"I agree," Stan said. He was feeling a bit light-headed. "I think I'll get out a while." The late sun was turning the cliff above the pool a soft orange. When he got out, his legs felt like two soft wax candles.

"Talk about relaxed," he said, sitting on a large rock. "I'm as limp as a dead snake."

Touisaint, dressed, returned and handed a note to Stan. Sir Warren crawled out of the pool. His body, like Stan's, was bright pink from the neck down.

"Here is Evita's address. She runs a hotel for officers and rich caballeros. A place for girling," Touisaint said, with a sly smile. "She wants you to know she has nice, clean girls. She does too, but they're too expensive for me. But take a look. Have a drink. Not many gringos get invited to Los Jubilo."

Stan never felt more mellow, but weak. He and Sir Warren snoozed on a large flat rock for an hour. They watched the light fade from the sky. Stan thought of Lynn, she was not as tall as Evita, but he was sure she was as beautiful.

"Old Touisaint has me curious," Stan said. He was unable to read the address in the dim light.

"Yes, indeed," Sir Warren said. He smiled and looked up at the first stars. "'Curiosity is one of the permanent and certain characteristics of a vigorous mind.' I too am curious, and I might add, a bit anxious."

Stan awoke and forced open his eyes, the left one seemed glued shut. His head split and his mouth felt fuzzy. He could see Walker nudging Sir Warren's leg with the toe of his boot. It was full daylight.

"We meet with the Governor in an hour," Jed said. "I figured you'd need coffee."

"I thought it was this afternoon," said Sir Warren. He sat up and put his head between his legs. Stan pulled himself up and leaned back against the wall. He watched Walker light a cigarette.

"We meet at noon, and it's damn near eleven," said Walker. He left the room. Jed Walker was a man who drank more than his share, but never seemed drunk. Stan smiled. It even hurt to smile. He looked at Sir Warren, who had fallen back asleep with his head between his legs. Stan had enjoyed the dinner and the wine, but it was the two decanters of tequila that sent he and his friends staggering home at two AM. He recalled most of their discussion was about the Buenaventura River. Did the river exist? If so, where was it? Walker insisted there had to be a major river that flowed west into the Pacific.

Stan got up and went slowly down the steps. His stomach was a bit queasy, and his head felt like a block of oak. Diamond brewed coffee at a small fire; Walker stood by waiting with two cups.

"Better have a shot of Diamond's mud," Jed said, filling the two cups and going back up to the room.

Stan rinsed his face in a basin of water Diamond had for him. He sat on the steps with his face in the towel. "Why did I do that?" he said; his body ached. Pepe brought him a plate with corn bread and a sliced apple.

"You'd better eat, Master Stan," said Pepe. He handed Stan a cup of black coffee.

"Thanks," said Stan. He was beginning to feel almost alive.

General Ciro Mier Biscusa came out from behind the Governor's desk and shook hands with his three visitors. He was not the swarthy, squat person Stan had visualized. He was tall and thin, a third generation Spaniard, proud of his family's bloodlines. His hand was firm, and his eyes were dark and piercing.

"Governor Armijo has been called to Mexico City. Until he returns I am acting Governor," said the General, returning to his seat behind the desk. He spoke slow and deliberate English. With his hand, he directed the men to the chairs arranged in front of his desk.

Stan listened while the General and Jed discussed the rendezvous and the trip south. Two bored military officers stood behind the General with the tri-colored flag between them. The room was large and whitewashed; several clerks worked in the far right corner.

One of the officers whispered into the General's ear.

"I have been reminded of another appointment," said the General. He moved closer to his desk. "Mr. Walker, before you leave Santa Fe for your trapping, you will deposit a note for five hundred American dollars, or equivalent goods with Colonel Ramirez in the Customhouse. The fee will be adjusted when you return with your pelts." The General then turned toward Sir Warren.

"I am told, Mr. Kent, you are from Scotland," he said. The General had a high forehead, and he reminded Stan of his algebra teacher at Dartmouth. He leaned forward and peered at Sir Warren.

"Yes, this is my first visit to Santa Fe. I wanted to see the city before I returned home. I travel with my clerk, Mr. Aldridge," Sir Warren nodded toward Stan, "and two others. We plan to return to

St. Louis after a brief visit."

The General studied Sir Warren and Stan, smoothing his long sideburns with his fingers. Stan was sure the General did not believe anyone would visit Santa Fe for pleasure. There had to be another reason.

"You," said the General standing, "will also leave a note for five hundred dollars with Colonel Ramirez and inform him three days before you depart from the city." The General came around the desk and shook hands.

The three friends walked out into the busy plaza. Stan sensed the disgust both his friends had for the arrangement.

"That is the first time I recall shaking hands with the thief who picked my pocket," Sir Warren said.

"Smile," said Jed, "until we sign a note for the Colonel. But I tell you boys. It's goin' to be a double pleasure to cheat the cheaters. A note ain't but a piece of paper."

"Amen. Let us get on with it," Sir Warren said, "and then find a pot of coffee. I think our strength is with time and patience. Anyway, I have a proposition for you, Walker."

"Ah, shit. I swear I've heard this tune before."

"While you're with the Colonel," Stan said, "I'm going to try to run down the army scout who was with my brother."

"Meet us back at the room before dinner," Sir Warren said. "I have got a proposition for you, too. We can discuss it at dinner."

Stan made his way across the plaza. He passed three Indians from the Rio Grande Valley. Their headbands supported large shoulder bags filled with dried, cracked corn. Stan wanted to talk to Nick Ryan. The merchant may have heard of Iron Paso. In the letter Paso had written Stan's mother, the scout said he was working the trails out of Santa Fe.

A crowd of men and women picked their way through the area where Ryan and his crew sold their goods. Stan stood and watched Ryan open a cloth-wrapped bundle; it contained ladies' white cotton hose. Two local women exclaimed over the material. Ryan turned to Stan.

"Give me a minute," Ryan said. He picked out two pairs of the hose and walked to two mounted Mexican soldier-guards. He handed each man a pair of the hose, chatted a while and returned to Stan.

"To stay in the plaza over night," Ryan said, "I'm required to hire men from the Governor's guard. It's a new one they've come up with since last year. I reckon this is my last run out here. I just hope I get out of town with money in my wallet."

"Looks like you're doing okay," Stan said.

"Two more days, and I buy a jug and get drunk. Gettin' here is one thing, the trick is gettin' out of town with a profit. . . how are you and the Scot doin'?"

"No complaints; I wanted to see the West. Sir Warren is a good boss, and Walker is a great guide. Did Sir Warren talk to you about us going back to St. Louis?"

"No," said Ryan. "Jed told me, back on the trail, the Duke would come back with me, but he's never mentioned it."

"He probably will," said Stan, "I think we'll be ready to go when you are. I'll ask him about it tonight, but what I'm interested in is if you know a scout by the name of Iron Paso?"

"Hell," Ryan said, with a big grin, "all of us who work the trails know Paso. He's the best scout goin' east or west."

"Where can I find him?"

"Last I heard he was in California, but ask at the Chapel of San Miguel. I think he has a sister who's a nun there."

Stan entered the small Chapel. It was dim and cool. An old woman in black sat near the front. With his hat in his hand, Stan walked down the idle rows of plain worn benches. He took a seat across from and behind the woman. She murmured a prayer in Latin. To the right of the plain altar, a door led to the rear. After a brief pause, Stan went to the door and rapped. Several minutes passed; Stan made a third effort. The door cracked opened and revealed a large bald man in a brown robe.

"What do you want, son?" he asked in Spanish.

"I'm sorry, but I don't speak Spanish," Stan said. "I'm trying to locate a man named Iron Paso. I was told his sister is a nun here at the Chapel."

The padre studied Stan for a long time.

"Why do you wish to see Senor Paso?" asked the father in English.

"He was the last man to see my brother alive."

"Come back in the morning when Sister Alita is available." Stan heard a voice from behind the padre, and the father turned to talk to someone in the room. The door eased open and revealed a short man with long gray hair held by a black head-band. He was dressed in well-worn buckskins.

"I'm Iron Paso," he said. Stan swallowed and he could feel his eyes water.

"My brother was Captain Dan Aldridge," said Stan. "I'm Stan Aldridge." Stan extended his hand and shook the small, firm hand of the scout. Iron introduced the padre. The two men were having coffee at a small table, and the padre pulled up a third chair.

"The Captain talked about you," Iron said. He looked at Stan through dark but friendly eyes. "We spent several good years together on the trail. I can still see him, that last day, smiling, then gulping down that sorry mule's blood." The scout looked at Stan and smiled. He had a strange smile. His mouth turned down. Stan could feel that Paso was the kind of man Dan would have liked and trusted.

"The Captain rode off on his horse, Valor, to find water. That night Sergeant Stockholm died and I buried him. Then me and that old mule followed the Captain. The mule died during the morning, but I made Middle Springs that night. I could tell the Captain had made the Spring and collected water. The Comanches got him on the way back to me and the Sarge."

"Sister Alita," said the padre, "didn't even recognize Raul, we don't call him Iron, when he got to the mission." The father got up and went into a back room for more coffee.

"I guess," Stan said, wetting his lips, "you never found his body."

"No," Paso said, "even if I had a squad, it would be nigh impossible out there on the Cutoff." The padre returned with coffee.

"There were eight of us when we left here for St. Louis," Paso said. "I was the only one to get back"

"What brings you to Santa Fe?" asked the priest.

"Dan had written about it, and I had a chance to come."

"Do you live in Santa Fe?" Stan asked, looking at Iron.

"Yes, but I was just talking to Father Joe about California. I've been offered a job to manage a ranch for a mission out there. Out on the trail my bones are starting to ache. My next trip west will be my last."

Stan lay on the park bench a long while watching the doves fluttering in the branches above. After Father Joe had left he and Paso alone, he had ask the scout to tell him all he could remember about Dan's last days. With Stan's questioning the sad events had unfolded. The session with the scout was difficult, but Stan felt more accepting of what life handed each person. He believed that Dan would want him to go on with his own lives journey, carefully making the most of each precious day.

Pepe told Stan he was to meet Sir Warren and Walker at the La Fonda Inn saloon. One huge room served as dining room, bar, and casino. It was still daylight when Stan entered. His eyes adjusted to the yellow haze of the smoke-filled room. It was early, and there were a few empty tables in the dining area at the left rear of the room. Above the din of the gamblers and drinkers, Stan heard a sharp whistle. It was Walker's. Stan saw Sir Warren waving for him from a table in the left corner. Against the wall behind their table were rows of wine barrels, stacked five high.

"Did you find the army scout?" Sir Warren asked. Walker slid out a chair for Stan with his foot.

"Yes," Stan said. "I was lucky. He had just returned from California."

"Ah, shit," Walker said, "we've just had a long discussion about that piece of land."

"I told Jed about Leon," Sir Warren said. His words were a bit slurred.

"Warren thinks," Walker said, grinning at Stan, "cause I know the Rockies, I can take him to California. . . it don't work that-a-way."

"Stan, order another drink," Sir Warren said. He got to his feet.

"When I get back we'll convince this goat to take us on west." Stan and Walker smiled. They watched Sir Warren pick his way through the crowded gaming tables and out the door.

"So you've heard about the brother?" Stan asked. He signaled a barmaid.

"Oh yeah, it's funny how things change. Sometimes I think you could sell the State of Pennsylvania to Warren." A young woman came with the drinks. She stayed a moment working her hand over the back of Stan's neck and ears. Her low cut dress was near his face.

"Somethin' tells me she likes you," said Walker, with a grin.

"What did you mean 'how things change'?" Stan asked. He felt his face flush a bit. He ignored the girl and she left.

"I've heard about brother Leon off and on during the past year," said Walker. He reached down and scratched his dog's head. "And it ain't been good. He's been kicked out of three or four schools, stole from his daddy, beat up his mother, and he's been in and out of jail. Leon is a real gem. So now Warren's all worked up to rescue him from this Russian whaler. He thinks the kid will straighten out after all this. Shit. Warren ought to go back to St. Louis with Ryan and forget the bum."

"I wonder what Leon has done with all his money?" Stan asked, holding his glass of claret half way to his mouth. Leon was not the brother he had visualized for Sir Warren.

"I think that's what bothers Warren most," said Jed. "Over there, all the family money goes to the eldest son. When Warren's old man died five years ago, Warren was given control of the fortune. The mother wanted Leon to complete his schooling before he got any family money. That never happened. The kid gets a generous allowance but continues to screw up. Warren feels he should've helped his parents more when Leon was a pup. Warren was already in military school when Leon was born. The kid has been a problem all along. I don't figure it will change just cause he's in the hands of a wild Russian."

An older man with a matching red vest and sombrero started to play fiddle at the end of the large mahogany bar near the dining area. The music blended into the din of the saloon. Stan watched Sir

Warren pick his way through the gambling area. It was dark outside, and there was not an empty table in the room. The room was well-lit by massive dusty chandeliers.

"We'd better get some food," Walker said, as Sir Warren took his seat.

"There's a barmaid out there," Sir Warren said, leaning toward Walker, "whose bed I'd like to park my shoes under." Stan chuckled. His boss never hid his need for women.

"Warren," Jed said, thumping his glass hard on the table, "let's get something to eat before your balls get roarin' out of control."

At the recommendation of the waitress, the three men ordered lamb chops, corn bread and red beans.

"I'm trying to talk Jed," Sir Warren said, turning to Stan, "into taking me to California, and I want you to come with us." While talking with Walker, Stan had anticipated the offer. He was thrilled by the chance to go west to the Pacific. He might even be able to track down Lynn, maybe it wasn't over.

"Warren," said Walker, leaning into Sir Warren's face, "Stan has to complete his schooling, and I have an obligation to Sublette and Campbell, and to the men. Shit. We can't just take off after every wild goose, even if I knew the route. Anyway, finding a Russian scow off California is a hundred to one. Shit, a thousand to one."

"If you knew Leon, you'd go," said Sir Warren, with a sigh. "He can be a real likable person." The waitress brought a decanter of wine and filled their glasses. "He's my only brother. I have to do this. I know Stan understands."

Stan watched Sir Warren and Walker study their wine glasses. He felt sorry for Sir Warren, maybe Jed was wrong. Both men looked older in the smoky yellow light. The lamb chops came on hot pewter plates.

"I could talk to Iron Paso," Stan said. "He rode with my brother. Mike Ryan said he's a good scout going east or west." Sir Warren put down his knife and fork and pulled up to the table.

"Damn, Jed, there is the man for us," Sir Warren said.

"Okay. He might be a good man," Walker said, "but the Company sent me and seven trappers down here to get beaver pelts.

It's our business, our livelihood, just like last season up in the Yellowstone. I can't spend months goin' to California, and next summer come to Sublette and Campbell with nothin' in the bag."

The three ate their meals in silence. The old man with the fiddle wandered through the area. He stopped at their table and sang a soft Spanish ballad. As he sang, Stan considered what Sir Warren had offered. A chance to cross the country and see the Pacific. It had been a dream of his boyhood, while reading about Lewis and Clark. But also, just maybe, he could see Lynn Monroe again. . . her father was a ship's captain with a business in California. Stan had never met a person from California before Lynn. Was it possible they might meet again? Would they feel the same? He was eager to go and help Sir Warren. Then he'd return to Columbia and finish his education. If he found Lynn, perhaps she would return with him? Or, had it been just words and dreams alone? Either way, he could be heading for California.

Sir Warren gave the singer a coin and talked into his ear. With a broad smile the fiddler stepped back and started a lively tune; his feet tapped and his bow arm flew. It was like the last time Stan had seen Lynn; they'd met at a noisy pub near the Columbia campus. A drunken medical student fiddled while other students sang crazy limericks. She had been a friend of a former Dartmouth colleague. He and Lynn left the pub early and walked for hours along the Hudson River. It was a magic night. He held her hand, and they kissed. But, mainly they talked about their future studies and becoming medical doctors, of working together and sharing a life, but she never had answered his letters. What had happened?

The fiddler completed his tune and moved on.

"What did you net last year on the Yellowstone?" Sir Warren asked. He slammed his hand on the table near Walker.

"About two thousand, I reckon. That's what made it to the bank in St. Louis."

"And," Sir Warren asked, "what does the average trapper have at the start of the rendezvous?"

"There's a big range there, but somewhere between two and five hundred."

"Listen up, you Missouri mule," Sir Warren said, rubbing his hands together. "At next year's rendezvous I'll make up the difference between your net and two thousand dollars. Stan will write it up. And, for each trapper who comes, I'll make the difference up to three hundred dollars. I'll give them each a note too."

Stan smiled. He liked these two very different men. Both Walker and Sir Warren sat back with folded arms and studied each other. A slight smile crossed Walker's face and he shook his head.

"All right," Jed said. "If we can get an experienced guide, I'll talk to the men."

Sir Warren leaped to his feet and pumped Walker's hand.

"'It is better to live rich, than to die rich,'" he quoted.

He then turned to Stan and held out his hand.

"You are coming?" he asked.

"You bet," said Stan, reaching out and shaking Sir Warren's hand. Sir Warren slapped him hard on the shoulder.

Sir Warren ordered more wine, and he put his hands on Stan's and Walker's arms.

"Thanks fellows," he said. "We'll make it to California and find the *Helenka* and Leon. I can feel it."

The three sat quietly; when they finished their wine, Sir Warren turned to Stan.

"Do you have the woman's address de Talon gave you?"

Stan and Sir Warren followed a wizened man, provided by the La Fonda bartender, down a labyrinth of narrow walled streets. The shadowed streets were empty, lit by a pale moon.

"How are we going to find our way back?" Stan asked, with a chuckle.

"I wish Jed had come," Sir Warren said. "He has a great sense of direction. I just hope this little fart knows where Los Jubilo is."

Finally the man stopped by the only doorway in a long stretch of high adobe wall. He placed his hand on the heavy wooden door, and he shook his head up and down.

"Not what I expected," said Sir Warren. He gave the man a coin, but he asked him to wait as he rapped hard on the door. Stan watched from the moonlit street. It was dark near the door. Sir Warren rapped several times before a small section of the door opened and he conversed at length in Spanish. Sir Warren dismissed the old man, who tipped his hat and disappeared into the black of the street. The door opened slowly.

"Come on," whispered Sir Warren. "I did not think we were going to get in. This fellow had to check with Evita."

"Good Lord," whispered Stan, as he passed through the doorway. Large hanging trees lined a torch-lit brick walkway up a slight rise to a massive adobe mansion. The two followed their guide across a large semicircular marble entrance through open doors into a spacious living room. As they passed through the room, to the right Stan heard music and saw people in a dusky barroom. They followed the stocky man down a dim hallway, and they were ushered into a small sitting room. The guide waved them into two over-stuffed chairs. The furniture was heavy and exquisite. Several rose-colored wall lamps lit the room.

"This is some place," Stan said. The heavy tapestry on the walls depicted nude women flying about on angels' wings.

"I've seen my share of fancy bordellos, and this looks like a winner. . . but the true test is with the flesh," Sir Warren said. He studied the figures and rubbed his hands together. An old man in flared pants and a short, braided jacket brought a tray with a decanter of wine and several glasses. Stan poured two glasses of the red wine, and studied the frozen smile on Sir Warren's face. A warm glow flowed through his body.

"I'm glad you came," Evita said. "I enjoy talking to people from out of town. However, I regret tonight I cannot take you to our ballroom." She leaned forward and lowered her voice. Stan could see, above her white blouse, the white swell of her bosom. "We have older members here tonight. They do not believe we should entertain gringos. But, the owners have let me handle these matters." Evita had shaken hands and taken a seat. Her back was straight and her legs, with white silk stockings, were crossed. She wore a white skirt embroidered with red and yellow flowers, trimmed with lace.

"On these occasions," she said with a beautiful smile, "I do not believe 'the wolf shall dwell with the lamb.'"

"Are we the wolves or the lambs?" Sir Warren asked.

"Ah, does it matter?" Evita adjusted her red and black mantilla, and she turned toward Sir Warren. "I must leave soon, so I will get right to the point. Assuming you're here for pleasure, Mr. Kent, do you have any particular type of partner in mind?"

"You assume correctly, and I assume you are not. . . available?"

"Correct," Evita said, "but thank you. We have younger and more beautiful women."

"Well then," Sir Warren said, holding his open hands in front of his chest, "perhaps someone. . . full-bodied."

Evita picked up a small bell and rang it. The old man appeared and she talked to him at length. Stan couldn't keep his eyes off her, and he was secretly pleased she hadn't gone with Sir Warren. She seemed to fair too be Spanish.

"Mr. Kent, please come with me," said Evita. She stood and turned to Stan. "Mr. Aldridge, I will be back soon. If you need for anything, ring the bell and ask Berto."

"If I don't see you," said Sir Warren, grinning at Stan, "come for me at noon tomorrow. We have lots to do. I will ask Evita to take care of you."

Stan leaned back and closed his eyes. He heard music coming from the ballroom. The lamb chops at dinner were tender and tasty, and the wine was smooth and not too sweet. He squinted at the rose-colored lamps and felt a soft tingle in his lower body. He was almost asleep when Evita returned with a dish of melon dipped in orange liqueur. He sat up, and she took a seat opposite him and placed the fruit on a low table between them. They sampled the ripe melon.

"Do you know why I invited you here?" she asked. She filled two new wine glasses.

Stan studied her; she was radiant. She had full red lips and a slight roman nose. The question surprised him.

"No, not really."

"My uncle mentioned you were studying at Columbia."

"Oh?" Stan did recall discussing his education with Touisaint.

"I studied," she said, wetting her lips with the wine, "there a year before I came out here."

"How did that happen?"

"It was ten years ago," she said. A distant look came into her dark eyes. "My father was here to make his fortune in silver. He had a good start, and he wanted me to visit him. So I did. I was twenty, and, you know, the world was my oyster. I was here four months when my father was killed at the mine. . . I never returned to Columbia or the East."

"I'm sorry, but it's nice out here," Stan said. He looked into her eyes and they returned from the past and softened. He felt his body tingle under her intense gaze.

"Yes, in a way," she said, brushing her dark hair back from her forehead, "but it is no Boston or New York." Stan felt an uneasy need ripple through him; she studied him with her dark eyes.

"Do you ever fantasize?" she asked. Her eyes were deep and fiery.

Stan didn't understand. Perhaps it was the wine. He needed time to think. He reached for the decanter and poured more wine. She stroked his hand.

"I'm not sure. You mean. . . like day-dreams?"

"Well yes, but. . . women may do it more, I suppose. It's like thinking, what might have been had you done things differently. . . For example, say I hadn't come West." Evita moved to the edge of her chair and smiled into Stan's eyes. She must be playing a game.

"You may think I'm crazy," she said, "but out at the pool, when I saw you, and Uncle said you studied at Columbia. I thought, what if I'd stayed in the East. . . perhaps, I'd have met a man like you, and today be married, with two children, and living near Boston." She laughed softly, and Stan smiled.

"Who knows? He might have been a wife beater," Stan said.

"No, no. I said he'd be like you," she said. Her eyes were locked on Stan's.

Evita stood and edged around the table. She placed her hands on each side of Stan's face, and she kissed him hard on the lips. Her tongue pushed into his mouth, exploring. Her hands dropped to his shoulders and he stood. Stan bent down and kissed her again. He felt her body press firm against him. A need surged through him.

"Come," she whispered, "you're the man I might've met. For this night you are mine."

5

I have never seen a mule that size," Sir Warren said. "It's from California," Paso said. "To come out with a mule like Jimbo, you start with a big daddy. They have donkeys at the Mission San Gabriel bigger than Indian ponies."

Stan and Sir Warren had ridden five miles west into the great valley of the Rio Grande to find the few dusty acres owned by Iron Paso. The three men stood at the weathered slats of Paso's corral. Stan saw the afternoon sun on the San Dia mountains far to the east of the city. Two other mules and a large horse grazed in a pasture farther out from the corral.

"Come," said Paso, removing a battered hat and wiping his forehead with a blue handkerchief, "it is hot for an old man." He led the two visitors into his low adobe home. Sparse yellow grass grew on sections of the flat roof. Stan ducked through the doorway. It was cooler inside the one room home. It was a clean, pleasant room, with a pounded clay floor and rough whitewashed walls.

"Please have a seat," Paso said. He went to a small stove in the corner.

"Ah, the ashes are cold. I thought I might brew tea," said Paso, raising up his arms in apology.

"No, no," said Stan, "water is fine." He and Sir Warren sat at the small table. Except for a bunk bed in the far corner, the table and four chairs were the room's only furniture.

"Senor Aldridge," said Paso, setting three cups of water on the table and taking a seat, "you did not ride out here just to say hello to the old scout of your brother's."

"Please call me Stan. Dan was twelve years older then me, our dad was lost at sea when I was four. Our mother never remarried. As you might imagine, Dan was more like a father to me."

"Captain Aldridge was a fine officer," Paso said. "All the men liked him, that's unusual." Stan saw a sad look in his dark eyes. "That was my last trip for the Army; they never did pay me," he said. He shook his head with his strange smile. The three sat for a time. Except for clothes hung by the bed, the only wall decoration was a large ivory-colored crucifix; Stan saw an open Bible on the bed.

"Sir Warren would like you to guide a small group to California," Stan said.

"When?"

"Soon as possible."

"Oh no. . no. . . perhaps in six months or a year," said Paso, studying Sir Warren. "But, tell me, why does he call you 'Sir' Warren."

"I am the Lord of a Scottish castle," said Sir Warren, with a slight smile.

Iron Paso looked at Stan, then at Sir Warren. He looked at the table top, shaking his head up and down, his lips pressed firm. Then he looked back at Sir Warren.

"There were many wealthy Scottish folks in the Carolinas. Most didn't care much for Indians or Catholics." Stan saw for the first time a hardness creep in Paso's dark eyes.

"I believe you could say," Paso said, "my grandfather was a Lord. The land was the castle of our people long as anyone could remember. Long before the white men came. My father was a man of peace, and he made the change to the ways of the white men. . . he thought. He was a lawyer in Charleston until he was forced to move his family west. He moved, and he died there with a broken heart." Iron Paso put his hands on the table and studied them.

"I am sorry," Sir Warren said. He glanced at Stan and nodded his head toward the door.

"It is all right," Paso said. He looked up at Sir Warren and Stan. "My sister and Father Joe have helped me over the years to deal with my bitter thoughts. . . 'What persecutions I endured: but out of them all the Lord delivered me. Yea, and all that will live godly in Christ Jesus shall suffer persecution.'"

Sir Warren and Stan stood up, followed by Paso.

"I'm sorry for your family," Sir Warren said, extending his hand. Paso shook hands, but without a smile.

"Do you know," Stan asked, ducking through the doorway, "of any scout who can help us get to California?"

Iron Paso walked with the two toward their horses.

"The man who taught me the trail," said Iron, "still lives in town, I believe. He might be able; his name is Joe Payne. Ask at a place called Los Pato."

"Let's find Ryan's dance," Stan said. He was concerned his boss was about to get too drunk. They had found the Los Pato, but the fat barkeep had not seen Joe Payne in weeks. The man thought Payne was dead, for he had been sick and very weak.

"All right," Sir Warren said, "Mike might know of another scout."

Stan knew that Mike Ryan planned to head back to St. Louis in three days. Mike had rented the town's largest dance hall, invited everyone, and arranged for a keg and a fiddler. Stan wasn't sure what to expect, but it must be better than getting drunk at the smutty Los Pato.

"Let's stop by and find Jed," said Sir Warren. "Maybe he's in a better mood." Earlier in the day, Walker told Sir Warren that in two days he and his men would head for the Gila River. Still, Stan thought, if Sir Warren could locate a scout, Walker would go to California as agreed. The idea of a possible waterway west gnawed at Jed Walker.

Walker was not at his quarters or the La Fonda saloon, so the two men found the dance hall just off the swarm of the plaza. It was a huge adobe structure, but the main room had a wooden floor and a beam ceiling. Two high, smooth wooden benches lined the white painted walls. A large crowd of men, more than Stan had expected, milled around the main entrance. They filled the street and a small bar across the street.

"Ryan must be inside," Sir Warren said. They pushed their way through the crowd. The size of the candlelit room surprised Stan. Women in their colorful clothes jammed the benches along the walls. The fiddler played, but no one danced. Stan smiled. It seems dances start slow everywhere. He saw the keg located in a corner near the fiddler. Nearby stood Ryan and his men.

"Enjoy the lull, boys," Ryan said. He handed both Stan and Sir Warren a cup of white whiskey. "It was like this last year, but once it gets going, watch out. Many of the locals say they won't attend a gringo's baile, but once the dancing starts they all show up. These folks love to dance."

Stan sipped his whiskey and looked at the rows of resplendent women, young and old. Each woman wore her best, and many seemed attractive in the uncertain light of the candles.

"Find one who locks the dark eye on you," Ryan said. "Then be sure she's not with an old woman. Those kind dance and go home to mama."

"Mike," Sir Warren said, "before you dance off, Walker and I need someone who knows the trail to California. There has to be someone in this town for the job besides Iron Paso."

"Far as I know," Ryan said, "there is only one or two packers who've gone each year to California from here, and I know Paso has gone the last two years. I'm sure there are horse thieves in town who know the trail. Half of the horses and mules here, I'll wager, have been stolen from out there. I don't know anyone. . . might try up at Taos."

One of Ryan's men selected a young woman and stumbled around the dance floor. Two more of his men whooped it up Indian style. Several Mexican men, in their best flared pants and short jackets filtered into the hall.

"Truth is," Ryan said, shouting above the noise, "I don't know much about west of here." More people were dancing. Ryan gave Sir Warren and Stan a nod and turned back to the keg where a large crowd had gathered.

Sir Warren took Stan's cup and headed to the keg for a refill.

The white whiskey slipped down easily. Stan moved off a distance and watched the mass of dancers. He saw Ryan's and Walker's men mix into the group. Most of these men danced with heavy feet, their nimble partners avoiding the heavy boots. Stan knew at a baile no introductions are necessary. Each man was eager to find a partner among the rows of tittering, preening and restless girls.

John Relle, one of Walker's men who came from the Bonneville crew, was an excellent dancer. He and his red and white skirted partner put on a whirling show, as did several of the indigenous couples. Stan always admired men who danced well. He recalled his Dartmouth song leader; the fellow had told Stan that he was nearly tone deaf.

"I'm going to drift about," Sir Warren said, handing Stan a drink, "and look for the dark eye." He tipped his hat and moved off. Stan might not see his boss until morning.

There was one young woman who caught and held Stan's eye each time she whirled by in the arms of her military partner. She was dressed all in white with a fine gold trim on her blouse and skirt. She was slender and taller than most of the others. She was gorgeous. It was a game they played as she danced by smiling. Her white shoes and stockings moved light and skillful over the waxed floor.

Stan found her location, and he went to refill his cup with the smooth white whiskey. This better be his last, the hall was becoming fuzzy in the smoke and flickering candle light.

Stan saw the woman surrounded by military officers. In her group there were a handful of other young women, and three older women in voluminous black shawls. All three older women nursed tiny yellow cigarettes between withered lips, as they kept a skeptical eye on the dancers. Stan stood nearby and sipped his drink.

A scuffle started across the dance floor. One of Ryan's men, a large man who worked with Ryan in the plaza, pushed a greaser to the floor. Several Mexicans surrounded him. Ryan and three of his men stepped in and resolved the issue. However, Stan sensed the thread of tension between Anglo and greaser increasing in the hall.

Sir Warren danced by gracefully. He gazed into his partner's eyes.

The girl of Stan's eye whirled by. She smiled at him, her eyes flashing. One finger of her free hand signaled him to come. She had a red paper rose behind her right ear stuck in her heavy black hair.

A second fight broke out near the keg; Stan did not see what happened, but he did see two of the officers who danced with the girl ready their knives. The music played on. The dancers continued.

"Get going," Sir Warren said. He danced by Stan, with his girl held close.

Stan decided to get another drink. He turned and almost ran over the girl.

"Do you speak Spanish, sir?" she asked him. She was beautiful. Her eyes and teeth shining with excitement.

"No, I'm sorry."

"It is all right, but hurry. Dance with me."

He held out his arms and she waltzed into them. He felt as if he carried a basket of flowers. She danced so well, so dainty. They danced off, just in time, for one of the officers came for her. Stan saw an angry look on the man's face. They danced off into the crowd.

"What is your name?" he asked.

"Veta. And who are you?"

"Stan Aldridge."

"Stan Aldridge, don't you like me?" she asked. Her eyes were like choke-cherries.

"Very much."

"Then why didn't you rescue me from those officers?"

They were by the keg, and Stan dropped off his cup. He held her tighter.

"Your eyes are so lovely, I could not move. I was frozen to the floor."

"Ah! I saw you go for more whiskey." She pinched his arm and stuck out her tongue, and they both smiled.

Someone grabbed his arm. It was Sir Warren. It was difficult to talk in the human swirl, and both couples moved on.

"Was he the Lord from Scotland?" she asked.

"Yes. How did you know about him?

"My father told us."

"Who is your father?" He wanted to kiss her. He saw several other couples embracing.

"General Biscusa." Stan felt a tap on the shoulder, and he turned. A stocky officer pushed him out of the way and danced off with Veta.

Stan headed for the keg. He wondered how he'd picked the daughter of the acting governor, but it explained her Spanish look, the officers, and the women in black. He took a swallow of whiskey and headed back for Veta.

Stan knew that she wanted to dance with him. He wanted to hold her. When he saw her, he tapped the officer on the shoulder and elbowed him off, then swept away with Veta.

"May I kiss you?" he asked.

"No! Not here. . . but, I think I'd like it." Her eyes sparkled in the candle-light.

"Does that officer mean anything to you?"

"No!. . . but he thinks he does."

Stan felt the tap, then the elbow, and away Veta danced. Another fight broke out near Stan. Through the pushing and shoving, he saw John Relle, so he went to help. John, known as Canada by Walker's men, was medium in size but wire hard. He'd flattened a Mexican. Three of the greaser's friends moved in on John. Stan pushed through and stood by Relle. One of the Mexicans drew his knife, and Cotton Crevier appeared next to Stan holding a foot-long blade, which he flashed skillfully. Ryan and two of his men pushed through to make peace. Relle danced off, and Stan and Cotton headed for the keg.

"Watch your tail, son," Cotton said, "this dance, or baile in Ryan talk, could get nasty before the last fiddle." He took a long swallow of whiskey and smacked his lips. "I'd say there are a good ten greasers for every one of us."

"But the women still like us," Stan said, looking for Veta.

"Oh, sure, that's what pisses the greasers," said Cotton. "Their women, like all I know of, fancy a change in color. Their crotch warms when they think of the big white pole," he chuckled, "or a shiny black, I reckon." Stan gave Cotton a slap on the back and headed through the dancers to find Veta. He was confident she wanted to dance with him. When he saw her, he barged in and danced off with her. The one stocky officer, he knew, was also intent on holding Veta.

"Why don't you tell the moose," Stan said, bending down and talking in her ear, "to find another girl." He brushed his lips on her ear. She smelled like lilacs.

"I have," she said, "but he does not think I should dance at all with a smelly, Anglo mule-driver." Stan chuckled. He danced Veta toward the door.

"Let's go out and get some fresh air," he said. He saw a look of concern on her face.

"For just one minute," she said. "Bella would kill me, leaving with an Anglo." A devilish smile crossed her face. Stan took her hand, and he pushed their way through the crowd and around the side of the hall. They passed two other couples who stood near the dark alley wall

When he stopped, she slipped into his arms. Her lips were moist and soft. They kissed first gently, then with hunger. From his knees up, Stan felt her body press into him. She allowed his hand to explore the upper crease of her firm buttocks for a moment before pulling it away.

"How are we going to get together?" he asked. He kissed her neck and ears.

"I will think," she whispered, "but we must get back."

They turned to go, the way now blocked by four dark silhouettes. Stan saw the epaulets of the officers, and fear bolted through him. "Uh, oh."

Veta talked to them in rapid and angry Spanish. One man, the stocky dancer, growled a reply and stepped forward, grabbing Veta's arm. Stan gave a hard chop to the man's arm. He heard the ugly snap of the ulna and a hoarse cry. The other three moved in. Stan whirled and gave the man on the right a vicious kick to the side of the head. He saw the glitter of a knife. It clanged on the bricks below. The man crumbled to his knees. Stan dodged and chopped the middle man hard to the neck with the side of his hand.

"Behind!" screamed Veta. . .Stan saw a moving shadow. . .

It was dark. A bell rang somewhere. Stan heard voices close by. He opened his eyes and saw a rainbow of color, but closed them again. Pain jolted through his forehead.

"Aldridge, can you hear me? It's Jed Walker."

"Yeah, Jed. Where am I?"

"You're in the Chapel of San Miguel. Someone clobbered you by the dance hall. The Sister thinks you're going to be fine. Cotton and Ryan brought you here and got me. You rest. I'll find Warren and we'll be back."

"Thanks Jed," Stan said, but he didn't open his eyes again.

Stan slept for two hours. He felt a cool rag on his forehead. He opened his eyes. It was not as bright and he saw the shadowed outline of the Sister against a stained glass window. It was afternoon.

"How do you feel?"

"Better."

"Good. I am Sister Alita. I want you to sit up and eat some soup I've made."

She helped Stan up and into a nearby rocking chair. The onion soup was good. Stan felt much better.

"You were fighting with the military. It was not wise. You could be jailed for months or taken to Mexico City."

"I was dancing with a girl named Veta. They didn't like it."

"Ah! Veta! Veta Biscusa?. . . You are handsome but dumb."

Stan smiled, it hurt, but he still smiled. He felt the back of his head. It was swollen and blood was matted in his hair. His ponytail may have protected him a bit.

Sister Alita was small and dark. Stan figured she was about his own age. She was pleasant, and frank. She gave him warm corn bread and cactus honey. It was good. They talked for an hour, about growing up in different worlds. Stan learned she had been stolen by the Kiawa when she was five years old. Her father and Iron journeyed to the Kiawa village and were able to buy her back.

"Raul often talks about your brother," she said. "It was sad."

"Is Raul going to take the job in California?"

"That is what he thinks, but Father Joe and I have asked him to wait six months, then see how he feels. He has a good life here, but he is one who has always wanted to see the other side of the mountain." She waved her hands up in the air.

"We'd like Raul to take us to California." She studied Stan with her hands on her hips. Her face was set and serious.

"No!. . . No. Raul is getting too old. It is a long and dangerous trip, and I'm sure it would be his last. I might never see him again." Stan looked into her dark eyes and saw a deep determination. He did not mention Sir Warren's brother, for Sir Warren had told no one but he and Jed, not even Diamond and Pepe.

Stan stood slowly, hiding the pain he felt. He enjoyed his talk with the Sister. He had not talked this long with a woman of his own age since his last talk along the Hudson River with Lynn.

"I can make it back to La Fonda. Diamond and Pepe will take care of me. Thanks for your help, Sister." He reached out and shook her small hand.

Pepe read the Spanish printed notice aloud.

"It is dated, September 10, 1833. 'The American, Stan Aldridge, is to leave Santa Fe within three days. If Senor Aldridge does not leave, or if he returns at any future time, he is to be arrested and charged with assault on officers of the Republic of Mexico. He will be taken to Mexico City for trial and sentencing.' It is signed 'Ciro Biscusa, Governor'."

"What were you thinking of?" Sir Warren asked, "a half dozen Mexican Army officers. . . old women in black hovering nearby. There were a dozen young girls who would have given you a night to remember. Even a geezer like me found one."

"Shit, Warren, he had a night he'll remember," said Jed, with a smile. "And he must have impressed the Governor's daughter, or he'd be in jail. That must've been some father-daughter debate to keep Stan out."

"I'm sorry about all this," Stan said. They were all, including Diamond, seated at a torch lit table in the rear of the hotel. "I guess I'll have to go back with Mike. I don't care to see Mexico City." Stan and everyone sat quietly.

"What about Leon?" Sir Warren said. He gave Pepe and Diamond a brief explanation of his brother's plight. Stan and

Walker studied the table top.

"My only brother's life is at stake," Sir Warren said, with a sigh. A breeze flickered the torches. "I ask you all for help. . . please. . . 'Clear your mind of can't.'" Stan looked around the table. Everyone studied their hands, even Sir Warren. Stan broke the silence.

"I want to talk to Iron one more time," Stan said. "Jed, will you go out with me in the morning?" Walker nodded his head. Stan's head hurt. He was ready for bed.

Stan stood. "Goodnight," he said and walked up the steps to his bedroll. On his pack was a note from Evita inviting him to Los Jubilo. Maybe tomorrow.

Stan made out Iron Paso currying a large horse near his corral. Stan and Jed turned west off the main trail and proceeded down the dusty lane leading to Paso's ranch. The sun edged over the eastern mountains painting the scout and his horse in shades of pale ruby and yellow. Stan turned in his saddle and looked east.

"It's a beautiful sunrise," he said.

Walker glanced over his shoulder.

"'Red at morn, trappers forlorn.'"

"We could use rain," said Stan.

"No," said Jed, with a smile, "I mean beaver don't move much in bright or colored water. It's trappin', not weather, I'm talkin' about. I like to trap when there's a heavy fog on the stream."

Iron Paso turned and looked their way. Stan saw him hold his hand up to shade his eyes, then turned back to his horse. The lane was lined with mesquite, but half the trees were dead or dying.

"Morning," Stan shouted, more to announce their arrival than as a greeting. Paso's horse's head jerked up at the sight of Walker's dog.

"Sit," said Walker. Ric sat while the two men rode on up to the corral and dismounted.

Iron Paso patted his horse and walked toward his visitors.

"Mornin'," said Paso, shaking Stan's hand. Stan introduced Walker.

"What happened to you?" asked Paso. The area under Stan's eyes and nose had turned blue-black.

"Night before last," offered Walker, "he was at a dance, and he danced with the wrong gal." Paso shook his head and smiled. Stan gave a sheepish smile.

"When we're young," said Paso, "we run into troubles—when we're old, trouble runs into us. Still, I'd rather be a young grasshopper than an old crow."

Walker chuckled. "You got that right," he said. "Trouble is, he tangled with the Governor's boys. It was Biscusa's daughter he was sparkin'. He's just got a couple days to get out of town or be locked up."

Paso let out a low whistle. "You mean Veta Biscusa?"

Stan nodded.

"Get out early," he said, "they'll be lookin' for you. Those boys don't want any Anglo sniffin' the General's daughter. We'd be lucky to see you in five years, if ever. If you need to bunk, come on out here, but it's serious. Be careful."

"Thanks," Stan said. Iron looked back up the mesquite path to where Ric sat

"Some dog," said Iron, "is he all right?"

"He's okay," said Jed. "I just thought your horse might not like him too near. It takes a while for animals to get used to him."

"That's a fine horse you have," Stan said. "He's a match for Midnight." The men studied Stan's and Paso's animals. They were both big and black.

"I reckon," said Paso, "I never told you this horse belonged to your brother."

"You mean that's Valor?"

"Sure enough is," said Paso, he sent a stream of tobacco juice between his boots. "About six months after I returned from our last mission, I went to Taos. One day I see Valor hitched out in front of a saloon. Owned by a squaw man, named Mercy. He said he bought him from the Pawnee. I paid double, but I finally got the animal from him."

"Bill's sister," said Stan, he turned toward Jed, "trained Valor for my brother." Then Stan turned to Paso. "Jed and Sublette are partners in the St. Louis Fur Company." Stan walked over and studied Valor. The two older men joined him.

"Don't you wish," Stan asked, "animals could talk?"

"Talkin' don't always help," Iron said, turning to Jed. "Call your dog in. Valor don't spook easy, and I want to see the critter." Jed gave a whistle, and Ric trotted in.

Iron Paso knelt down and put a hand on each side of Ric's head rubbing the dog's ears. Ric liked it and licked Paso's face.

"May need it," said Paso, standing, "but I'll pass on the bath. He's part wolf, I'd guess."

"Half," said Jed, "not many strangers greet him like that. I like a man who's easy with animals." Paso gave his turned down smile.

"I like animals, and they like me, I reckon. I'm best with mules; they seem to give most people trouble. Can I offer you gents coffee?"

"No thanks," said Jed, "we have to get back to town. Stan and I wanted to talk to you about California. I've agreed to go if we can find a good scout. Both of us want to help Warren."

"You mean 'Sir' Warren?" asked Paso, his face turned cold.

"No," said Jed, with a chuckle, "he's just Warren to me. But he's a fine man. I figure he can't help he was born rich. Shit, look at me, I wasn't born handsome as Stan here. That's just the way life is." The men studied Ric. The dog came and nudged Paso with its head. Paso obliged by scratching it.

"I told him I'm not interested. . . What's he want to do anyway?" Paso asked. "Hunt grizz?"

"His only brother," Stan said, "has been shanghaied and is held off the coast. Sir Warren thinks he'll be killed if he doesn't get there with ransom money."

"Shanghaied?"

"It's like bein' captured," said Jed, "and held as a slave aboard a ship." Both Valor and Midnight shook their heads restlessly. A slight breeze rustled the mesquite.

"His only brother, you said?"

"Yes."

Stan saw an odd look soften Iron Paso's weathered face. The Catawba's eyes grew distant.

Iron turned and walked to Valor, and he started to curry the animal.

"I need to think. . . where can I find you boys?"

6

Stan crossed the Rio Grande at Espanola. Following roads developed by Indians centuries before, he led a ten mule caravan up the west side of the river to where it joined with the Rio Chama River, just below San Juan Pueblo. From there, he followed the bottom land of the Rio Chama to the frontier outpost of Abiquiu. He passed the moldered ruins of the first capital of New Mexico, named San Gabriel by the Spaniard Juan de Onate. The native village there had been a flourishing pueblo for over two centuries before the arrival of the first white man.

This was Stan's third two-day trip over the ancient trail. Iron Paso led the first trip. Paso told him that here in Abiquiu, founded by the Spanish government in 1754, they would see the last white faces until they reached California. From this staging area, Iron Paso would lead Walker's and Sir Warren's groups west.

"This bunch was a tad easier to handle," Cotton said, as he, Stan and Boatswain Brown unloaded the mules.

"We're just more experienced," Stan said. Stan felt good about the role he'd played in convincing Iron to lead them to California. When he'd left the east with Bill Sublette, Stan never dreamed he would get an opportunity to travel to California and the Pacific. He was thrilled, for himself, and especially for Sir Warren.

"I don't reckon," said Brown, leading a mule into the corral, "I'll ever like workin' with these buggers." Ben Brown was Stan's age and spent four years keelboating on the Ohio and Mississippi Rivers.

"Don't start fightin' with 'em," Stan said. "Iron says they'll be our trail buddies for two months."

"Damn, Cotton," said Boatswain, "I thought you fellows told me this'd be easier than settin' traps."

"Walker told us what to expect," Cotton said. "You can still get out, but, I say, this beats wadin' to your bung in ice water. Besides, Sir Warren guarantees we all get to next year's rendezvous with money in our pockets." The men led the last of the mules into the corral, owned by a friend of Paso.

Cotton and Ben headed for town. At a dusty cantina there, they'd find warm beer and local white whiskey. Stan rode three miles down into the Chama Valley to a ranch where Iron and Walker arranged for the purchase and slaughter of one hundred fifty head of sheep. The thin cuts of meat dried on wooden racks. The old rancher, who spoke no English, showed Stan the many racks layered with meat. It would be ready to pack in two more days.

Heading back to Abiquiu with the sun sinking, Stan led Midnight through the cottonwoods along the Chama. He'd let the animal feed on the leaves and shore grasses while he took a needed bath. Across the river a deep arroyo cut in from the north. Paso had said that from its multi-colored cliffs natives had found the huge prehistoric bones of giant animals.

Stan smiled as he entered the cool water, which moved southwest from the continental divide, for he thought of the small chain around his neck. The chain held a tiny gold cross, and Diamond fastened it for him. It'd be difficult for him to remove. Stan wasn't much for jewelry, but he'd wear the gift for a time. Diamond thought he should. A servant girl had given an envelope to Diamond marked only with his initials SA. The chain was wrapped in a piece of paper containing only the initials VB.

Stan left Santa Fe the day after he and Walker talked to Iron Paso. He did not return to the city. Chances were, he'd never see Veta again, or Evita. Ah. . . that was life. His thoughts turned to the Old Spanish Trail and the trip to California. A man never knows what life has hidden away for him. . . perhaps now he'd have a chance to find Lynn, and find out what had happened. Perhaps their dreams weren't dead. He'd had a few girl friends, some nice girls too. . . but, Lynn seemed more than a girl, she was. . . a person too, and a friend. He couldn't put his finger on why that was important, or what exactly it meant. But he could feel the difference.

Three days later, Paso and Walker led the party of thirteen men and one woman along the Chama River northwest out of Abiquiu. The frontier outpost had been founded as a buffer against marauding Indians. Traveling with them were forty-two mules and horses, and five beef cattle. Iron told Stan it was, he figured, some twelve hundred miles to the Mission San Gabriel in California.

"Do you think," Sir Warren asked, "we'll need all that dried mutton?" Walker pushed back his hat, and raised his eye brows.

"I reckon Paso knows what he's doing," said Jed. "He says we can't rely on findin' game. In three trips, he's seen buffers only once." Diamond handed Walker a glass of wine.

"Better squirrel this tonic," Walker said, sipping his wine. "You won't see more 'til California."

"I want a good start for the trip," Sir Warren said, "'Life is very short, and very uncertain; let us spend it as well as we can.' This way we will lighten the load while we tighten our belts. Besides, I suspect Paso does not approve of my method of travel." Both Stan and Walker smiled. Stan wondered if Sir Warren Kent and Iron Paso would ever be more than tolerant fellow travelers.

For Stan, the routine of the first ten days on the trail was similar to the trip into Santa Fe. He seldom saw Iron Paso, and Walker joined them only at dinner for a glass of wine. Stan traveled with Sir Warren's party at the rear of the caravan. They forded the Chama at El Vado, and they continued northwest to avoid the large canyons and hostile Indians to the south. The party passed through the open gateway between two mesas, called Puerta Grande. They then labored over the Continental Divide at an elevation of seventy-six hundred feet. The Divide separated the waters of the Rio Grande and Colorado River.

"This is the last of our wine," Sir Warren said. Diamond handed a glass to Jed. Their camp was in the cottonwoods along the San Juan River.

"Salut," said Stan. The three men touched their glasses. Stan felt a deep bond developing with each of these very different men.

"Iron said we're coming into Ute territory," Walker said, laying his hat by his chair and running his hand through wire-like hair touched with gray. "He claims there are three tribes. Two of the three can be dealt with. . . usually. Just give 'em a thing or two for passing through their land. The third might be trouble."

"Trouble? What kind of trouble?" Sir Warren asked.

"He called, their chief, Arrapeen, a 'crazy mule,'" said Jed.

"Coming from Iron," Stan said, "it doesn't sound too good."

They'd slaughtered the first cow, and Stan and Sir Warren were finishing their ribs. Jed had eaten with his men.

"Just have everyone stay alert," Jed said, "and keep the group tightened up." He pulled his chair up to the table.

"Warren," he said, "Iron would like to have Stan work with him and me a couple hours each morning—after we get started, that is." The yellow leaves of the cottonwoods appeared orange in the fading light. A slight breeze rustled them, and a few glided softly to the ground. For the first time, Stan felt an urgency to get Sir Warren to California.

"Fine with me. . . Stan?" asked Sir Warren.

"Sure. What does he want me to do?" Stan asked.

"He don't say for sure," said Walker, "but he's still got Army in him. That ain't all bad. Tell you the truth. . . he wants someone who can take over and work with him if somethin' happens to me." Jed gave a grin and wiped the stubble on his face. "We've tried a couple of my boys. Iron tells me they may be good trappers, but he's lookin' for a young lieutenant type. I know he likes Stan."

"Fine," said Stan, shaking his head with a slight smile, "but he knows I'm a medical student not a West Pointer."

"He knows," Jed said. "He wants you to know the routines. He also knows you get along well with my men, even Labrosa. Besides, he wants you to know Moki and Vanko."

Moki, a stick-thin Hopi Indian, worked each trip west with Paso. He was an interpreter. The rotund Jack Vanko, a Ukrainian muleteer, was working his way to California.

"I think the Catawba," Sir Warren said, pouring the last of the wine into Stan's glass, "knows a good man when he sees one."

"Hear, hear," Walker said. He raised his glass. Stan felt a slight blush up the back of his neck, but he was pleased. Dan would have been proud of him. His brother wanted Stan to consider West Point after Dartmouth. But after Dan's death, Stan chose medical school. For a time he questioned whether he should have gone to the Point, but he loved medicine. He was sure Dan would have understood.

They moved on for several days across open, rolling country. Pinyon, juniper, oak, and sagebrush outlined the often rocky hills. Stan enjoyed riding out in the mornings with Walker and Iron. He listened and he learned.

It was early on the fifth day after Stan started riding with the two leaders that the Utes appeared. They were assembled along a low ridge that led toward the Animas River. A mile or more ahead, Stan could see the trees along the river. The ground where Walker halted the caravan was open with scattered sagebrush and scrub oaks.

"Recognize the group?" Jed asked.

"Ute, maybe thirty. Can't tell who," said Iron. "Moki?" he asked.

"Arrapeen," said the Hopi. He looked through a small telescope.

"Damn," Iron said, "better tighten 'em up."

Walker and Stan brought the single line caravan into three side-by-side columns. They had, at Iron's suggestion, practiced the maneuver three times before.

"Everyone," Walker said, riding back through the columns, "get your rifles ready, but, lordy be, don't shoot until I tell you. This is Ute country, and it ain't a place for us to have a war."

"Stay here," Walker said, as he and Stan rode back to Iron and Moki, "and just keep everyone cooled down. I'll ride out with Iron and Moki, and see what in hell we got. Maybe we can give 'em beads and blankets and be on our way. . . and maybe not."

Stan rode back to the group and waited at the side next to Cotton and Isaac Labrosa. Since their fight, Stan got along with Isaac as well as anyone, except Cotton Crevier. They all sat and watched their three emissaries ride out through the sagebrush and dried gramma grass. Walker's dog Ric tagged along. There was a breeze from the north, a hint of fall was in the air. One hundred fifty yards out and almost half way to the ridge the three stopped. Walker, who was in the middle, raised his right hand. After a time, three braves rode down from the ridge. It was hard for Stan to tell much about the Indians. From time to time the sun reflected off their jewelry or weapons. He thought two of the three, who met Walker, carried rifles.

Half an hour dragged by. Stan moved to the other side of the group near Sir Warren. The restless animals stirred and shifted. Stan thought about Captain Bonneville's comment regarding the number of trappers lost last year to Indians. He checked his rifle carefully.

"I count twenty-nine of them on the ridge," Sir Warren said, "and we do not know if there are any on the far side."

"Looks like the powwow is over," said Joe Lapoint. Stan watched their three men turn their animals and walk back toward the group.

Walker addressed the group in a loud firm voice: "It is the Ute tribe led by Arrapeen. He was all smiles and friendly, too friendly. Iron and Moki say he's a mean horse thief and slaver. They're comin' in and we'll give them blankets and beads. Keep your rifles in your hands, and watch all the pack animals. If you see anything suspicious, don't shoot, but speak up loud and clear. Iron believes he'll want to trade for rifles. There could be trouble, cause we ain't got rifles to trade."

Stan and Cotton helped Walker pull out five wool blankets and ten strands of beads. They spread two blankets in the grass where Walker would smoke a pipe with Arrapeen. All six men who met would share the pipe.

Stan watched the Utes canter across the sage plain. Dust rolled up in the morning sun and trailed them. They stopped fifty yards out from the caravan and their three leaders advanced to sit with Walker, Iron, and Moki for the pipe ceremony.

Stan could see that Arrapeen was a large man with a heavy square body, thin hooked nose and angular face. Most of the braves had round full faces, with flat, wide noses. All wore their hair in double braids that hung down their chests, some to their waists and beyond. The bulk of their hair fell straight down the back. Paso had told Stan that the colorful beaded bands on shirts, leggings, and sashes indicated each brave's war achievements. Most wore a feather or two held at the rear of the head by a hide strap. Arrapeen was the only brave who wore a fourth feather. Few braves carried rifles, most carried lances or war clubs; these hung from their saddles by a thong loop. Stan saw many decorated and painted shields.

"Fine animals they have," Cotton said. "Bet my trip-stake, they stole them in California." The horses appeared larger and stronger than the ones Stan had seen with the Indians at the rendezvous.

After the lengthy pipe-smoking, Walker gave the blankets and beads to Arrapeen. Jed and Iron then walked back and circulated through the uneasy caravan. Everything went well they told Stan, but both Jed and Iron found Arrapeen too accommodating. Everyone was to stay alert while the braves meandered through the area.

"Ready up," yelled Walker, standing in his stirrups. He told Stan to bring up the rear and hold a tight single-file formation. The smell and dress of the Utes made the horses and mules skittish. Iron and Vanko moved up and down the line helping the men with the animals. Jed and Moki took the lead. Two young braves rode up by Stan eyeing his rifle. Stan gave one a friendly smile, but the man just looked at him with dark eyes and spit in the ground. This encounter wasn't over. Arrapeen and his men trailed along for a time, then Stan was pleased to see them gallop off over a rise to the north.

The caravan forged across the knee-deep Animas River without any sign of the Utes.

"I doubt," Iron said, riding back beside Stan, "if we've seen the last of him." They left the cottonwood and willows along the river and entered low hills marked by desert juniper, hackberry, and pinyon.

"According to Jed," said Stan, "you don't think much of Arrapeen."

"Before today, I'd never met the man, but he has a reputation. It can't be all beer hall talk. The chief we met today reminded me of a root gatherin' squaw. It don't add, somethin's wrong."

At mid-afternoon Arrapeen and ten of his braves rode out of the north. Eight of the Utes led an extra mount. They rode right up to Walker, Iron, and Moki. The caravan halted and a lengthy discussion ensued. They met fifty yards in front, and Stan could see little from his position. His mouth was dry. He took a small swig from his canteen. It didn't help.

Finally, Iron rode back and signaled Stan to come forward. Paso passed the word that Arrapeen wanted to trade horses for rifles. Walker refused. He told the Ute leader the white men had no extra weapons and needed no horses.

"Come with me," Iron said to Stan. "You can help keep the men informed. The true Arrapeen has showed up." They rode forward to a position behind Walker and Moki.

"Him say," Moki interpreted for Walker, "no trade for horse, then you must pay with five rifles to cross Ute sacred land." Stan saw Arrapeen and the other braves had painted a white stripe under each eye. Their faces were determined, and their dark eyes moved slowly from man to man.

"We come," Walker said, "as friends of the Ute nation. We take nothing from the land, and we have given our gifts of blankets and beads to Chief Arrapeen.

Arrapeen gave a gruff reply.

"He say, blankets are buffalo dung. Beads horse piss. He take rifles," Moki said.

"We have no rifles to trade or give."

Stan watched Arrapeen's face stretch tense and white, his black eyes ablaze. The Chief's white-faced horse pawed the ground. Arrapeen and five of his braves carried rifles. Stan saw the others held lances or clubs. All the braves packed bows and arrows.

The Chief spit out low hissing words. He shook his left fist at Walker.

"Go back. You no cross Ute land."

"We come," Walker said, "as friends, but we will not turn back."

Arrapeen's face was a mask of hate. He turned and addressed his men.

"He tell men, prepare to die," Moki said. Stan tightened his grip on his rifle. He could be dead in minutes. He took a deep breath. Had it been like this for Dan alone on Santa Fe Trail?

Arrapeen drove his heals into his mount and the animal pushed roughly out between Walker and Moki, and Stan and Iron. The Chief, high-stepping his animal, circled the caravan. Walker moved back to the head of the column and yelled.

"Don't shoot unless he shoots me or I give the order."

Arrapeen came back toward the head of the column. His horse pawed the earth, tossing its head. The Chief moved his fidgety horse in close to Walker's men and their animals. Without warning, he lowered his rifle with one hand and shot one of the pack mules in the neck. Midnight jumped slightly, but Stan's grip was firm.

The animal fell to the ground thrashing wildly. John Relle, who held the wounded mule, flew into the air, thrown by his bucking horse. Several animals up and down the line kicked and bucked. Cotton Crevier jumped down and blasted a second shot in the head of the dying animal.

"Hold your fire," yelled Jed, as everyone struggled to bring order to the column. It reformed ten yards from the dead mule. Arrapeen returned to his men.

"Iron, Stan, Moki, let's go," ordered Jed. Walker's sweaty face was pale and tense in the dusty afternoon sun. Stan felt a wave of fear ripple through him as they rode out toward Arrapeen and his men. He shifted his grip on his Gibbon.

Walker rode right up to Arrapeen, his horse bumped the Chief's mount.

The Chief was all smiles.

"He say, now you need trade for horse," interpreted Moki. Several of the braves laughed.

"Tell him I came as a friend, but he has acted like a fool," Walker said. He kept his eyes fixed on Arrapeen. Walker let Moki speak. The Chief's face darkened. Jed continued. "We are crossing Ute land, and will do no harm to it, but if he kills more of my animals or men, I will kill him." Again he let Moki interpret. Several of Arrapeen's men scoffed at the remark, but Arrapeen and Walker stared at each other in silence.

Arrapeen spit out a brief remark.

"He say, he welcome the day you try to kill Arrapeen."

"Tell him," Walker said and Stan felt a strange chill in his friend's voice, "to part friends we must part equals." Moki used his hands to convey Walker's meaning. A small dust devil drifted in near the men and then raced off through the grass and sage to the south. Stan blinked his eyes for a moment, but he saw Walker raise his rifle and shoot the nearest rider-less horse between the eyes. The animal collapsed to the ground with a thud, dead. A brave, who had the horse secured to his waist, landed hard on its rump. Everyone's weapons were ready, but no one moved for a long minute. A slight smile crossed the Chief's thin cruel lips, and he spit out words and gestured with his hand. He turned his horse back toward his men.

"He say, you cross his land today. He get rifles another day."

Walker turned his horse back toward the column.

"Let's go," said Jed, "we've got miles to make up."

For three days they rode northwest, doubling the guards at night. They saw no Utes. They followed a small creek through grassy swales and narrow meadows. Paso told Stan that this was the land of the prehistoric Anasazis, who for hundreds of years built villages on the mesas and in the open country. On the morning of the fourth day, they crossed a fork of the Mancos River. Between the two forks of the river was a Ute encampment. Walker, knowing they were scouted each day, stayed on the trail Paso knew. They passed within three miles of the Ute's camp.

"Where do you think they are?" asked Stan.

"They're here," said Iron. "When they want us to see them, they'll show."

The caravan picked its way through a boulder-strewn stretch along the north fork of the Mancos.

"How far until we cross?" Jed asked.

"In about three miles it opens up," said Paso, "and there is a shallow stretch."

They passed through a shady grove of pinyon and juniper. When they emerged, Stan saw the Utes. He judged there were thirty to forty braves. The Indians carried rifles, lances, and war clubs, and had painted two white stripes under their eyes. Many rode painted animals. The area between the two parties was an open field of sand and sage, lined on each side by a series of heavy boulders.

"Shit," Walker said, with a thin smile. "I knew we'd have at least one more test. Stan, form three columns. Tell the boys to sit easy, but ready."

Stan signaled to tighten up the line, and he helped with the process. He repeated Jed's orders to each small group. He checked his rifle. He felt for his knife. He pulled down his gray bollinger. Yes, he was ready. He took a position near Sir Warren. His mouth felt chalky.

"The Chief is all smiles," Sir Warren said. They watched three Indians approach Jed, Iron, and Moki. "But I don't like that paint. Paint is for war or celebration. Somehow, I do not think that Jed or Arrapeen plan a celebration." Stan saw Arrapeen's white-faced mount had black circles painted around each eye and two stripes across his snout.

"That's some grin on Arrapeen," Stan said, "but his friends aren't smiling. It may be sinful to think another person is total evil, but with him, I believe it'd be a mistake to think otherwise." The Chief wore a large, bead-decorated sash over his shoulder and across his chest. His two companions wore large, circular, quilled chest ornaments. Stan saw the tips of Arrapeen's head feathers were painted red.

After a brief discussion, one of the braves rode back to the main group. Iron dropped back to talk to Stan.

"Jed has told him," Iron said, "in every possible way we have no rifles to trade. The man persists. Now he wants to trade slaves."

"Slaves?" Sir Warren asked.

"Yes," Paso said, "years ago the Utes discovered there was a good market for slaves in Mexico. The Spaniards offered horses and white-man goods for slaves. I'm told there is still a good market down there." They watched the Ute brave return. He led three half-starved dirty young men. The slaves were hobbled by lengths of rawhide, and they were pulled forward by straps tied around their necks. Repulsive welts covered their bodies.

"Maybe Piutes or Diggers," Iron said, "but they could've been captured or bought from any tribe."

Stan watched as Arrapeen got down from his horse and towed the three slaves to Walker. Again there was discussion; Stan saw the smile leave the Chief's face, and his hands and fists gestured at Walker and Moki. The wind grew and there was a chill in the air. Dark clouds rolled out of the northwest.

Arrapeen shouted orders to his brave, and the captives stumbled back to the main group. The brave returned with two women and three naked children. One of the women carried an infant. The entire group looked starved and dirty. They shuffled along trance-like. All were tied by the neck except the baby.

"Good God," Sir Warren said, "this is worse than Africa or Charleston."

Arrapeen, again with a big grin, marched the group in front of Walker. Stan couldn't hear, but Arrapeen stepped back and grabbed the younger squaw. Stan figured she was about sixteen. The Chief yanked her head back by her hair, and he forced her to look up at Walker. Grinning, he tore open her shirt revealing her small breasts. There was more discussion. Stan saw the Chief's face fade white, consumed with rage.

Without warning, Arrapeen turned, tearing the infant from its mother's arms. He marched with dogged steps to a large boulder about twenty yards from the group. He carried the screaming infant by one tiny leg. Large, scattered rain drops started to fall. When the Chief reached the boulder, he swung the child in a giant arch and thrashed its head against the rock surface. Its skull snapped with a hollow pop. The baby was dead. Arrapeen tossed its limp body into the sand.

Sir Warren leapt from his horse and raced toward the Chief. Walker spurred his mount to cut off the Baronet. Raising his lance, the Ute brave who'd brought the slaves moved to protect Arrapeen. As Walker reached to grab Sir Warren, the brave threw his lance. It headed for Sir Warren, but it tore into Jed's lower left arm. The Chief stood face to face with Iron Paso, who'd spurred forward with Walker. Stan leaped from his horse to cut off the second brave, racing with a knife toward Sir Warren and Walker. He collided with the brave. Both men were knocked into the grass.

Stan and the brave leapt to their feet. The two men circled each other with knives in hand. Both the Utes and Walker's group moved forward with weapons ready. Except for Stan and the Ute brave, the parties remained at a stand off. Diamond and Pepe came to Walker's aid. Stan saw an eager look on the brave he faced, and he heard the Chief yelling.

"He say," shouted Moki, "let them fight. Winner get rifle or slave."

"Stan!" yelled Paso. "Can you take him?"

"I'm fine," Stan said, his voice sounded strange to his ears. Raindrops swirled through the group.

"Don't worry, Iron," shouted Isaac Labrosa, "Stan can take him."

"Get him, Stan," yelled Cotton. Stan felt himself taking deep short breaths.

The brave, lips curled back, charged Stan. Stan side-stepped him and delivered a solid backhand to the man's neck. The brave was powerful, and fast for a heavy-set man. From the corners of his eyes, Stan saw the two groups had closed off both ends of the narrow passage. He also saw Sir Warren, Diamond, and Pepe working to remove the lance from Walker's arm.

Stan and the brave circled. The Ute was now more cautious, feinting with his knife but not charging. In a sudden, unexpected move, the Ute jumped forward feet first, whipping his powerful legs. The brave's legs caught Stan below the knees, flipping him hard to the ground. Stan rolled free, as the Ute leapt for him, knife raised. Stan rolled back the other way, and the brave's knife plunged into the sand where Stan's chest had been. Both men leapt to their feet; again they circled. Each gasped for breath.

The mounted Utes started a rhythmic war chant, and Stan heard shouts of encouragement from Walker's men. Stan felt sweat and rain running down his face and neck. He knew he was in a fight for his life. Sweat from the Ute caused white paint under the brave's eyes to make trails down his face.

Feinting with his knife, Stan whirled on his left foot sending his right foot hard into the left side of the Ute's head. The stunned brave staggered, but he did not go down. Stan charged forward, driving his right heal into the man's face. The brave's nose and upper teeth collapsed in, and he shot backward, hitting the ground unconscious.

Stan stood looking down at his opponent. The only sounds were the wailing of the slave mother and the wind-whipped rain drops.

"Scalp the bastard," yelled Labrosa, and several others. The sorrowing mother was silent. All eyes were on Stan. He picked up the Ute's knife, and he kneeled by the brave. The man's face was pulpy. Tiny bubbles of blood and water wheezed out from what remained of his nose. There was a sharp, rancid odor. Stan pulled out one of the brave's oily braids; plunging the knife, he nailed the hair to the wet, sandy grass.

He got to his feet, and Walker's men gave a mighty cheer. Black clouds whirled overhead. A heavy rain pelted the area.

The Ute lance with its hammered metal point and feathered shaft lay in a dark pool of Walker's blood. The pelting rain stopped, leaving a fine mist among the surrounding boulders. Stan kneeled by his friend and checked the tourniquet Diamond and Sir Warren had applied. The wound was appalling.

"Warren says you gave the Ute a new nose," Jed said. His voice sounded gravelly and his face was ashen. He forced a thin smile.

"Yeah, they're working on him now," Stan said. He loosened the tourniquet, which was the upper part of Sir Warren's shirt. Sir Warren and Diamond also knelt by Jed. Blood again started to flow from the wound. Stan tightened the tourniquet.

"Looks like you'll be ridin' the point," Walker whispered, laying his head back, "for a few days anyway."

The Utes placed their still unconscious brave over the back of his horse, covered him with a blanket, and cantered off.

"I'll check the arm," said Stan. Walker nodded his head and closed his eyes. Diamond adjusted a saddle blanket to pillow his head.

The lance had entered the back of Walker's left arm three inches up from the wrist. Stan kept a calm face, but he swallowed hard. The broad metal point had rammed between the radius and ulna, shattering both bones. The lance must have also severed the main vein or artery, or both. The laceration was a tangled bloody mess of broken bone and torn tissue. It was the worst arm wound Stan had ever seen. He looked across Walker's body at Sir Warren. The Baronet's eyes were dilated, pleading. Diamond's coal-black eyes mirrored the same helplessness. They looked to Stan for help.

"We'll camp here tonight," Stan said, searching his mind for the best ways to handle the wound.

"No!" Jed said, in a firm voice. "We've got to get distance between us and that crazy bastard. Wrap the arm, and fix me a sling. You can doctor tonight."

"Jed, for Christ. . . " started Sir Warren.

"Let's not waste time," interrupted Walker. He struggled to sit up with Diamond's help. Stan knew it was useless to argue with Walker, and he was probably right about Arrapeen . Anyway, he didn't think Walker could travel far. The arm was a mess, but after this, Stan would have to take charge.

With Walker's arm wrapped and in a sling, the caravan moved northwest for three long hours. Stan was amazed that Walker could hold to the saddle. As Stan rode he reviewed in his mind the structure of the arm and the treatment of similar wounds. One weekend at school he had assisted Dr. Millard with a similar leg wound. A dock worker had been accidentally harpooned. Stan wished Millard was with him now, and that they had Walker in the University Hospital.

"We'll camp by the creek up ahead," Iron said. Stan looked at Walker, but Jed's chin rested on his chest. He appeared barely conscious clinging to the saddle horn.

"Good," Stan said. "Find out if any of Walker's men have worked with similar wounds before. I'll get Jed comfortable and take a better look . . . but it's bad, real bad."

"I've seen my share," Iron said, "of messed up human flesh."

They made a bed for Walker back under the cottonwoods and willows near the creek. The bottom-land near the creek was fertile and covered with fine grass. Cotton brought Jed's bed roll to Sir Warren's camp. Diamond bathed Walker's face with a wet towel. His dog, Ric, lay nearby with its head on its paws.

"I reckon the boss," Cotton said, "best stay with you folks. Iron told us Jed's arm is tore up bad. I'll help if need be. I've had to do some doctorin' over the years."

"Thanks, Cotton," Stan said. "It's a bad one, we'll probably watch it for a day or two. Ask Iron to come over."

"He's havin' us cut poles for carryin' Jed," Cotton said." He returned up the creek to the main camp.

Sir Warren and Pepe started a fire to heat water.

"Dear God," Sir Warren said, looking up into Stan's eyes and gripping him hard on the shoulders, "I wish that were me over there." He glanced to where Walker lay. Stan looked into his boss's eyes. His face had aged and his voice cracked. "Can you save the hand?"

"I'll clean it up and have a look as soon as the water's ready," Stan said. "I want you, Iron, and Diamond to see what you think, too." He removed Sir Warren's hands from his shoulders. Stan wanted to know if anyone had ever seen a wound like this one, but he knew that he must take charge. What would Professor Millard do if he were here?

"Christ," Sir Warren said, "I'm no good around blood. If Diamond and Pepe had not been there I would never have gotten the lance out of Jed . . . Dear God, what have I done?"

"Don't blame yourself or anyone," Stan said. "Just help Jed get through this." He turned and watched Iron ride up with the young Indian squaw behind him.

"Ah shit," Stan said, "what are we supposed to do with her?"

"You won her," Iron said. He dismounted with a slight grin. "I figured she'd better stay with Diamond." The rawhide cords still hung from the girl's ankles and neck. Sir Warren started to help her off the horse, but she shook him off and jumped down.

"Diamond better give her a bath," Sir Warren said. "She smells."

"I've got whisky," Iron said, opening his saddle bag, "for Jed."

As Iron handed two whisky bottles to Stan, the young squaw jumped onto Valor. She kicked her heels into the animal and headed out through the trees. Iron gave a shrill whistle, and the horse stopped. The girl tumbled over its head. Valor returned to Iron. The squaw lay trembling in the grass. She cowered down as Iron, Stan and Sir Warren ran to her.

"She's not hurt," Stan said, "she's just scared."

"Yep," said Iron, "she figures she going to get a whipping."

Stan watched Iron talk to the girl with signs. He pointed to Diamond and to the creek. After a bit, the girl got up and headed for the creek.

"She might run off," said Paso, "but I told her we were her friends. It will take a while. If she stays, I'll have Moki find out where she came from. Now let's look at Jed's arm."

The men carried hot water and Sir Warren's face towels to where Walker lay. Diamond got to her feet, and spoke to Sir Warren.

"She said he was in bad pain," Sir Warren said, "but he is now asleep or unconscious."

"I'll put a strap around his upper arm," said Stan. He knelt by Walker. "Getting these towels off will likely start the bleeding, and he can't lose much more blood. Have Pepe dilute the whiskey, fifty-fifty. When he's conscious we'll give him a cup. He needs fluids."

"Jed, can you hear me? It's Stan, Stan Aldridge." There was no response. Walker's head wasn't hot, but his pulse was weak.

"Iron, your knife is like a razor," said Stan, "help me cut away these towels. Diamond, you tighten the strap if the blood starts." The three knelt by Walker. Stan positioned the bandages so Paso could cut through the blood saturated towels, which covered the entire hand and arm. Stan positioned the arm palm up.

Iron cut the blood-saturated towels, and Stan peeled them back starting at the elbow. Jed's arms were hairy and muscular. At the wound, the copious blood had fused the towels with the mangled flesh and bone. Stan carefully separated the bandages. The dark blood of the outer wrap mingled with a pale ooze from below. Blood started to pulse from the upper area of the wound. Stan nodded, and Diamond tightened the strap.

Two small splinters of bone and strips of tissue adhered to the bandages as Stan worked them off the wound.

"Cut it," Stan said. He had trouble freeing a tendon from the dried crusty wrap. Iron clipped it off, and Stan continued to uncover the hand. Walker's waxy pale fingers were wrapped around his thumb. His hand had shrunk, and, except for dried blood around the nails and between the fingers, it was a grim gray-blue.

"There's no blood getting to the hand," Stan said. Iron nodded his agreement.

"I'll say prayers," Iron said, "but I'd say the arm has to come off. The sooner the better." Stan signaled for Diamond to loosen the tourniquet, and he looked for Sir Warren. Sir Warren was standing back by the fire with Pepe.

"Sir Warren," yelled Stan, signaling him to come, "take a look at the arm. I want your opinion. Iron, ask Pepe to get Cotton."

Iron stood up and let Sir Warren take his place. The Scot's face was colorless. His lips were thin blue lines.

"God have mercy," said Sir Warren. He took a couple deep breaths and stood.

"You and Iron decide," Sir Warren said. He mopped his brow.

"Diamond," Stan asked, "what do you think?" The black woman talked rapidly with Sir Warren.

"She has seen injuries like this," Sir Warren said. "One of the men lived. The others died. She has never heard of an amputation. They don't do that in Africa. The native who lived had a shriveled hand, which fell off after two years."

Walker gave a sigh. He was regaining consciousness.

"Jed, this is Stan."

"Yeah Stan, what's happenin'?" Walker asked. He struggled to rise, but Stan held him down.

"We're checking your arm," Stan said.

"Damn," said Jed lying back. Ric came and licked his face. Iron rubbed the dog's head and pushed him back.

"How's he been?" Jed asked.

"Real good," said Iron.

"Ric, you do what Iron and Stan tell you," said Walker. "Shit," he lay his head back and ground his teeth. Stan saw sweat about Jed's lips.

Cotton and Pepe came up.

"Pepe, get the whisky," Iron said.

"Could use a tad. Whose is it?" Walker asked. He stared up into a cloudy sky.

"I packed some," Iron said. "Makes good trail medicine." Pepe brought a cup of the whisky, and Iron and Diamond helped Jed up while he drank from the cup. He drank it all.

"Good, Paso," Walker said, lying back. "I like a Bible man who ain't afraid of whisky. Now let me see this arm."

Iron and Diamond helped Jed into a sitting position. Walker's face showed not a thing as he studied the wound.

"Christ," he said with a sigh. "Got any more whisky?" Stan signaled Pepe to refill the cup. Everyone watched Jed drain it. He reached out and rubbed his dog's head. Ric's silver tail beat the ground.

"Well, Doc," Walker asked, his voice was hoarse, "what do you think?"

"I don't need to tell you," said Stan, looking into Walker's eyes, "it's bad . . . we may have to take it off." Iron and Diamond lay him back down. He again studied the clouds for a time.

"No," he said in a whisper. "I ain't goin'ta be a man with one arm."

"Hell, boss," Cotton said, "I know'd a fellow who did right fine with one arm."

"Shut up, Cotton," Walker said, closing his eyes. Stan looked at Iron for support. The scout nodded for Stan to step to the side, and the two walked off.

"I think we have a day or two," Iron said. "We'll stop early tomorrow. Who knows, miracles do happen." Stan agreed they could delay. He was relieved for now, but he didn't believe in miracles.

Just after midday, two days later, the caravan was nearing Sandstone Creek. Stan rode with Paso in the lead. They moved through an area Paso called the Great Sage Plain. Iron had fashioned a hide stretcher to carry Walker over rough or rocky areas, but most of the time he rode a travois pulled by his horse. Diamond rode the animal. Ric walked at his master's side. Diamond set the pace; she picked her way along the sandy trail made for her through the sage and pinyon. The Indian girl followed on Diamond's mule. Stan knew the young squaw had found a friend, hardly letting Diamond out of her sight. Walker was semi-conscious or unconscious most of the time, but he had taken a bit of Pepe's stew and whisky.

"Master Stan," said Pepe, riding up beside Stan, "Diamond wants you to look at Master Jed. He's talking funny." Stan rode back, concerned he'd let Iron and Sir Warren talk him into delaying what was now inevitable.

"Where's Bill?" Jed asked, when Stan walked up.

"Bill?"

"Sublette! Bill Sublette, for Christ sakes. And who's the nigger woman on my horse?" Iron and Sir Warren rode up and dismounted. Stan put his hand on Walker's forehead. It was hot.

"Ah, Spider," Jed said, looking at Iron, "get the whisky. We'll be in St. Louis in a couple days, and I'll get his damn arm looked after."

Paso removed a whisky bottle from his saddle bag and handed it to Walker. Jed's hand shook. He gulped the spirits.

"I'm Iron Paso." Walker took more whisky. He studied Iron with a peculiar look, then closed his eyes.

"Let's get to the creek," Iron said, "and you can check him." They rode on. Stan knew the arm must come off. He could see the tangle of cottonwood and water birch along the creek. Fifteen miles to the north was the hazy outline of the La Plata Mountains, and to the southeast trailed the areas distinguished landmark, Ute Mountain.

Under an old cottonwood, Diamond fixed a place for Walker, while Iron and Stan proceeded to unwrap the arm. Walker remained unconscious. Dried reddish-brown stains streaked the bandages, but it was the putrid odor that caused Stan to look up into Paso's dark eyes. With a grim look the scout nodded his head.

The twisted hand was shrunk, and it seemed as if a thin plaster coated the bones. From the wrist to the wound the skin was a slick olive color. The open wound was a grisly rainbow of streaks covered with a viscous, tawny syrup-like liquid. Near the elbow the arm expanded to half again its normal size.

"How much whisky is left?" Stan asked.

"A bottle and more than a half," said Iron.

"Good. I want to go when we're ready," Stan said. Iron nodded agreement. Stan had reviewed the amputation procedure in his mind many times during the last three days. At school, he and two other students were given a woman's leg to work with in the surgical lab. At the time, he thought they were lucky to have the leg. They could practice more cuts on a leg than on an arm. He recalled the sound and sense of the saw on the cold bone and the crude jokes told by his fellow students.

Stan talked to everyone who would help, one on one: Pepe and Sir Warren would build two large fires and have plenty of hot water, and Pepe would wrap and bury the severed arm; Iron would provide two good knives, have Sir Warren's bone saw ready, and be at Stan's side; Diamond would have the clean towels and whisky, and she'd help Stan wash the arm with whisky and wrap it after searing; Cotton would have two, broad skinning knives red hot for searing the arm, since he had done the task twice before he would do the searing; Isaac Labrosa would help hold Walker.

Walker regained consciousness. He drank the whisky, but his eyes were vacant and he did not respond to Stan. Stan hoped they hadn't waited too long. Jed drifted into unconsciousness.

They placed Walker on a large buffalo robe near the fires. Stan positioned him on his back with the injured arm nearest the fires. Iron straddled Walker's knees and held the injured upper arm at the shoulder. They extended the wounded arm out from the body. Cotton was at the side to hold the bandaged hand and lower arm. Labrosa knelt above Walker's head and held him at the shoulders.

Stan moved in between Iron and Cotton with his chosen knife and Sir Warren's bone saw. He lay the saw on a towel.

"Diamond," called Stan, "you take Cotton's place. Cotton, you make sure your knives are red hot." Diamond replaced Cotton, and Stan tightened the hide tourniquet. He would cut through the major muscles of Walker's upper arm. Stan glanced at Iron, Labrosa, and Diamond and nodded. Everyone's pupils were wide, full.

With his left hand holding the arm near the tourniquet, Stan started the cut through the skin and muscle. Walker's body gave a slight flinch at the start of the incision. A deliberate river of blood flowed onto the robe. It surprised Stan how quick the razor sharp knife reached the bone. He picked up the saw, and worked it down through the rent.

The placement of the saw is critical he thought, as he started his cut.

With a wrenching cry, Walker's legs shot up, and Iron crashed into Stan. Walker's right arm flailed wildly. Stan fell into Diamond. Nearby, Walker's snarling dog hit the end of his rope thrashing. Jed started to rise. Isaac Labrosa gave him a solid head butt and Walker fell back unconscious.

"Almighty damn," Stan said, picking up the saw, "he's still strong enough." Stan worked fast: the butcher's saw bit into the bone.

"Hold it up," Stan said to Diamond. He made the last cut with the knife. The arm fell free, but the blood oozed on.

"Okay, Cotton," said Stan, "he's all yours." Stan and Diamond moved aside. Diamond handed the severed arm to Pepe. Cotton Crevier crouched with two red-hot knives, one in each hand. Paso helped position the stump of the arm, and Cotton seared one half of the open wound and then the other with the knives. There was a sizzle and fetid ivory clouds curled up. A tremor shook Walker's body. Ric started to howl. Stan and Diamond moved in with the whisky and bandages. The char of the stump looked dark and fried. Diamond looked at Stan; she gripped his arm and smiled. Tears ran down her face. Stan sighed. It was over, but was it a success?

They camped on Sandstone Creek for three nights. Then, with Walker on the travois, they continued northwest.

"Jed hasn't said a word to me," Stan said. He and Iron Paso led the caravan northwest, climbing from the Sage Plain toward Piute Springs. Here, Stan was told, for hundreds of years the Anasazi Indians, before the Spanish arrived, had practiced dry farming. The soil and climate were ideally suited for growing beans, winter wheat, sunflowers, and dry land alfalfa.

"He says a few words to Diamond," said Iron, "and I guess that's it."

"Sir Warren talks to him," Stan said, "but he just stares off into space. The arm is doing fine, and he's getting stronger. He's told Diamond he wants to get on his horse tomorrow." They make their way up Piute Draw, a spillway for the spring.

"He's a proud man. The kind others depend on," Iron said. "This is the first time in a long while he has needed help. It will take time."

"You're right," said Stan. "And he's a physically proud man, He may feel vulnerable with only one arm."

"Jed will be fine," Iron said. "All he needs is time. 'To every thing there is a season, and a time to every purpose under the heaven: A time to kill, and a time to heal; a time to keep silence, and a time to speak.'"

The days turned into weeks. The group turned to Stan for leadership. Stan did not choose to be their leader, but he accepted his role. He tried to think what Dan would do, and it helped him through. The weather grew colder, with frost in the mornings. Jed remained solitary, and rode at the end of the caravan, behind Sir Warren's group. His arm healed, but he took his meals alone.

Paso now turned the group southwest with the great canyon of the Colorado River well to the south.

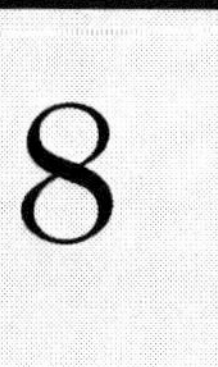

Stan, Iron, and Moki paused in the shadows of the canyon, encased by an eerie silence. Midnight was tense and fidgety, pawing at the rocky canyon floor. For the last half hour the three had wound through a narrow, red canyon. It was a shortcut Iron used after they crossed the Sevier River, an area known as Hurricane Cliffs.

"What is it?" Stan asked. All remained silent, there was no sound but a slight tremor. Solid red rock formed the towering walls of the one-hundred foot wide canyon.

"Up north," Iron said, "I'd say buffalo." The three were a half mile in front of the caravan. From the rear they heard a horse galloping up the canyon.

Jed Walker raced toward them. Stan was shocked, for although Jed's arm had healed in the past six weeks, he remained silent and solitary.

"Stan! Iron!" he yelled. "It's gotta be horses comin' down the canyon." He reined up in front of them. "Let's go, we could lose every damn pack animal." The four turned and raced back down the canyon. A wave of fear flowed through Stan, but he was relieved to have Jed back in control. Since the arm came off, it had been a difficult six weeks. The early spirit of the trail had been lost by the accident and the grind of daily travel through a barren land.

When they reached the caravan, Stan and the others helped the men secure the pack animals to scrub trees along the north canyon wall. The rumble intensified and their animals grew more restless.

"Pass the word," Walker said. "If anyone can't handle their animals, and they break loose and start runnin' with the herd, just ride on out with the flow. Don't try and turn back."

Stan moved up and down the line to help secure the animals and pass the word. Wave after wave of hoofs pounding on stone echoed down the canyon. Mules kicked and horses bucked.

"We sure picked a hell of a time to come through," Cotton said. He tried to quiet a kicking mule. Stan grinned, but he moved down the line toward Sir Warren.

Suddenly, Midnight rose up on his back legs and snorted. Stan gripped the reins tight and held his hat down. A ribbon of fear jolted him as he quieted the horse. Stan moved in to the wall face at the end of the caravan.

"We'll be lucky," Sir Warren shouted, "if we don't lose half our animals." The sense and sounds now overwhelmed them. Stan fought to re-secure a pack mule.

The living mass stormed around the bend one hundred-fifty yards to the west. Two drunken men rode in front of the herd. They yelled and waved their arms as they passed. The frantic horses thundered after them. The animals were of every size and color, a frightening quilt of browns and blacks, with grays and paints. How they raced in so dense a pack amazed Stan. With the charging beasts came a choking cloud of copper colored dust, it mingled with the stench of the herd. Many animals passed within ten yards of Stan. He could see the flare of their nostrils, and a wild glare in their eyes.

Stan took his eyes off the stampede to look up along the wall at the caravan. There, frantic men tried to hold their animals to the canyon wall. A deep primal urge drove the frightened animals of the caravan to join this wild race for freedom. They struggled to break free. Stan kept a powerful grip on Midnight, and he watched two pack mules pull loose and race by with the herd. One of Sir Warren's mules broke free. Both Sir Warren and Pepe had the animal's rope for a brief moment but neither was able to hold the frenzied beast.

Pepe's mount bucked, all four hoofs left the canyon floor. Its tether broke, and the old Spaniard lost his grip. His horse was desperate to join the mad stampede. Pepe held hard to the saddle horn and swung off. But his left boot caught in the stirrup. He was committed, it was too late for him to pull back up. The crazed animal charged on, dragging the frantic man.

The Indian girl, who stood nearby, ran to Pepe's aid. She yanked at his boot, but she was flung aside by the bolting horse. Pepe's head and arms bounced off the red shale of the canyon floor. As Stan pulled the girl to safety, he heard his friend's muffled screams. Pepe disappeared down the canyon, lost in the dusty tangle of hundreds of racing hooves and legs.

In five minutes the herd passed, and, except for a dusty tremor and the mournful chant of Diamond, it was quiet. Stan tore his tether loose and headed out as Walker rode up.

"Warren," yelled Jed, "help Iron and the boys get out of the canyon. Stan and I will ride ahead." Stan and Walker galloped after the herd. There was still a chance. Pepe was liked by everyone. He was always friendly, always helpful. Stan knew Jed felt the same as he, and to Diamond and Sir Warren, Pepe was family.

Soon, one hundred yards from the canyon's mouth, Stan saw a white and black object crumbled in the settling dust of the ruby-brown floor ahead. It was the twisted remains of Pepe Ortago.

Walker dismounted and untied his saddle blanket. Stan went to the body, which lay in a broken curl, all except the left leg that lay against Pepe's back near his head. Stan stood up. He felt weak and lightheaded.

"Are you okay?" Jed asked.

"Yeah."

"We'll wrap him up," said Jed, "all mighty. . . Diamond, Warren, and the girl don't need to see this." Tears push up into Stan's eyes.

He looked away several times as he helped Walker straighten and wrap the body; much of Pepe's face had vanished, but his ivory teeth remained in place. The two men placed the well-wrapped body near the canyon wall, and they rode out through the mouth in search of the missing animals. Stan felt as if there was nothing fair about this life, but he would, he must, push on. He rode by Walker's side over a flat plain of reddish sand and scattered clumps of sagebrush and dwarf junipers.

"The herd will be along Little Creek," Jed said. "There's miles of grass there, and water."

"What about those two men?" asked Stan.

"A couple drunken horse thieves," Jed said. "There'll be ten or more others comin' along, I reckon. The bastards knew they could run them through the canyon and still round them up at the creek."

"They didn't look like Indian ponies," Stan said.

"Shit," Walker said, "they got those critters in California, or I still got two good arms."

Stan gave his friend a startled look. It was the first time Walker mentioned his arm.

"I'm rollin' a pretty fair cigarette," Walker said, with a grin. "I reckon I'll make it . . .you did right, Stan . . .if that means anything."

"Yes, thanks," Stan said. He peered into Jed's eyes. Walker gave him a wide grin. Stan grinned and looked away. He didn't want Walker to see his face or his watery eyes. Good Lord . . .if it means anything!

As Walker figured, the herd was spread out along the creek two miles from the canyon mouth. The two men who led the stampede were at the creek, but neither spoke English. Stan and Jed found Pepe's horse and the three mules from the caravan and headed back to the canyon. They'd camp on the creek and go though the canyon in the morning.

The sun edged up over the Cedar Mountains to the east. Stan removed his hat, as did most of the men who stood scattered around the grave site. Diamond sang in a deep and soulful voice. Sir Warren stood by her side. He had hardly spoke since Pepe's death. Stan did not understand Diamond's words, but her voice was spellbinding. The horsemen from their nearby camp walked closer to listen; all the caravan's men stood in stony silence. Her fine voice filled the still desert air. When Diamond finished, she and Sir Warren knelt by the grave. Iron Paso stood there with his Bible.

"'But we see Jesus,'" Iron read, "'who was made a little lower than the angels for the suffering of death, crowned with glory and honor; that he by the grace of God should taste death for every man.'" Paso read on, and Stan pondered the trip . . . Walker's arm and Pepe's death . . . he hoped Leon Kent would appreciate this someday . . .the worst had to be behind them.

"I'd get fifteen head," Iron said. He told the group they could expect no game ahead.

"Do you think that's enough?" Walker asked.

"Twenty is all you get," said Peg-leg Grant. "I can get three times this price in Santa Fe." Grant was a filthy little man who led the horse thieves. Stan saw tobacco juice leak out of the corner of his mouth and onto his sheepskin vest.

"Paso tells me," said Grant, "you're huntin' some rich kid." He chuckled and spit juice. "But I know you bastards are fixin' to run horses east, same as me." He studied Iron, Jed, and Stan. The four mounted men had discussed the purchase of horses in an open, sandy area back from the creek.

"One more thing, Paso," Grant said, chuckling, "those Californio's balls are all a blazin'. We buried four of their men gettin' through Cajon Pass. You ain't goin'ta get no Sunday welcome out there."

"We'd better get our horses," Walker said, he didn't hide his dislike of Grant, "and get movin'."

"Do you know anything about the Monterey or San Francisco bay areas?" Stan asked. The one legged man studied Stan through puffy eyes.

"Never been there," he answered, "but Old Ham claims he worked the docks there for quite a spell."

"Does he speak English?"

"Shit yes, he's half limey hisself."

Walker and his men separated the twenty heads, under the watchful eye of Peg-leg Grant. Stan and Paso rode to Grant's camp and found Old Ham.

The elderly man sat with his pipe by the fire; he wasn't grimy like his boss. He wore a black fez with a red tassel on his curly gray hair, and there was a twinkle in his eyes.

“I’m workin’ my way East,” said Old Ham, after introductions. He did not stand; Stan and Paso sat on either side of him. No one else was at the fire. “Have a sister in Savannah, and I ain’t doin’ Cape Horn again. Jesus, Lord, I was never so sick.”

“Peg-leg told us you worked around Monterey and San Francisco bays,” Stan said.

“Twelve years, good years too,” said Old Ham, “but the last couple, the fog seemed to settle into my bones. The water and air there can be a cold, hard mother. That where you boys headin’?”

“Yes,” said Stan, “we’re looking for a ship, the *Helenka*.”

“Oh,” Old Ham said, lighting his pipe and studying Stan, “she’s a greasy Russian sealer. I know that scow. What you want with her?”

“We believe our friend’s brother is being held on her,” Stan said.

Old Ham chuckled. “That don’t surprise me none,” he said. “Those docks aren’t a place for choir boys, or their mommas either.”

“Do you know anything about the *Helenka*?” Stan asked. Two of Grant’s men came to the fire to get coffee.

“No, not much,” Old Ham said, “she’s just one of a bunch that stays along the coast each year and hunts seal for the China market. She’ll come into Frisco at times for general supplies. I’ve never seen her in Monterey, but haven’t been there in four, five years. I’d imagine she visits the Russians up at Bodega.” He knocked out his pipe and stood.

“Is her crew all Russian?” Stan asked. He and Paso got to their feet.

“Hell, most are I reckon,” said Old Ham, “‘cept their Captain, a man named Whitelaw. He’s a Brit, and I’m sorry to say he’s slimy as they come. You’ve gotta’ watch your pockets when he’s about.”

“Is he a new Captain?” Stan asked.

“No, no, he’s been on that scow long as I can remember.”

They moved on southwest through the Beaver Dam Mountains and into the basin of the Virgin River. Stan moved back and worked with Sir Warren. Jed took over as trail boss. It was a parched land, and, when they found bunch grass in an arroyo or at a spring, they would let the animals feed. The men ate dried mutton, and, about every fifth day, they slaughtered a horse. Except for three occasions, Paso found water each night.

"If I would have known what this country was like," Sir Warren said, "and all that has happened, we would be back in St. Louis." He and Stan gnawed on their jerky dinner.

"It will pay off," Stan said, "when we get Leon off the ship. Iron says it'll be only about two more weeks and we will be in California." The young Indian squaw, whom Diamond named Little Rabbit because of her twitching nose, served them water.

"Still," quoted Sir Warren, staring off toward the Virgin Hills, ". . .'He is no wise man that will quit a certainty for an uncertainty.'"

Walker rode up and dismounted. He removed the dust from his trail hat by beating his leg with it.

"Keep a watch tonight," said Jed, taking a seat at the table. "We saw a few Diggers following us along the trail. Paso said the little bastards aren't too smart, but they'll steal you blind."

"How do people live out here?" Stan asked. "We haven't seen any game for hundreds of miles." Walker's dog came and lay by his master's chair.

"Shit, you find yourself a giant ant hill," Walker said, with a gleam in his eye, "then smear your hand with yucca juice. Jam that sweet hand in the hill and let it set for a second. Then pull it out and start lickin'. A dozen dips, a couple thousand ants, and supper's over."

"Good Lord, Jed," Sir Warren said.

"We're going to move slow," Jed said, "along the river. Give the animals a chance to feed and build up. Paso says this is the best feed we'll see until we get into California." Scrub mesquite and cottonwood grew along the river, with plenty of reeds and bunch grass. They heard two rifle shots.

"The boys have seen a few rabbits," said Walker. "I told them to get them if they could."

"Rabbit would taste good about now," Sir Warren said, "we'll keep an eye open."

"What about the Diggers?" Stan asked.

"Paso says the dirty buggers are on all fours most of the time lookin' for roots and insects," Walker said. "They don't have horses, and their weapons are sticks and stones. Unless there is a lot of them, we'll be okay. Except, they'd love to steal a horse, or anything they can get their hands on."

"They need horses," Sir Warren said, "then they can head to buffalo country and get decent food."

"Shit," said Jed, "if they stole a horse, they'd eat it." Walker pulled out his cigarette materials and rolled and lit a cigarette.

"Mercy, Jed, that is good," Sir Warren said.

"And fast," Stan said. Walker grinned and winked. Stan knew he was proud of his handy work.

More shots came from up river.

Late the next night, Stan heard shots at the main camp. He, Sir Warren, Diamond, and Little Rabbit took turns on watch. They saw no Diggers near their camp. Little Rabbit was an intelligent, quite young woman, devoted to Diamond. She had become a useful member of Sir Warren's group.

"The boys shot a couple Diggers last night," Paso said. Jed had asked Stan to again ride the point with him, Iron, and Moki. "Cotton found blood, but they had carried away the bodies."

"Shooting Indians wasn't too smart." Stan said. They left the river and were on a long, waterless jornada of twenty miles, to a place Iron called Muddy Springs.

"No," Iron said, "you're right, these boys don't realize the buggers can be dangerous. On my first trip out we lost two men. We never did find their bodies. The fools went lookin' for squaws. The Diggers killed and likely ate them."

They plodded on hour after hour. The land was dry and parched. It reminded Stan of the bed of a giant furnace. He saw no Indians. Perhaps, they had been left behind.

It was later afternoon when they approached the top of a long gradual rise. The animals became uneasy. Water was the central thought of the men and their animals.

"The spring is two miles on the other side of this rise," Paso said.

When they reached the rise, Stan saw the welcome sight of

grass and mesquite. But there were other odd formations, perhaps outcroppings of rock, around the spring.

"What is it?" Stan asked. Moki pulled out his small telescope and studied the scene.

"I can't believe it," Iron said. He shaded his eyes with his hand.

"Diggers," Moki said, "many Diggers."

"All mighty damn," Jed said. Stan saw the outgrowth was not rock, but hundreds of Indians sitting and squatting in the sand. His mouth felt drier.

"Is there any other water?" Jed asked.

"Las Vegas Springs is a good thirty miles," Iron said, "we wouldn't have a horse or mule standing. This is it."

"Okay . . . Stan," Jed said, "get the men ready and stay with them. I'll get the beads, and we'll have a powwow. Somehow or other, we get to this water."

The caravan formed three columns. Stan and Sir Warren sat and watched Walker, Iron, and Moki ride down toward the spring. When the Indians saw the party approach, they swarmed like ants into a mob to meet them.

"There do not seem to be any Chiefs," Sir Warren said. They watched the three men ride toward the milling throng. Stan's lips were starting to crack. Tonight he would get a little oil from Diamond.

"Paso hasn't seen much social structure. The old men usually lead," Stan said.

"There have to be three or four hundred of them," Sir Warren said, wetting his lips from his canteen. "You know what is scary is, if they wanted to take our three men, they could do it in a minute." The sun sank to the crest of the Spring Mountains far to the west.

"You're right," Stan said. "I'm glad they're still in the stone age. If they were Utes and we killed one of them, we'd be dead men."

After about fifteen minutes of talk, Paso turned and rode back to the caravan.

"We ain't gettin' anywhere," Paso said, talking to Stan and Sir Warren, "They don't understand what a rifle can do. They just laugh. It's just a funny lookin' stick to them. They say we can't have water because we killed two of their men. Walker wants you two, and Cotton, to come back with me. He wants to demonstrate what a rifle can do. We hope it'll put fear in 'em. They're all standin' there with sticks, looking at us like we're supper."

"I guess the beads didn't work," Stan said.

"They tried to eat them," said Paso. "When they couldn't, they lost interest. What they want is food, and we don't have any to spare." Paso yelled for Cotton to come forward, and he explained the situation.

"The boys are havin' a time holdin' those critters," Cotton said. "They smell water. Can't say I blame 'em for wantin' to run for it." The four men checked their rifles and rode toward the powwow.

The Diggers who moved in close to Walker and Moki skulked back as the four men approached. Stan saw they were small, scruffy people. Most were naked. Some wore rabbit skins. Most men and women carried digging sticks. These were used to locate roots and insects, and, if lucky, a lizard.

"Cotton," said Jed, "set up a couple logs. I want to show them what a rifle will do." Stan dismounted and helped Cotton prop up two, four-inch diameter logs that lay in the sand. The men held up the logs so the Indians could see they were smooth and unblemished. As he helped Cotton, Stan smelled the dusty bodies and waste of the tribe.

When Cotton and Stan mounted, the Indians came in and picked up the logs.

Moki tried to make them understand, but the Diggers would not stand back from the log targets. Three times Cotton and Stan set up the targets, and three times they came in and picked them up.

"We'll just stand by," Stan said, "Sir Warren, shoot before they move in." Stan and Cotton stepped back a few steps, and Sir Warren fired. With the rifle's crack, the Indians threw themselves flat into the sand, cowering and moaning. Many further back in the crowd, ran into the thicket of the spring or into the desert.

Stan picked up the log split by Sir Warren's ball. He handed it to the Diggers as they regained their feet. Their eyes were like choke-cherries, half hidden by oily hair. They jabbered, some laughed and others danced.

"I don't think they get the connection," Stan said, remounting. "The rifle is a noisy stick that splits logs."

"Maybe," Moki said, "they need see blood." Sir Warren raised his eyebrows, and he looked at Stan.

"There are two vultures," Iron said, "in the mesquite." The large birds were perched at the edge of the thicket.

"Warren, what do you think?" Walker asked. It was about eighty yards to the trees.

"If we could move in a bit," Sir Warren said, "I will use Stan's shoulder for a prop."

Jed led them in ten yards, but the Diggers yelled and threatened with their sticks.

"This is okay," Sir Warren said, and he and Stan dismounted.

Moki got nearby Diggers to look up at the vultures.

"Give it a go," Walker said. "I don't know. The buggers aren't smart as Ric."

Stan stood with his left hand over his right ear, while Sir Warren used his shoulder as a prop. The Baronet's shot was on target. Feathers flew and the heavy bird crashed through the trees to the ground. Again, most of the Indians fell to the ground in fright. The throng parted as Stan and Sir Warren walked to the thicket and retrieved the dead bird. On their way back, Stan held the bloody vulture high by its legs for all to see. The crowd parted, but to Stan, they seemed unimpressed by Sir Warren's shot.

"The bird act was no better," Sir Warren said. The sun was down and a breeze came in from the west, rustling the leaves of the mesquite.

Many of the Digger women and children did not return to the spring after the shots were fired, but a core of one hundred militant men remained. From these, a group of five advanced to talk to Moki and Walker.

Stan, Sir Warren, Iron, and Cotton moved in behind Moki and Walker. Stan saw the mass of Indians were fanning out to encircle them while their leaders talked. The crowd had changed. They now moved slow, crouching, with their sticks held out from their bodies.

"They want our horses," Jed said, turning his head back to the men behind him, "or they say they'll kill us."

"Hell, they say," Cotton said. Stan and the others could feel the difference as the Diggers closed in.

"A hundred hungry men," Jed said, "can do a lick of damage. Cotton, come up here." Cotton moved his mount to the other side of Moki. Three of the five Diggers confronting Walker were naked, the older two wore rabbit loin clothes. All the Indians were armed with heavy sticks, which they started to shake menacingly.

"We'll shoot the two with loin clothes," Walker said. "They look the oldest. You take the one on the left."

"Okay," Cotton said, readying his rifle. Stan tried to swallow. His mouth was too dry.

"You are not going to shoot the devils are you?" Sir Warren asked.

"Shut up, Warren," Jed said. "Ready, Cotton?"

"Yap."

"Fire."

The two buffalo rifles roared into the quiet evening. The pair of Diggers tumbled back hard and hit the sand with gaping holes in their chests. The Digger Cotton shot hit the ground pumping a stream of blood into the air. The one Jed shot gave two desperate kicks, then died. The other three blood-spattered Indians lay flat trembling. Most of the other Indians had dropped to the sand. A few further back took off running.

Moki yelled at them, waving his arms.

The three cowering men scrambled to their feet and with a few others dragged off the mutilated remains of their companions.

Back by the caravan a rifle shot was heard, and Stan saw two mules break loose and run for water. The thirst-driven animals charged right through the few scattering Diggers.

The Indians were a chaotic mass.

The entire caravan came charging down the hill. Many of the men firing their rifles. Leading the charge was Walker's dog, Ric. The Diggers retreated in all directions.

The battle for the spring lasted four minutes. Seven Indians were killed. The hundreds of others disappeared into the desert. The caravan took Muddy Spring, and they rested there a full day. Walker's men buried the Indians.

9

Stan leaned over, his eyes shut. The urge to vomit passed. His forehead was moist. It felt clammy-cold to his hand. He grinned, shaking his head, and looked out of the corners of his eyes at Paso. The scout chuckled.

"The last time I was with Captain Aldridge," Paso said, "we shared a cup of mule-juice. He took it better."

"I'm alright," Stan said, with a weak smile. "Dan was West Point. If drinking blood was the thing to do, he'd drink blood and smile. For me . . . I sure hope we find water at the next hole."

"This is the first time there was no water at Salt Springs," Paso said, taking a swig of horse's blood from the cup. He handed the cup back to Stan. "There'd better be water at Bitter Springs. If not, we won't have a horse or mule alive when we reach the first California water."

Stan held the cup, but he didn't look at its dark, tepid contents. He focused on a nearby group of cactus and yucca plants. What was he doing here? With luck, the caravan would be out of the Mojave by the next night. He took a third mouthful and forced it down. Walker and his men were mounting up. If he drank anymore he would be sick. He handed the cup back to Paso and headed for Midnight. The trail stretched out and disappeared across the desert, a magnificent, but solemn and dreary sight.

Four days later, the world was bright again. The caravan made camp among a stand of oak along the San Gabriel River. They had traveled more than a thousand miles since Santa Fe. Sir Warren bought two beef cattle and a barrel of wine at Rancho Cucamonga. The winter grasses of California were spring-like green.

"This morning, on the trail," Sir Warren said, "I remembered where I heard the name Whitelaw before." Stan reached across the table and filled Sir Warren's wine glass for the third time. "He was my cadet leader a while during my first year in the guards at Cambridge."

"I suspect," Jed said, "there're a sack full of Whitelaws livin' in old England."

"Whatever happened to him?" Stan asked. The late day sun painted the San Bernardino Mountains a faint orange, and Stan mellowed with the first red wine he'd tasted in weeks.

"He was booted out of school," Sir Warren said, "for stealing rifles."

"Sounds to me," Stan said, "he could be the same one Old Ham told us about."

"His name was Hayden," Sir Warren said, "Hayden Whitelaw. After he left school, it was rumored he had propositioned three of the male recruits."

"That's some school, Warren," Jed said. "But Paso thinks we might find word about the *Helenka* at the plaza in Los Angeles. If not, we'll head for Monterey, but first we get supplies at the Mission and give the men and animals a few days rest."

The following day, they rode over mile after mile of grassland. First, they passed through a massive herd of cattle. Then came the horses. Both herds numbered in the thousands and were guarded by armed vaqueros.

"I'm glad we have Paso," Stan said, riding beside Sir Warren. "These guards are armed and mean looking." Several of the guards greeted Paso; the word spread to let the party pass.

"I suspect," Sir Warren said, "they have to deal with the likes of Peg-leg Grant." The caravan was leaving the grassland and entering strange groves of trees.

"What are these?" Stan asked. The trail wound through row after row of them.

"Olives," said Sir Warren, "and I see oranges up ahead."

The pale feathery leaves changed to dark shiny ones, and Stan saw the first buildings of Mission San Gabriel Archangel. The Mission was much larger than he expected. Huge and sprawling, it was more of a town than a church. Paso stopped the group in a stand of oak and cottonwood. They were near a bridge over an irrigation ditch at a south entrance to the Mission. The Mission formed a square, the massive chapel faced east and the guardhouse west, with workshops and quarters on the north and south.

"The walls," Sir Warren said, "have a Moorish look to them." He and Stan sat on ground covered with oak leaves. They watched a dozen men, across the ditch, tanning hides in open pits. "It reminds me of southern Spain." Walker and Paso walked over the bridge and disappeared behind the long side wall of the Mission. Stan rested his head against the trunk of an oak and studied the cloudless sky.

"For mid-November," Stan said, "I like this weather." One of six bells in a giant tower along the church wall rang.

"It is much like southern Spain or France" Sir Warren said. "But I worry now about being able to find the damn Russians, or Whitelaw, or whoever, and freeing Leon." Sir Warren sighed. "Lord knows, it was not an easy trip."

For the next three nights, they camped along a stream two miles west of the Mission, and Stan silently puzzled over where Lynn Monroe might be. He also could tell that Sir Warren was growing more and more impatient, for they would soon know if their efforts to find the *Helenka* were for naught.

Father Joaquin Carrillo was head of Mission San Gabriel, master of thirty-three hundred people, fifty thousand animals, and a territory larger than the state of Rhode Island. He was a scholarly man with a deep interest in medicine and surgery.

"If I understand," Father Carrillo asked, waving a fly off the table and peering at Stan through silver rimmed glasses, "you don't think much of bleeding a patient for any reason?"

"I can't think of a situation where I'd recommend it," said Stan. The Father had invited Stan to lunch, the main meal at the Mission. "Many doctors in the States think it weakens the patient." Stan ate a spoonful of the spicy beef stew. It was excellent. Two priests seated across from Stan finished their huge plates of stew and mopped them with corn bread. Stan judged from their pear-like shapes both padres enjoyed their food. Neither of these men spoke English. Stan, replying to Father Carrillo's questions, had eaten only a third of his stew.

"Have you ever worked with smallpox?" Father Carrillo asked. He was a thin handsome man with a shaved head. He sat at the head of the table; his sister Laura Dia Aznar sat between him and Stan. She was an attractive woman in her mid-thirties.

"Hermano, enough," Laura said, "let the doctor finish his meal." She addressed the Father by her childhood nickname for him. Stan understood, from the previous day, she lived in Mexico City. She sat across the table from him then, and her penetrating eyes consumed his every move.

"I'm not a doctor, yet," Stan said. He moved closer to the heavy oak table to concentrate on his stew. A young Indian girl came into the room and filled everyone's goblets with a rich red wine.

"You have the commanding look," Laura said, leaning aside to survey Stan, "of a doctor in charge. Anyway, hearing the story of the amputation of your friend's arm has made you a doctor to me." Two of the Mission bells began to ring.

"Ah, you were right, Laura Dia," said Father Carrillo, "I have talked too long. The three of us, doing God's work, must attend another local meeting on secularization. Change is coming, Mr. Aldridge. Mexico City is eager to get their hands on our land and animals." The three Fathers stood up. "I shall see you, my friend Paso, and the others before you leave tomorrow. Laura Dia please take care of our young guest." With a smile to his sister and Stan, the Father swept out of the room. He was followed by his two portly companions.

"Your brother," said Stan, tasting the wine, "is an interesting man."

"Hermano could have been whatever he wanted," Laura said. She angled her chair to watch Stan finish his stew.

"In ways he is a fool," she said. Three candles helped light the table, for the room's only natural light came from two oblong windows high up in the fifteen-foot high wall.

"Why do you say that?" Stan asked. He finished his stew with the corn bread.

"He could have been rich," Laura said. The Indian girl returned with the wine decanter; she started to clear the table. "But he is poor. . . without real money."

"Money isn't all there is," Stan said, pushing his plate back.

Laura chuckled and shook her long auburn hair. "You are young," she said. She spoke to the Indian girl in Spanish, and the girl left the room. She closed the door.

Laura filled their goblets with wine. She picked up hers.

"Here's to the final days of Hermano's mission," Laura said, holding her goblet toward Stan. He picked up his goblet and the two containers touched. "It will soon be only Hermano's church." They each tasted the wine, and Stan looked into her dark eyes. They seemed to draw him into them. After a time, he looked away into a flickering candle and felt a flush creep through his lower body.

"Who is going to get the land and the animals?" Stan asked. Laura leaned her head back and laughed, revealing the pale skin of her neck and the first rise of her breasts. Her dress was black, but glittered with silver spangles and buttons. While not a beautiful woman, she was sensual.

"The official plan," Laura said, moving her chair closer to Stan, "is to give most of it to the Indians. But the wealthy families are already arguing about who can buy what and when from them. I am here to protect the Aznar interests. It is not easy. My husband is a stupid man, and my brother is an honest man." She threw up her hands and smiled. "But we'll make out."

"I'm sure," Stan said, he sipped his wine, "you will get what you want."

"I hope so . . .but," she said, moving closer to Stan, "this is not a time to talk of land and horses." A slight smile came to her face; Stan looked into her rakish eyes. She reached out with her hand and placed it on his leg. A bolt of awe and desire quivered through him. She began to stroke the inside of his thigh. Stan looked into dark, fiery eyes. He felt blood surge to his loins.

"Have you," she whispered, she wet her lips with her tongue, "done this before?"

Stan's mind was a whirl. "What do you mean?" he asked.

"Have you made love to a married woman?"

"No." Stan took a deep breath as her fingers inched along his swell.

"That is fine," she said. Her fingers moved slowly back and forth. "We will have a splendid afternoon. Do not worry. . .Hermano forgives me."

"You tell Father Carrillo?" Perhaps, with the wine, he was confused.

"He knows," Laura said, "that fifteen years ago our dear father married me to Beinvenido Aquilino Aznar. It was to increase and insure our family money. Parts of my life are fine, but much I miss. You are a young man. . . enjoy what life offers. I'm sure Hermano knows I want you. . . he knows me too well to have missed that." Stan felt his body tingle with need.

She removed her hand from Stan's thigh, and she unbuttoned the top buttons of her dress and displayed one of her breasts. Laura stood up and moved close to Stan. She brought the firm breast to his face. She smelled of jasmine. He kissed the aroused nipple for a moment and then stood up. They kissed, and he felt her tongue explore his mouth. Her body was glued to him.

"You are ready," she whispered. "Come to my quarters." She laughed. "For what I have in mind, a table is not the place."

It was nine miles from the Mission to El Pueblo de los Angeles. The road from the Mission to the town's plaza was a century old.

"Are you sure we don't need Iron?" Stan asked. He and Sir Warren rode out of the Mission, and Stan remained concerned about Sir Warren's ability with the Spanish language.

"I am certain," Sir Warren said, "I can handle the language. Besides, both Paso and Father Carrillo said anyone who has worthwhile information about the *Helenka* will speak English. . . Paso got us here. I do not wish to obligate him further."

"Chances are," Stan said, he tightened the grip on the pack animal he led, "we will have to go north to find Leon. Father Carrillo and his sister told me few ships come down here. Monterey and San Francisco Bay are where they go for supplies. Some come here to pick up hides, but that's about all. They said it's ten miles from the town plaza to the ocean, and there isn't a real harbor there."

"You seem," Sir Warren said, "to have learned a lot from the good Father's sister." Large fields of grapes spread out on both sides of the road.

"We had a good chat," Stan said, "after lunch yesterday." He looked north toward the San Gabriel Mountains, but in his mind he saw Laura's nude body. He questioned the afternoon, but he'd enjoyed it.

The grapes gave way, and the road wound through a forest of oak, white alder, and sycamore, at times with a heavy thicket. Two miles into the woods, they heard from ahead shouts, laughter, and two shots.

"Now what?" Sir Warren asked. They came to a halt.

"Sounds more like a party than a fight," Stan said. They saw nothing, but boisterous, confused sounds continued from the road ahead.

"Let us find out what is going on," Sir Warren said. He positioned his rifle across his saddle horn. The two rode forward. The road turned to the left. Soon, Stan saw seven fancy dressed vaqueros dragging a large object along the dusty road. The shouts stopped when the party saw the two gringos. One vaquero, who Stan took to be the leader, turned and rode back toward them. The handsome man held up his hand in friendship.

"Hello, you speak the Ingles?" he asked. Both Stan and Sir Warren nodded. The man rode a fine chestnut horse adorned with silver and embroidered trappings. His rich leather saddle displayed embossed birds and flowers.

He smiled and extended his hand. "I am Carlos Pastora, the rancho chief." Both Stan and Sir Warren introduced themselves. His hand was firm and workman-like.

"You go pueblo?" asked Carlos, who wore a red bandana, and a gray wool hat lined with silk and held on with a chin strap.

"Yes," said Sir Warren, "we are here in your country to find my brother. . . my hermano." Stan was fascinated by the man's dress. He wore a green and gold silk scarf, white, embroidered cotton shirt, and an ivory, silk-trimmed, open jacket. His pants matched his jacket, and a red sash circled his waist.

"Ah si. . . we go pueblo and today fight parir," he said, pointing to the object dragged by his men, "and toro, bull. . . you come along, si."

With Carlos in the middle, the three rode toward the other vaqueros, who moved on, with their dust-clouded load. Sir Warren and Carlos attempted to communicate in Spanish, and Stan tried to make out what the men were dragging. He saw what looked like the tail of a steer or bull.

"I think," Sir Warren said, looking around Carlos at Stan, "they are taking a bear into town to fight a bull."

"Si," said Carlos, with a proud smile, "bear to fight bull."

"I see the tail of a bull," said Stan.

"A steer, I believe, was used for bait," Sir Warren said. "They have the bear tied to the top of it."

"A live bear?" Stan asked. He peered into the haze of dust ahead.

"Yes," Sir Warren said, "they roped it when it came for a steer they killed."

They again rode through lush, open land of vineyards and groves of olives. At one point, in an open field, Stan and Sir Warren rode up beside the captured animal. They saw its wide, dust-covered head and snout. The eye they could see was wild and filled with fury.

"I have seen several bull fights in Spain," Sir Warren said, "never a bull and a bear. This should be good." Ahead, were the first low adobe homes of the pueblo.

A noisy crowd gathered and trailed along, as the proud vaqueros dragged their prize catch right into the town plaza. The town was small compared to Santa Fe. It consisted of a church with two dozen flat-roofed adobe houses and other structures clustered around the central square. Everywhere were horses; they were cheap, and none of the men walked. Groves of fruit trees and gardens spread out in all directions from the plaza. Besides the grapes, Stan saw pears, apples, and peaches, and Sir Warren pointed out pomegranate trees.

"Are we going to this fight?" Stan asked. He and Sir Warren sat on their horses, under an old cottonwood tree. They watched the crowd gather near the bear. Three young boys poked sticks at the beast.

"I would not miss it," Sir Warren said. "Besides, Carlos said everyone in town will be there. This is the first decent bear they've found in six weeks." Stan wanted to see the match. He had seen two cockfights and a dog fight near New York City. Still, he knew that these affairs spoke to a darker side of human nature.

"Did Carlos know anything about the *Helenka?*" Stan asked. There was a commotion on the far side of the plaza, and Stan turned and watched three mounted vaqueros lead a feisty, black Iberian bull across the Plaza.

"There is a fighter," Sir Warren said. The men struggled to control the animal. "Carlos mentioned a man in the hide shipping business. He is from the States but owns property near here. We will look him up in the morning."

One of the vaqueros, dressed in red and silver and on a gray horse, sounded a long brass trumpet. He led while three other mounted vaqueros dragged the bear out of the plaza. They were followed by the crowd and the men restraining the bull.

Stan and Sir Warren rode with the anxious crowd. It moved west for a quarter mile into the bright afternoon sun. Their destination was a circular fenced arena dug out of the side of a small knoll. The design allowed most of the spectators to sit on the hillside and watch the action below.

"Unless the bear is half dead," Sir Warren said, he and Stan tied their animals in a stand of white alders near the arena, "it should be able to handle that bull. It is typical of the type used in most bullfights. Carlos said they have fights here every Sunday."

"It has a wicked set of horns," Stan said. They walked by the Iberian and scrambled up the knoll. "There must be close to three or four hundred people here."

Tallow workers, farmers, hide merchants, Indians, fancy dressed dons and their women, and dozens of children and dogs milled over the knoll and near the arena.

Stan led the way to an open area near the top of the grassy knoll. The view was excellent. The three mounted men dragged the bear into the arena, and labored to free it. At opposite ends of the arena, teenage boys manned two heavy gates.

"I don't think those fellows ever get off their horses," Stan said. "I haven't seen one walk yet." The crowd clamored, and the grizzly got to its feet, sniffing the air. It rose up on its hind legs and roared. The crowd went silent. With grace and speed, the beast took three steps forward and swung its heavy arm. The long gray claws racked a vaquero's horse and the man's heavy, leather legging and ornate garter flew onto the arena's dirt floor. The horse reared up with a frightened bellow, blood ran from its torn flank.

Quickly, the other two men roped the grizzly by its hind legs and pulled it off its feet. They circled the arena dragging the snarling bear. The crowd cheered, and their companion rode his wounded horse out of the arena.

"They're good with ropes," Stan said. "They had that bear under control in a hurry." The vaqueros maneuvered the bull into the arena.

"That is a grizzly for sure, "Sir Warren said, "and it has to weigh a thousand pounds."

Three vaqueros led the bull to the side of the arena near the crowded hillside. They held him until the bear was again freed on the opposite side. When both animals were free, the men rode out of the arena. The gates closed, and the crowd grew silent.

The grizzly came to all fours and shook its massive head, as if to clear its brain of the last thirty hours of hell.

The enraged bull, meanwhile, was trained and focused. The animal pawed the ground. It spotted its dusty, silver-tipped target. The Iberian lowered its head, and the black beast charged across the hard-packed arena floor at full speed. The bear heard the hooves and saw a black blur through its weak eyes, but it turned too late.

High on the knoll, Stan heard and felt the dreadful impact. The bear crashed into the fence, and the crowd roared. The bull staggered back, stunned by the unexpected mass of its target.

The grizzly rose to its feet. Its mission clear, to kill. It stood on its rear legs and straddled humped-backed toward the bull. Blood oozed from a gore in the bruin's flank. The bull made a short charge. The animal's front feet left the ground and it drove its head and shoulders at the bear's chest. But the bear turned just enough to swing a massive paw. In an instant, the gray claws rolled up furrows of hide along the bull's throat and shredded its left ear. The bull bellowed with rage and tried to pull back, but the silver-tip had the bull's tender snout with both its powerful front paws. The bruin's claws formed an awesome vice. The grizzly maneuvered the helpless Iberian onto its back. Kicking in hapless rage the black bull lolled out his tongue. The bear with its big dog-like mouth seized the black tongue and tore it from the bull's mouth. The bull struggled to its feet bellowing in agony. The bear, on all fours, leapt at the bull's throat. The grizzly's pig-like snout and powerful jaws tore open the bull's neck. The black bovine collapsed backward in a shower of its own blood. The crowd fell silent. They watched the ravenous silver-tip tear open the side of the still-living bull.

"Good Lord," said Sir Warren, "I have never seen the likes of this."

"Now what?" Stan asked.

The answer came as they watched three vaqueros lead a second bull into the ring. The crowd cheered. This animal was larger than the first with a streak of brown along its back and shoulders.

This animal, like the first bull, immediately spotted its foe. The grizzly became accustomed to the noise and confusion of the arena, and it enjoyed its first good meal in days.

The bruin's back was to the bull, but it sensed the rumble of its foe's charge. The silver-tip stood up and started to turn its concave face toward the charging bovine. But it was too slow, the bull's huge head and shoulders drove into the middle of the bear's back. It was a crushing blow. Stan heard the gruesome snap of the spine. Both animals tumbled over the dead bull and rammed into the fence. The crowd was on its feet screaming.

The bull struggled to his feet, but his horns were still impaled in the back of the bear, and he could not pull free. The grizzly lost the use of its rear legs. It roared in agony and beat the air with its front paws. The bull shook free, and it commenced goring the fallen bear with powerful head butts. One of its horns tore into the silver-tip's neck, but the bruin fought with desperate fury. It managed to grab the bull's snout with its still powerful claws, and suddenly, it held the bull's throat in its mighty jaws. With a pitiful bellow, the bull pulled free. It staggered back, a river of blood flowed from its throat. Trembling, the bull dropped to its knees and rolled over, kicking, dying. The grizzly gave a muffled roar and lay slowly back, rotating its giant paws.

The boisterous crowd cheered when Carlos Pastora rode into the arena; he high-stepped his horse, circling the fallen grizzly. Then, still mounted, the chief vaqueros reached down and drove a long sword into the bear's heart. The crowd was in a frenzy.

"We won't forget this for a while," Stan said. He and Sir Warren watched the crowd surge down through the arena. "But, frankly, I don't care to see it again."

"I would not want to miss it," said Sir Warren, with a slight smile, "but, 'I wonder what pleasure we humans can take in making beasts of ourselves.'"

Later, Stan and Sir Warren watched teenage boys carry the grizzly's head, mounted on a tall pole, through the plaza.

10

The grizzly's head titled skyward and its black lips curled back over massive teeth. With a frightful roar it stood on its rear legs and straddled toward Stan. A damp fog of musk enveloped the beast. Stan reached back for his knife. It was there but it felt withered, and it crumbled in his hand. Walker's dog, Ric, leaped over Stan's head and disappeared into the bear's mouth. It was too late; the grizzly's massive paw seized Stan by the shoulder.

Stan snapped opened his eyes. It was a half-hour before sunrise. A man's hard boot was on his shoulder shaking him awake. Near his face, he saw the man's other coarse-hide boot and the butt of a rifle. He sat up. The man who woke him wore a sombrero and a faded blue military jacket. The squat man had a round face and large black mustache. He spoke to Stan in Spanish. Stan got to his feet, trying to clear his mind; he saw Sir Warren sitting on the ground across from the cold gray fire pit.

"What's going on?" Stan yelled to Sir Warren. Stan counted three other uniformed men in their camp, all with rifles. Sir Warren got to his feet, and he spoke to the man who woke him.

"They say we stole a horse," Sir Warren said. The sharp edge of the San Bernardino Mountains was developing to the east. Unable to find rooms in the pueblo, Stan and Sir Warren made camp two miles west of the plaza.

The entire wall shook when Sir Warren entered the jailhouse and the door slammed shut. He took a seat on the floor beside Stan and sighed. They heard the guard slide the wooden latch back in to place.

"I hope my message gets to Jed," Sir Warren said.

"I should have known better than to use one of those horses we bought from Grant," Stan said.

"It is a good horse," said Sir Warren, "and Jed told you to take it. I did not even know it was branded, and what are the odds of a woman from Rancho Cucamonga spotting it." The two men sat for a time leaning against the wall of the twelve by twelve foot room. There was one other prisoner in the small jail. Stan figured he was a local drunk. The man's smell was offensive, but he had not moved since Stan entered the room two hours before.

"The corporal-in-charge," Stan said, "won't make a decision. It doesn't matter if Jed and the Father bring our papers and the proof of purchase Jed got out of Dog log." Their cell mate sat up and looked at Stan and Sir Warren through half-closed, bloodshot eyes. His straw hat lay on the floor. Black strands of greasy hair hung down his face.

"You are probably right," Sir Warren said, "but the Captain will be back tomorrow or the next day." The drunk staggered to his feet. He leaned on the door and pounded it with his fist. After a time, he stopped and seemed to be asleep where he stood.

"I hope," said Sir Warren, "Jed and the Father can get us in better quarters until this is resolved." The man stood at the door snoring. "What concerns me now is time. I've read Leon's letter, maybe fifty times, and I figure I have about three weeks left to contact the *Helenka*. Whitelaw or Ivanvo, whoever is in charge, could be ready now, all loaded with skins and oil. He might give me an additional two weeks at most. After all, what could he expect, a letter posted in Boston regarding a vessel off California. If he pulls anchor and heads for China, this trip was an awful waste. And I will never see Leon again." Sir Warren leaned his head back against the cell wall and closed his eyes.

"They'll wait." Stan said, "Greed has no time limit."

"Let us hope," Sir Warren said. He opened his eyes and gave

Stan a weak smile.

The drunk started a half-hearted pounding on the door. Soon he stopped, and Stan saw urine wet the man's left pant leg. The steamy liquid poured into his moccasin and out onto the floor.

"Ah shit," said Stan, "I hope you're right about the better quarters." Sir Warren yelled at the drunk in Spanish, and the man went back to the place near his hat and lay down.

"Think of it," Sir Warren said. "Leon may be living everyday like this, or worse. . . have I told you what Dr. Sam Johnson said about life on a ship. . . 'Being in a ship is being in a jail, with the chance of being drowned.'"

Stan leaned back and closed his eyes. He should get some sleep. He might be able cause sleep by reviewing their trip from Santa Fe. But with each step of the trip, his thoughts circled back to the fact that if they didn't find Leon, it all would be a tragic waste, especially for Sir Warren.

The drunk left the jail before noon, but it was near midnight before Jed arrived with the papers and a note from Father Carrillo. Stan and Sir Warren were released an hour later. The corporal allowed the men to return to Stan and Sir Warren's original campsite. However, he confiscated all their weapons, including Walker's. They were to remain in the area.

"I'd like," Jed said, adjusting the steaks on the fire, "to smash that corporal's smilin' mouth. He's a cocky little man who's been given authority for the first time."

"His Captain should be back," Sir Warren said, "maybe tomorrow, and clear up this mess."

"Don't count on it," said Jed. He tossed a bone to Ric. "Father Carrillo said the Captain does everything by the book. If it ain't in the book, he goes to his boss in San Diego for direction."

"We have the paper on the horse," Stan said. "That should satisfy him." He poured the two older men wine from the jug Jed brought.

"I hope you're right," Jed said, "but while I was packing, Father Carrillo looked at our other papers. He thinks a couple things might be problems."

"What are they?" Sir Warren asked. Both Stan and Sir Warren

turned and eyed Walker.

"The papers for me and my boys," Walker said, "say we will trap the Gila River area and return to Santa Fe. There is nothing about California. And there's a note on Stan's papers sayin' he assaulted Mexican officers in Santa Fe and is not allowed back into the city."

"Damn," said Sir Warren. "Is there a consul in town or someone to help straighten this out?" Sir Warren did not wait for Jed's reply. "If I do not get to Monterey soon, the bastards may sail, and that will be the end for Leon." Everyone carved their steaks.

"Father says we have a man in Monterey," Walker said, "but there is no one in Los Angeles or San Diego. He thinks a Yankee ship captain, near here, named Monroe might be helpful."

"He is the fellow," said Sir Warren, "the chief vaquero thought might know about the *Helenka.*"

"Did you say Monroe?" Stan asked. He knocked over his wine glass. It had to be Lynn's father. There couldn't be another ship captain named Monroe in California.

"Yes," said Jed. "Do you know him?" Stan wiped up the wine.

"No, but I know his daughter. Her father is a ship's captain out here somewhere. It has to be him."

"My, my, Stan, I have not seen you like this," Sir Warren said. "Might she be more than a friend?" He leaned back with tight lips and studied Stan.

"I met her in New York City," Stan said, feeling a little foolish, "we talked a lot. . . about medicine and things. She was going to consider returning to Columbia and study . . .she sailed for California with her father last spring."

"It sounds romantic, two young doctors studying and working side by side," Sir Warren said. He studied Stan with a huge smile on his face. Stan shook his head with a slight smirk, but he didn't mention the lengthy unanswered letters he had sent to Lynn.

"Shit, Warren, Stan probably has a dozen girls back East," said Jed.

"'Every man's affairs, however little, are important to himself,'" quoted Sir Warren. "Besides, love becomes stronger when we realize it might be lost."

"Pass the Scot the wine," Jed said, mashing out his cigarette with his boot. Stan filled all the glasses, but he knew that Sir Warren had noticed that he was thrilled at the prospect of seeing Lynn.

Young oak trees lined the last quarter mile of the road, that led into Captain Monroe's sprawling adobe ranch. Fanning out, in the morning sun, from the road and oaks on one side was a grove of citrus; on the other side was a large placid pond. The size and beauty of the place amazed Stan.

"I didn't think we'd get much further without a welcome," Walker said.

Stan saw two armed vaqueros riding down the road to meet Walker, Sir Warren, and him. Both guards rode large black mules. The older man, with his broad hat tied beneath his chin, took the lead. He held up his hand in friendship, but eyed Walker's dog with suspicion. His companion remained several yards back with his rifle across his saddle.

"Good morning," said the elder vaquero. He spoke a fine English. "Is the Captain expecting you?" Walker signaled Ric to sit.

"No," Walker said. "We have come from the States, and we need to talk to the Captain."

The older man studied the three visitors. Stan considered mentioning Lynn, but decided not to. It might just complicate things, Lynn had nothing to do with their visit.

"Do you have weapons?" he asked.

"No," Walker said. "They have been taken by the Corporal at the pueblo."

"Ah, I see," said the man, with a smile. He spoke to his friend in Spanish. "Please follow me." They followed the older man toward the ranch; the younger vaquero brought up the rear. Stan had no idea that Lynn came from this type of background.

The tile-roofed ranch was built in a deep 'U' shape. The main two-story structure formed the bottom of the 'U'. The open area was a landscaped garden of flowers and shrubs. It contained a well, and a fish pond. Stan and his friends left their horses with the younger man and followed the older vaquero through the garden to the main entrance. He directed them to sit on a patio bench near the main door. He entered the house. Stan did not feel like sitting and remained standing, flexing his shoulders back and forth. His mouth was dry.

"I would say the Captain is doing well in California," Sir Warren said.

"This is nice," Jed said, "and well kept." They didn't wait long before the Captain appeared. He was well-built, of medium height, with steel gray hair. He wore an open white shirt with black pants.

"Marco tells me" said the Captain, with a slight Boston accent, "you're from the States. Welcome, I'm Doug Monroe." Stan liked him, his hand was firm and his smile genuine. "He also said you have been in town and met the Corporal." He chuckled. "So I have a general idea why you are here. Come into my study. I want to know what's happening back East, and I'll see what I can do to help."

Walker left Rio on the patio and they followed the Captain They crossed a two-story high, marble-floored entrance way. Second story rooms came out on a railed hallway above the entrance. The Captain's study was in the rear of the building. The carpeted study opened onto a patio and a private, walled-in garden. The Captain took a seat behind a large desk from where he could view the room and the patio. His visitors sat in white wicker chairs in front of the desk. The Captain served them a strong unsweetened limeade, and they chatted about the trip West and President Jackson's popularity in the East. Walker and the Captain did most of the talking. Stan's thoughts were on Lynn.

"Do you have a daughter named Lynn?" Stan asked when there was a lull in the conversation. He couldn't wait any longer.

The Captain looked surprised and studied Stan.

"Why, yes I do. . .your name was Stan wasn't it?"

"Yes sir, Stan Aldridge."

"How do you know Lynn?" the Captain asked. His eyes never moved off Stan.

"I met her in New York. I'm a medical student at Columbia." Stan looked into the Captain's sharp blue eyes. He saw them smile and soften.

"Lynn studied in the city for two years, and, indeed, the field of medicine is her. . . hobby. I'm sure she'd like to see you, Stan. She's out riding with her mother. They should be back before you leave." The Captain turned and looked at Sir Warren.

"This is a beautiful place," Sir Warren said.

"Thank you," said the Captain. He sat back in his chair for the first time. "It's the result of what I call 'leather dollars'. For the last ten years, I've taken hides from the ranchos and missions back to New England." Stan heard voices and horses from the rear of the ranch. "The boot and shoe business is still crying for them. It's been good for me, but there are a lot of good opportunities out here. What we need is more Yankees to move in. Then maybe we can do something about this crazy government. It's a situation where everyone wants power, but they don't want the responsibility that comes with it. Every decision creeps up line and becomes lost in the maze of Mexico City."

"Douglas," called a woman's voice outside the study, "you must see what Lynn has." Two women entered the room, startled to find visitors.

The three men turned and got to their feet. Captain Monroe stood and came to the front of his desk.

Stan's eyes froze on the flashing black eyes of Lynn Monroe.

"Hello, Mr. Aldridge," Lynn said.

"Hello, Lynn." She was beautiful.

"I understand you know Mr. Aldridge," Captain Monroe said, having completed the introductions of Lynn and his wife Elisa.

"We met in New York," Lynn said.

Lynn and her mother had been riding, and they were dressed like twins. The women both wore tight, tan pants with white blouses. Broad white hats were tied under their chins. Lynn carried a baby rabbit, and when she shook Stan's hand her flashing dark eyes sent a jolt through him.

"That's remarkable," Mrs. Monroe said, studying Stan. "I don't recall you mentioning him." An odd feeling passed through Stan.

"I had a lot of friends, Mother."

"But, you remembered his name," Mrs. Monroe said. She gave Stan another long look, then turned to the Captain.

"Douglas Monroe," she asked, with her hands on her hips, and with a slight Spanish accent, "what are we going to do with you?" She turned toward the three visitors. "Just two days ago, we ladies asked 'The Captain' to please let us know when he expected visitors. You can see what good it did."

"Mrs. Monroe," Sir Warren said, "the Captain must not be blamed, for we rode in unannounced." Stan's eyes were on Lynn Monroe. Even with a glisten of sweat under her small, turned-up nose and above her full lips, she was a beautiful woman. Their eyes met again and held; her dark eyes drove into him. She offered him a slight smile before she turned back to her mother.

"Don't defend him," Elisa Monroe said, she waved a hand at Sir Warren. "He could've had Marco tell us. Then we wouldn't have barged in here like a couple horse thieves."

"You two," Stan said, "would never be mistaken for horse thieves." The Captain's wife turned toward Stan.

"Thank you, young man," she said, and looked back at her daughter.

"Douglas, invite the gentlemen to lunch," Elisa said. "We're going to clean up." The two women filed from the room.

"Well I've got my orders," said the Captain.

"I don't know much about the *Helenka*," said Captain Monroe, nursing his coffee at the head of a heavy oak table. "She flies a Russian flag and runs seal oil to China. I've seen her in San Francisco Bay at times during the past three years, but I've never met the Captain or any of the crew that I know of. I suppose she goes to Bodega Bay quite a bit, too. The Russians have a fort near there."

A middle-aged Indian woman, dressed in a black and white uniform, carried in a large soup tureen shaped like a swan. She placed the tureen by Mrs. Monroe, who sat at one end of the table, opposite the Captain.

"The first thing," Jed said, seated on one side of the table with Sir Warren, "is to clear up this mess about the horse. Then we need to get north to Monterey."

"I think I can help with the horse," the Captain said, "but permission for your party to go to Monterey may be difficult." Mrs. Monroe ladled out a hot tomato bisque, and her daughter, who sat on her mother's left and next to Stan, stood and served the men.

"Why would they object to our going to Monterey?" Sir Warren asked. Stan watched Lynn serve his friends across the table. Their eyes met and she smiled. He needed to talk to her alone. She seemed friendly but something had changed.

"Mexico City," said the Captain, "realizes their hold on Texas, Santa Fe, and this part of upper California is weak. Hell, we're sixteen-hundred miles by pigeon from Mexico City. The English and Canadians, plus the Russians, are shoeing in from the north, and people are coming west from the States. The Mex don't like it, especially if it's a group of armed men from the States."

"My men are simple trappers," Jed said. He wiped his soup bowl with piece of corn bread.

"I know, Walker," Monroe said, "but the Mex won't believe you." Everyone finished the soup and Mrs. Monroe and Lynn served each a dish of fresh fruit.

"Mr. Walker," Lynn asked, "may I ask how you lost your arm?" Jed and Sir Warren gave a brief description of the Ute incident.

"Mr. Aldridge," Mrs. Monroe asked, "had you ever performed an amputation before?"

"No," said Stan, with a smile, "except on cadavers." The Captain chuckled.

"That's wonderful," Lynn said. She turned and studied Stan.

"Lynn is our family doctor," said the Captain. He looked at his daughter with pride.

"She's always been interested in medicine and surgery," Elisa said. "As a child she would bring home wounded birds and animals. Now, many of the Indians in the village and at the mission come here for her help."

"Not just the Indians," added the Captain. "Father Carrillo has come at least twice to consult with her."

"Have you decided to go back to school?" Stan asked.

"No" said Lynn. She fixed her dark eyes on Stan. "I read a lot. There are no medical schools here. I've just had those two years in New York City, but it was liberal arts."

"Are you," Mrs. Monroe asked, looking at Stan, "going to finish your medical schooling?"

“Oh yes,” he said, “and Lynn should too.”

Mrs. Monroe turned to Sir Warren and asked how long he planned to remain in California. As they were getting up from the table Stan asked if Lynn was going to return to New York and go to Columbia.

“No, I’ve decided not to.”

“Can we talk alone?” Stan asked. Mrs. Monroe came between them and put her hand on Stan’s arm.

“I hope you can visit again before you head East.”

Lynn was friendly but seemed to look to her mother for what she should do or say. It had been months, but Stan felt there was still a spark there.

Three days later, in a stuffy barracks room on the plaza of Los Angeles, the men met with Captain Eduardo Rodas. Rodas was not the man Stan expected. He couldn’t say why, but he didn’t like the man. He was young, well built, and almost too handsome. He was also a politician, for he kissed Father Carrillo’s hand and his left hand gripped Captain Monroe’s shoulder while he pumped his hand with a hardy welcome. Captain Rodas spoke English with a slight Spanish accent. He was a polished and well-educated military man. During the small talk about the Mission and Captain Monroe’s family, Stan gathered Captain Rodas held a special interest in Lynn.

“Gentlemen,” Rodas said, raising both hands into the air, “we have not met here to discuss the secularization of the Mission or the hide business. Time is of value to all of us. Please be seated.” He went behind a small desk and took a seat. The corporal stood behind him near the Mexican flag. Stan and the others took seats on plank benches in front of the desk.

“I was fortunate,” said Rodas, “to review these issues with my superior before I left San Diego.” This surprised Stan. He hadn’t thought much of the corporal, but somehow the man had gotten the information to the Captain. Rodas opened a single sheet of paper.

“First,” Captain Rodas said, with a slight smile, “you are to pay Senora Diega of Rancho Cucamonga a sum of five pesos for her horse, which you bought, but was nevertheless stolen property.” The smile left his face and he turned toward Jed. “Second, Mr.

Walker, you and the seven trappers in your party are to leave California within one week by the same route you came. You will report to the Mexican authorities in Santa Fe, as agreed to. Third, Mr. Aldridge, you are to leave California within one week, or I will be forced to arrest you for the assault on Mexican officers in Santa Fe." Stan sat up shocked.

"Captain," Sir Warren said, coming to his feet, "may I say something?"

"Please take your seat," said the Captain. There was a sharp, unpleasant change to his voice. "I will first read the orders I have been given, but understand I have no authority to change them. And I have no intention of doing so." Under the glare of the Captain, Sir Warren took his seat.

"Mr. Kent," continued the Captain, his voice and eyes softened, "you are granted six weeks to complete your personal business. At that time, or anytime before then if you leave Mexican California, you are to report to government officials here or in Monterey. While you are in California, you will be considered a ward of Captain Monroe." Captain Rodas folded the orders and placed them in the inner pocket of his blue jacket.

"Is it possible," Jed asked, "for me to apply for a permit to trap in your territory? We came here to escort Mr. Kent. We have not trapped since we left Santa Fe."

"No," Rodas said. He placed both hands on the desk. "This was reviewed with the General; his thoughts were, you should complete your agreement made in Santa Fe. You have permission to trap the Gila River area. No additional grants will be made."

"Eduardo," said Father Carrillo, standing, "Mr. Walker and his men are only interested in beaver pelts. We or the Indians have no use for them, and he could show you his catch before leaving."

"I'm sorry Father," said Rodas, standing, "I have my orders."

"Captain," Sir Warren said. He got to his feet, as did Stan, Jed and Captain Monroe, "Mr. Aldridge is in my employ and is vital to my mission. I will assume full responsibility for him."

"Gentlemen, gentlemen," said Captain Rodas, waving his hand back and forth, "I have no liberty to change these orders, and I will not. The orders are final and will be carried out as written."

11

Stan, nude and wet, shivered as he spread his blanket on the grass near the river. He came here almost every day. His favorite spot was a mile from camp. He lay down out of a northwest breeze. He'd picketed Midnight near a stand of alders. There, the horse could feed on new winter grasses. The sun was warm down out of the wind. Stan studied the clear blue California sky. A hawk circled high above.

In two days he'd be heading back East. Odds were he'd never see California, the Pacific, or Lynn Monroe again. At first, Jed talked about starting east then going north to trap despite Rodas's orders. Stan realized it was he who had ended the idea. Father Carrillo told Walker if he and his men were caught, they would be escorted out of the province, but if Stan were caught, he'd be sent to Mexico City. Captain Monroe agreed with the Father, and Jed changed his mind. They would all head back toward Santa Fe. It was a shame, but both he and Walker knew they'd better not fool with the Mex.

He'd looked forward to helping Sir Warren and seeing Monterey and San Francisco bays. Stan was also curious to meet Leon Kent, Sir Warren's troubled younger brother. Chances were he would never see Sir Warren or Diamond again. Still, he'd seen more of the West than he thought he would when he left New Jersey. The hawk dropped lower, but still circled above.

Stan thought of his brother Dan. He often did during quiet times like this. Dan had been like a father. He understood why his brother loved the West, the open beauty, the unknown touch of danger. Above, a half dozen crows were attacking the hawk.

Dan would have been proud of him, the way he handled the amputation and his role while Walker recovered. If Dan had lived, perhaps Stan would have gone to West Point, but the Point was more what Dan wanted than he. Stan enjoyed the study of medicine, and he was confident one day he'd be an excellent physician. The hawk retreated off to the south with two crows in pursuit.

It all would have been different if he hadn't left the dance hall with Veta Biscusa. There was that word "if"" again. He didn't want the word to be a part of his life story: if only this, if only that. Was he in love with Lynn? He didn't know. He did know he felt sick to leave her so soon after finding her again. Still things had changed between them, and now he would never know what had happened and why. It still hurt, he wanted Lynn. The hawk disappeared and the sky was again serenely blue. The wind died and it was warm.

"Senor Aldridge."

Stan opened his eyes. He didn't know how long he had slept. The sky was a faded blue. He sat up and tried to determine what was happening. Captain Monroe's lead vaquero, Marco, stood nearby.

"I'm sorry to wake you," Marco said, holding his hat in his hand, "but the Captain, Father Carrillo, and your friends need you back at the Mission." Stan felt foolish sitting nude on the blanket. He got to his feet and started to put on his clothes.

"Is anything wrong?" Stan asked. He didn't recall a meeting with Captain Monroe, and it was too early for dinner at their camp or at the Mission.

"No, no, but I think it has to do with the pox. The Senorita will explain it to you on the way back."

Stan pulled on his pants and looked toward Midnight. He saw Marco's mule, and Lynn stood by her horse with her back toward Stan. Stan rolled up his blanket, and he and Marco walked back to Lynn and the animals. Lynn wore red-trimmed buckskin pants and a red blouse, her broad, black hat tied tight under her chin.

"Sorry," Lynn said, walking toward Stan and extending her hand, "we had to wake you." What a smile. Her hand was warm and soft.

"I hadn't intended to sleep at all," Stan said, with a shy smile. "What's happening?"

"Captain Rodas came to Father Carrillo this morning," Lynn said, as Stan secured his blanket to Midnight, "and reported there is a smallpox outbreak in the valley east of Monterey. Father is considered to be one of the most knowledgeable medical men here in upper California." The three mounted and rode out through the trees toward the Mission road.

"And you," Stan said, he studied Lynn riding next to him, "are his able first assistant." He wondered if he should ask her if she had received his letters, but it wasn't the time.

"Well," said Lynn, with a shrug, "I wouldn't put it that way, but we do exchange books and consult with one another on our patients. Since spring we have met twice a month to improve and help each other. It's hard. I'll have Dad buy new books when he is back East." They reached the Mission road, and Marco rode ahead of the two younger people.

"Have you ever dealt with smallpox?" Stan asked.

"No," Lynn said, "but about thirty years ago it wiped out many Indians and whites in this area. Captain Rodas told Father there is a real concern in Monterey and in the valley."

"It is deadly," Stan said. "What they've tried back East is a vaccination program, but it is for prevention. If you get the pox, you hope it's a weak strain and just sweat it out." They passed Stan's campsite. Stan waved to Diamond and Little Rabbit, and they proceeded on to the Mission.

"Have you ever done any of the inoculations?" Lynn asked. They saw the Mission ahead; the tile roofs gleamed in the later afternoon sun.

"Yes, "said Stan, "but vaccination is different from inoculation. The trick is getting the right medium to inject." When they reached the Mission, Marco took the horses, and Stan and Lynn headed for Father Carrillo's quarters.

"We are all here," said Father Carrillo. He sat at the head of the bare dining room table. "Perhaps it is best, Captain, if you review your message from the Governor-General." The Captain had barely acknowledged Stan, but had given Lynn a lusty smile.

"Late last night," said Captain Rodas, he cleared his throat, "I received a message from Governor-General Jose Maria Echeandia, in Monterey. He reports there is, east of the Capital, a serious outbreak of smallpox. They believe they have isolated those infected, who are Miwok Indians. The Governor is concerned. I understand, as a young boy in Sinaloa, he lost some family to the pox."

Captain Rodas paused to examine the two page message he received from the Governor. Stan looked at Lynn but her eyes were on the Captain. Stan couldn't believe she could like that man.

"Some time ago," said Rodas, studying the papers, "Governor Echeandia heard, from an English sea captain, that there is a method for the cure of smallpox. Therefore, he has sent this message throughout the province, and he has asked each of us, with local responsibility, to try and locate someone familiar with this cure." Captain Rodas looked up. He folded the papers and placed them in his inside coat pocket. "That is why I came to you, Father Carrillo."

"Thank you, Captain," said the Father. He placed his hand on two books before him. "I have read work done by Doctor Jenner in England, and also, by a Benjamin Waterhouse at Harvard. They have found that persons who have cowpox or mild cases of smallpox become immune to the disease."

"Lynn," asked the Father, "is that what you understand?"

"Yes," Lynn said. She looked across the table at Stan. "But Mr. Aldridge has performed the procedure."

"Good. Mr. Aldridge," the Father said, holding his hand out toward Stan. "That is why we ask you here."

"Well," said Stan, as he pulled his chair up to the heavy table, "first, what has been developed in England and the States is not a cure for smallpox. It's a prevention procedure. The technique involves a vaccination. It's like an inoculation but without the risks. People have died after inoculation with the disease medium, but that's not been the case with vaccination. What happens is a healthy person is given a mild case of cowpox. The person than becomes immune, we believe for life, from smallpox." Stan looked around the table, which also included Jed, Sir Warren and Captain Monroe.

"Once a person has full blown smallpox," Stan said, "there is little you can do except make them comfortable. If that's possible." Stan looked at Captain Rodas. "Your people took the right steps in imposing a quarantine. Smallpox is very contagious."

"Can you perform this inoculation?" Father Carrillo asked.

"Yes," Stan said. He felt all eyes on him. "What I'd do is the vaccination. I won't get into it here, but as I mentioned, vaccination is a safer procedure than inoculation. I'd work with cowpox. I've been vaccinated, so I'm safe from smallpox. Does anyone know if there is any cowpox in the area?"

"What is it?" Lynn asked.

"It's an irritation to a cow's udder," Stan said. "It often spreads to the hands of the milker, but it's not too serious. It was Dr. Edward Jenner, as Father said, who found people who had cowpox didn't get smallpox."

"I've never heard of it," said the Father. "We don't have too many dairy cows out here. Lynn, have you seen anything?"

"I've seen a rash," Lynn said. "I suppose it could be cowpox. Just last week, I was at the Gomez's ranch to check on Rosel's broken leg. Her two older sisters had a hand rash they thought came from milking their uncle's cows. I didn't think much of it."

"We get our cream from Gomez," the Father said. "Is it alright?"

"Oh yes," Stan said. "Normally cowpox isn't too hard on the cow or the milker, and the milk and cream are fine, although there wouldn't be much production while the cow is sick. I'd like to visit the Gomez farm."

"Can you teach this procedure to others?" asked Captain Rodas, peering hard at Stan. Stan admitted to himself that he didn't like the pompous Captain. The man had a way of talking down to everyone.

"Yes, but it's not a simple procedure," Stan said. "If we can find cowpox matter for the media it'd be easier. With matter taken from a human with active smallpox, even an experienced person can kill people. What I'd do is inoculate cows with the agent taken from a smallpox patient, and I'd work from the developed cowpox. It means a two week delay."

"If I have to get the vaccination," Sir Warren said, "I want Stan to do it."

"Yes indeed," said Father Carrillo, with a chuckle. "This is more than I'm ready to handle. What do you think, Lynn?"

"I'd like to learn more from Mr. Aldridge," Lynn said, "but until then, I'd better stay with broken legs and bee stings."

"Captain," said the Father, he turned to Captain Rodas, "if anyone can help the Governor-General, it is Mr. Aldridge."

"There is no way," Captain Rodas said, folding his arms across his chest, "I will send a man who assaulted Mexican officers to Monterey. I don't understand why he wasn't locked up in Santa Fe." Everyone looked at the Captain in stony silence.

"Captain," Sir Warren said. He leaned over the table with his hands on the edge. "Let me tell you about the 'assault' charge recorded in Mr. Aldridge's papers." All eyes turned toward Sir Warren. "Stan and I went to a dance in Santa Fe. The dance, by the way, was given by a Yankee trader from St. Louis. During the dance Stan and General Biscusa's daughter stepped outside for fresh air. Outside the dance hall, Stan was forced to protect the young lady who was pulled away, against her will, by a half dozen drunken Mexican officers." Stan looked across the table at Lynn. Her face was firm as she studied Sir Warren.

"Do you mean Veta Biscusa?" Captain Rodas asked, glaring at Sir Warren.

Stan smiled to himself. It seems everyone in Mexico knew Veta. Walker started to make a cigarette.

"Yes," Sir Warren said. "She's one beautiful young woman, and, for some reason," he looked at Stan and smiled, "she took a fancy to Mr. Aldridge. As I said, when she and Stan left the dance they were accosted by the officers. A fight resulted. The next day, Miss Biscusa sent Stan a small gift for his aid. Show them, Stan." Stan held up his head and pulled out the small gold chain around his neck. He looked across the table at Lynn and smiled, but she just stared at him with her lips pressed together.

"Mr. Aldridge should have known better than to dance with a General's daughter," Captain Rodas said. Stan stared into the

Captain's dark flashing eyes.

"I thought Veta wanted to dance, and she did," said Stan. "I didn't know who she was at the time."

"Stan," Jed said, he leaned back in his chair and lit the cigarette, "the Captain means a gringo ought' know better than messin' with the Mex General's little girl."

"We'd better get back to our discussion of smallpox," Father Carrillo said. "While we would like to help, Captain, it seems the one who could make a difference is Mr. Aldridge. It's up to you. . . and of course, Mr. Aldridge."

"Captain Rodas," said Stan, looking at the Captain, "I regret the incident in Santa Fe. . . but if I was forced into the same situation tonight, I'd react the same way. Those officers were drunk and out of line." Stan turned to look at Father Carrillo. "I don't need to remind anyone smallpox is a killer. If it breaks loose in the province, many people will die. I'd be happy to help."

"Does anyone have anything more to add?" the Father asked

"In a few days," Captain Monroe said, "I will sail for Monterey. I can take anyone who would like to go. I'll be picking up hides along the way, but I'd be there in a week."

When the meeting broke up, Stan overheard Captain Rodas tell the Father that, if he changed his mind, he would return to the Mission in the morning. Captain Rodas gave a small envelope to Lynn and left without a further word. Stan figured he wouldn't change his position.

In the courtyard, Captain Monroe walked up to Stan and extended his hand.

"If I don't see you again," said the Captain, "good luck on your trip East and your medical career."

"Thank you," Stan said. "I doubt if Rodas will change his mind. Anyway, I don't know how good my sea legs would be going up the coast with you."

"You'd be fine," said Captain Monroe. "In two months I head for Boston; that's a real test for the legs and stomach."

"Cape Horn," said Stan. He looked at the Captain with admiration. "That must be an adventure." Lynn Monroe came and took her father's arm and the three walked toward the horses. Father

Carrillo, Sir Warren, and Jed followed them.

"Are there any books you'd recommend on smallpox, Mr. Aldridge?" Lynn's voice and manner was cool. Stan hoped it was the presence of her father.

"Nothing special comes to mind," Stan said, "but always get the latest publications you can. Jenner's work has caused a lot of excitement, and new studies come out each year or two. For background, there is a book on the life of Jenner. It's by a man named Baron. . . When can we go to the Gomez farm?"

"Early tomorrow."

"We're not going to get much from these two," Stan said. The tail of the cow whipped him across the face. "Damn." He and Lynn struggled to squeeze matter from each inflamed bluish postulate. They'd found the udders of two of the six Gomez cows infected with cowpox. The two cows were somewhat indisposed and produced little milk, according to Gomez.

"This is just enough," Stan said, studying the small vial, "for about twenty people. Wash your hands good or you could get milker's rash. I had chicken pox, all over the place, and it was hell. Cowpox rash is similar."

"Yesterday you didn't show any sign of a rash," Lynn said, with a grin on her face, "that I could see."

"No, it was several years ago. . . What did you mean, you could see?" Stan asked.

"I have to admit," Lynn said, "I found you yesterday by the river, but I thought it better if Marco woke you."

"Well thanks a lot," Stan said, his face blank. "How long were you there?"

"Long enough," she said, lifting her chin.

"Have you thought at all about us?" Stan asked. He looked at her, but she looked at him in a blank and questioning manner.

"Not really. What about us?" she said. She avoided his eyes.

"Oh nothing. . . forget it," Stan said. He looked away so as not to show the hurt.

What the hell, if she could pretend that she had forgotten what they had planned back in New York, so could he.

Stan staggered across the starlit deck to the leeward rail. On hands and knees he vomited into a dark churning sea. Relieved, he lay back on the damp deck of the one hundred-twenty foot brig *Norwood*. He'd felt dreadful in the stuffy hold below. Sir Warren and two of the ship's mates were snoring as Stan felt his way up the ladder to the deck above.

He felt better, and he lay on his back and watched the stars roll back and forth. They disappeared and reappeared among the numerous sails of the full-rigged vessel. He closed his eyes and listened to the song of wind and water, to the creak of the blocks and the slap of the jib. He smiled. He was glad the others had not seen his sickness. Damn, what an awful feeling, a listless hell. At midday, they would pick up hides off the coast. He'd be ready.

He moved back out of the fine spray near the rails to an area by the forward mast; he'd spend the night there, on deck. When the heavy roll started after midnight, it disturbed the bilge water and a swampy smell filled the hold. Stan awoke knowing he was going to be sick.

It was four hectic days since Captain Rodas decided to let Stan go to Monterey, as a ward of Captain Monroe. According to Father Carrillo, a second message came from the Governor-General requesting skilled help in controlling smallpox "at any cost." It was this message that spurred Rodas. There had been two testy meetings, for the problem became, how would Stan, Sir Warren and his brother Leon return East without the help of Jed Walker. Stan stood firm; he wouldn't go to Monterey without Walker. In the end, Captain Rodas agreed Walker and his men could trap the valley to the north until Stan returned to the Mission.

Stan awoke to confusion overhead in the rigging. There was a sharp horizon of rolling hills to the east. The sea calmed and finger-like clouds turned red over the eastern horizon. They were near the place where they would pick up the hides.

"This will be the last of 'em, Captain," shouted the mate; he steered the long boat toward the beach. Captain Monroe lifted his hand in reply. The *Norwood* rode at anchor a half mile out from a small, sandy beach. Stan saw men on the cliff throwing dried hides down onto the beach below.

"How many hides are you picking up?" Sir Warren asked.

"Looks like it'll be close to three hundred," Captain Monroe said. "This ranchero is one of our best sources. His hides are cleaned and cured. That's what we like."

"Do you mean sun cured?" Stan asked. He watched the glistening oars of the long boat flash in the late afternoon sun.

"No. All of the missions and ranches stake and sun dry their hides," said Captain Monroe, "but not many brine cure them. For the shipment to Boston, the hides must be brine cured, or you end with a moldy mess on your hands."

"If they are only dried," Sir Warren asked, "who does the brine cure?" The three men watched the crew wade ashore from the long boat, which was anchored out beyond the breakers.

"We do," said the Captain. "We do it down near San Diego." Diamond and Lynn came up on deck and stood at the rail near the men. Diamond has a way of taking young women under her wing, thought Stan. White Rabbit stayed at the Mission, but Lynn insisted on coming. Stan knew both her father and mother objected, but in the end, Lynn prevailed. Lynn had traveled with her father before. It wasn't the travel the parents objected to; it was the smallpox. But Stan was glad she came, for he could use all the skilled help he could get. Lynn and Diamond were the only women on the ship. He would work with Lynn like any other young woman. He wasn't going to show he cared.

The afternoon sun warmed their backs, while the group watched the boat crew load the hides. The crew carried the folded, stiff hides, one by one, on their heads out through the breakers to the long boat.

Lynn came and stood next to Stan at the rail. "Mr. Aldridge, is there a way," she asked, "you could show Diamond and me the vaccination procedure before we get to Monterey?" The loaded long boat pulled toward the brig.

"Sir Warren asked me the same question," Stan said. "It's a good thought; tomorrow I'll go through the whole procedure with all of you." The long boat was alongside, and men brought the hides aboard for storage in the main hold.

After the unloading, several of the boat crew, who'd handled hides since sunrise, removed their shirts and shoes and leaped into the ocean. They wouldn't stay long in the frosty water.

"Everyone out," yelled the mate, "we've got to get the boat aboard and up anchor. The tide's goin' out." The men started climbing back into the long boat.

"I wouldn't mind a dip myself," said Stan, half to himself. He watched the last two men swim to the boat. The first of the two, a young man with reddish hair, put one hand on the side of the boat. With a sudden jerk, he disappeared beneath the surface.

"Shark!" yelled the second man, struggling to get into the long boat.

"Shark! Shark!" shouted the two crewmen. They pulled the second man to safety.

The stricken man broke the surface his arms flailing.

"Help!" he screamed, but again disappeared below the surface. The mate unlocked one of the long oars and pocked it into the water near where the man disappeared.

Stan removed his stiletto from his belt, and leaped feet first over the rail. He watched his moccasins hit the water ten feet from the long boat. The water was clear, but it was shockingly cold. It tore his breath from him.

Stan saw the shadowed bottom of the long boat, and, under it, fought the desperate young man. A seven-foot long shark clamped its powerful jaws on the man's lower leg. Stan could see the brute's slate colored snout shaking back and forth, forcing his victim into submission. With the knife in his mouth, Stan reached the man and his attacker with three powerful breast strokes. The man broke the surface a second time as Stan passed under him. The crewman's free foot kicked hard into Stan's shoulder. Removing his knife from his mouth, Stan passed under the wicked, crescent-shaped mouth that gripped the sailor's leg.

Stan was now along the white under belly of the beast. He stretched out toward the shark's tail and drove the six-inch long blade in to its hilt. Stan pulled forward with all his strength. The water clouded dark with blood and gut. Stan slashed twice more into the soft milky under pillow. Looking up, the water churned a strange reddish green, and it was alive with whipping snake-like viscera. A desperate need for air strangled Stan as he fought upward; he broke the surface gasping. He saw the mate and others pull the sailor into the boat. The man's face was pale and his eyes like dark blue gems, but he was alive. The shark, near death, still clung to the seaman's leg. The mate jammed a knife into the beasts deep eye; the dying shark dropped loose and floated, still quivering, past Stan. Stan dropped his knife into the boat. He hung on the gunnel with both hands, still gasping for air.

"Get him aboard," yelled Captain Monroe from above. "There may be more out there." Three sailors pulled Stan into the long boat. Stan lay back and closed his eyes; he heard a cheer from above.

12

Stan held Lynn's arm firm as he applied the needle. It was over in less than a minute.

"It wasn't bad was it?" he asked.

"That's it?"

"Yep," he said, he wiped her arm with a piece of whisky-dipped cotton. "We'll know in seven days if it took. If it did, a red ring will develop around it." Stan had reviewed the vaccination procedure with Lynn, Diamond, and Sir Warren. He'd vaccinate Lynn and Sir Warren, and Lynn would vaccinate her father, Diamond and the first mate. They would hold the remaining material until they met with the Governor.

"There is Point Pinos," Captain Monroe said. The blue Pacific sparkled calm in the noonday sun. Stan and Sir Warren stood at the starboard rail with the Captain. They watched the approach of the cypress-green California coast.

"The coast here," Sir Warren said, "doesn't look as barren as in the south. Down there reminded me of northern Africa."

"I agree," said the Captain. "This is a great area. I have property here, and I'd like to build and move up, but Elisa wants to wait." They rounded the Point and saw the first of the white homes and red tile roofs of Monterey.

"What is her concern?" Sir Warren asked.

"Well," chuckled the Captain, "Elisa, like many women, fancies herself a match maker. She's also a good friend of Nalda Rodas, Captain Rodas's mother. They think Eduardo and Lynn are a great match, and he has asked to court her, which is the Spanish custom. I think it's a good match myself, we'll have to see how it works out. . . .but it's pretty well set. Gentlemen, please excuse me. We'll anchor soon." The Captain moved off toward the wheel deck.

Stan turned away from Sir Warren. He felt the blood drain from his face, and there seemed to be a sack of lead in his stomach. It explained a lot. The very close Spanish mother, the handsome Captain. He was upset with himself. There had been nothing, no understanding, between him and Lynn. He studied the white wake of the brig. He shouldn't care, but he admitted he thought about Lynn in a very special way, and it hurt. He couldn't tell her how he felt, not how.

Stan was thankful his boss hadn't noticed his face.

"There's not another ship in here," said Sir Warren, he studied the harbor. "No *Helenka*. . . but who knows, maybe there's a place where we can get a drink."

The Captain anchored the *Norwood* close in, and Stan rode the first boat ashore with the Captain, Lynn, and Sir Warren. The day was bright and pleasant, the bay calm as a mountain lake. The Mexican flag flew from the small square presidio, and the sound of parade drums rolled across the water.

"It looks like we have more than our normal customs officials to welcome us," said the Captain. "I feel the Governor-General is involved." Stan saw several military officers at one side of the small group on the main dock, and soldiers with horses and a carriage waited at the rear of the dock.

"Eduardo told me he'd let the Governor know Mr. Aldridge and I were with you," Lynn said. Stan studied the planks of the boat's deck.

"Captain," Sir Warren asked, "would the customs people know about the *Helenka*?"

"I don't believe they deal with sealers," the Captain said, "but there's an inspector named Tito who knows about most ships' comings and goings. Talk to him."

"By the way," Sir Warren said, "I thinks it is important Stan's situation, like my own, be explained to the American consul before either of us leave town."

"Yes indeed," said the Captain. "I became a Mexican citizen years ago when I married Elisa. There are a lot of us out here like that, but we're still Yankees at heart. The consul, Ralph White, knows it too. Both of you will get to talk with Ralph today or tomorrow, before you go anywhere."

The Captain was right. Two officers from Echeandia's staff were at the dock to escort them to his quarters. While the Captain made arrangements with the customs officials for the inspection of his ship, Stan and Lynn watched two young boys feed huge manatees off the dock. To one side, Stan saw Sir Warren had found the inspector named Tito. The Captain's first mate, a veteran named Henry Stearns, would go back to the ship with the customs officials. The Governor's open carriage waited to take Stan and the others to the presidio.

"Tito was up to San Francisco Bay just three days ago," Sir Warren said. From the carriage, the four saw the bay through wind-shaped cypress trees. "The *Helenka* was in the harbor."

"Great," Stan said. He looked into the Baronet's bright eyes.

"The problem is," Sir Warren said, "he heard the ship will head for China within a week. He does not know about Whitelaw, but he claims the first mate is named Ivanov. When Leon wrote, he must have thought Ivanov was the captain."

They came into a large open square with a half dozen cannons in the center. One-story adobe buildings surrounded the square.

"Tomorrow," Sir Warren said, "I head for San Francisco Bay. You can meet me there. We have made it." Sir Warren gave Stan a slap on the knee.

Jose Maria Echeandia was a thin, juiceless man with dark suspicious eyes. The Captain told Stan that Echeandia was from an old Spanish family. Moorish designed, carved and gilded pieces furnished his spacious office. After the introductions, he took a seat behind a heavy desk. Stan and the others sat in the front.

"Senorita Monroe," Echeandia said, "I'm sure you are excited about your courtship with Captain Rodas." Lynn put her hand to her chin. Her mouth opened, but no words came out.

"It will work out fine," said Captain Monroe. "They're just getting started."

"These things take time," said the Governor, smiling at Lynn. "The Captain, like your mother, has fine Castilian blood. It will make a strong family line." Stan thought he saw a slight smile cross Captain Monroe's face. Lynn pressed her lips together and nodded.

"Mr. Aldridge," Echeandia said, he turned his dark eyes on Stan, "before I ask you to explain your vaccination procedure, I would like to have Dr. Chavez join us. He is my personal physician and my advisor on medical matters."

Dr. Rufo Chavez was a middle-aged man with a patch over his left eye. He sat with a bored look on his face while Stan described the principles and practice of smallpox vaccination. Walker would have labeled him a pompous ass.

"Let me see if I understand," said Echeandia. "You believe, if we could somehow vaccinate everyone in this province, we would no longer need to worry about smallpox. Is that correct?"

"I didn't put it quite like that," Stan said. The Governor had listened carefully and asked well-directed questions. "But that can be done, yes."

"What about infants?" Lynn asked. She had taken numerous notes when Stan reviewed the procedures on the *Norwood*.

"I'm not sure," said Stan, "perhaps when they reach a certain age, they'd be vaccinated."

"What do you think about all this?" Echeandia asked Dr. Chavez.

"The English medical people," Dr. Chavez said, only his mouth moved, "are always in a squabble over each other's work with chickens, dogs or rabbits. Most of the time, their results are no better than reading the bumps on the patient's head. Dr. Jenner has brought a cow into the laboratory, likely with the same results."

"This procedure," Lynn said, with a fiery glint in her eyes, "has been well-tested during the past several years."

"Senorita," Dr. Chavez asked. His voice was low and he still slouched in his chair. "Where did you, indeed, where did you and Senor Aldridge receive your medical training?"

"The Governor requested help," Sir Warren interrupted, "and these two volunteered with information from America and other progressive nations."

"Yes, yes," Echeandia said. He raised the palms of both hands toward the group. "Both Dr. Chavez and I are aware much work has been done with smallpox. Rufo knows it is more than bumps on the head." The Governor paused and broke a thin smile. "Still, we are concerned about starting here in the Capital, so Dr. Chavez has a plan." He turned toward the Doctor. "Explain it to them."

Dr. Chavez sat up in his chair. He adjusted his short, green jacket of silk, and ran his index fingers over his thick black mustache. Stan was glad Walker was trapping. Jed would put a fist in the man's face.

"As Senor Aldridge admitted," said Dr. Chavez, "this procedure can be dangerous; people have died. All of the area's prominent citizens live in Monterey. They must be protected." The doctor was then seized by a series of coughs. "Jose, could you ring for water?" he asked.

"People have died," Stan said, "from an inoculation of smallpox pustulate. I don't know of anyone who has died from a vaccination of cowpox medium."

The water came and Chavez continued, ignoring Stan's comment.

"We have isolated the current outbreak to a group of Miwoks near the San Joaquin River. Senor Aldridge would gather his medium for vaccination there. Then he would vaccinate a group of say fifty to one hundred Indians from the nearby Wintun tribe." The doctor paused to drink more water.

"If the vaccination appeared successful," a slight smile appeared on the Doctor's face, "the protected Wintun's would be mingled with the Miwoks. We would soon know if this vaccination procedure is both safe and effective."

"It would also," Echeandia said, "give you technical people a chance to gain valuable experience with the entire procedure."

"We can't infect other humans with a deadly disease," Stan said. "Besides, I just said smallpox pustulate is too dangerous." Stan felt a warm glow creep up his neck. What are they thinking?

"Certainly not," Lynn said, moving to the edge of her chair.

"Now, now," said Echeandia, holding up his hand, "if the procedure works, like you two say, no one would be harmed." There was silence while each person stared into space. Stan couldn't believe Chavez was proposing such a test on humans.

"Remember," said the Doctor, slouching back in his chair, "both the Miwok and the Wintun are an idle, shiftless people, poor for even simple labors."

"You seem to put them," Sir Warren said, leaning forward to look at the Doctor, "in the same class the English doctors do dogs and rabbits."

"I want to help," Stan said, "but I can't participate in this."

"Nor I," said Lynn. Echeandia's face was gray.

"Senor Aldridge," said the Governor, he leaned toward Stan with his arms extended and hands flat on the desk, "you said you wanted to help, but you disagree with our suggestions." His voice came low and strained like wind through tall pines. "Pray tell us, what you would be willing to do." The Governor forced a thin smile.

"I meant no disrespect," Stan said, moving forward in his chair, "to either you or Dr. Chavez."

"Nor I," interrupted Lynn.

"In fact," continued Stan, "my idea was similar to Dr. Chavez's, except we'd use cowpox pustulate, and not mingle the sick and the healthy. First, I'd collect the agent from the infected Miwok, and we would inoculate dairy cows. Then, I'd vaccinate and train a team of persons you select to do the field vaccinations. It takes seven days to determine if a vaccination has been successful in each person. At that point, you would have a trained staff capable of doing the vaccinations. I'd recommend vaccinating here in Monterey first. You can do what you want. But remember, this is a contagious disease, difficult to quarantine. Time is important. The pox can break out here or anywhere, anytime. . . tomorrow perhaps."

"I have arranged for you to be taken into the valley at dawn tomorrow," Echeandia said. He leaned back in his chair, closed his eyes and rubbed them. "You will be at the Miwok village by dark.

We will have the cows for you to inoculate when you return in three days." He opened his eyes and studied Stan. "Remember you are a ward of Captain Monroe, who will remain here until you return."

"Governor," Sir Warren said, "I'm sure Captain Rodas has informed you I am looking for my brother." The Governor gave a slight nod. "One of your customs officials has informed me the ship holding him is in San Francisco Bay. I plan to leave for there tomorrow."

"Senor Kent," Echeandia said, "we have been more than generous in permitting your group to trap for beaver, considering the lack of proper passports." He got to his feet. "You are to remain in Monterey with Captain Monroe until Senor Aldridge returns from the valley. Perhaps then you and the Captain can proceed to Yerba Buena."

"But-"

The Governor, without a further word, swept out of the room, followed by Dr. Chavez.

"I have the distinct feeling," Captain Monroe said, he got to his feet, "our Governor-General questions whether a party like yours came all this way to look for a lost brother."

"Does he think we're a group from the U.S. government?" Stan asked.

Captain Monroe shrugged, "It wouldn't surprise me. Texas is in trouble. Who knows what's next. . . Santa Fe. . . maybe California? Echeandia don't trust his mother. He's got two more years, and he doesn't want trouble on his watch. But with Stan leaving at dawn, we'd better find Ralph White before dinner."

Stan and his four escorts headed due east over the Diablo Range. Corporal Hector Gil was in charge. He woke Stan before 3:00 AM, and the men rode hard for two hours, through a fine mist, before the first dull light appeared in the east. The pox marked Corporal could speak English, but there was no time for conversation. Corporal Gil was intent on reaching the Miwok village before dark.

The mist stopped, but the sky was a low, heavy gray. The rolling hills of the range were a strange green, almost treeless. This was not New Jersey.

"Are you from this area?" Stan asked. They'd stopped to water their horses at a small stream.

"No, no," said Corporal Gil, "me home Durango, in old Mexico."

"I'd like to visit there someday," said Stan. The Corporal studied Stan and a slight smile came to his face.

"Maybe no," Corporal Gil said. "Where your home?"

"In the U.S. near New York City." Hector Gil broke into a broad, nearly toothless smile.

"I have been there," Corporal Gil said, "to New York City." Hector was a man you couldn't help liking when you saw his smile.

"Well I'll be," said Stan. "How'd you get there?"

"Around the Horn," said Corporal Gil. "Me sail for ten and two years."

They pushed down into the broad San Joaquin Valley. Here the landscape took a more Eastern look with plenty of alder, sycamore and oak, and, along the streams, willow and cottonwood. The Corporal rode alongside Stan whenever possible.

"Have you had the pox?" Corporal Gil asked. They rode through an area of scattered trees.

"No, but I've been vaccinated," Stan said. "It's a new way to keep people from getting it."

"The four of us here," said the Corporal, "have all pox when we small. Could you do. . . this thing for my wife and children?"

"Sure," Stan said, "how many kids have you got"

"Ocho. . . you say eight."

They reached the Miwok village at sunset. It was a village of dome-roofed dugouts along the eastern shore of the San Joaquin River. The Corporal halted the group on the western side of the shallow, stony river. The sky cleared, and the late sun colored the village a mustard yellow. Stan saw no life, no smoke, not even a dog. Far to the east rose the white tips of the Sierra Nevada Mountains. The Corporal and his men jabbered in Spanish.

"There," Corporal Gil said, "five soldiers here. They to keep people in village. They be maybe nearby. We go across here." Stan followed the Corporal. They picked their way around the stones and boulders; the water was never more than four feet deep. About half way across, the stench hit Stan. The Corporal halted and tied a bandana over his nose and mouth. Stan did likewise.

When they approached the low cutbank of the eastern shore, Stan's horse shied to the left. To the right, just below the river's surface, were the bodies of two Indians. They were both men; one lay on his back, eyes bulging from his swollen face.

"Sometime," Corporal Gil said, "sick ones jump in river to die."

Stan swallowed hard and followed the Corporal into the village. Everywhere were bones and litter: clothes, weapons, utensils, firewood. In one cold fire pit were the remains of a white dog with a black face. The unskinned animal was partially cooked and a hind quarter removed.

"Where are your men?" Stan asked. He was amazed people could live in these conditions.

"They camp back out of smell. We go there now."

Corporal Gil led the group through a narrow trail of oak and underbrush to an open area. They traveled less than a half-mile, and the smell was again overwhelming.

"What is this?" asked Stan. He tightened the bandana over his mouth and nose.

On the far side were the stacked, swollen bodies of eight Miwok men and women.

"They bury dead here." There were several places where the earth had been dug and covered, and they passed a huge smoldering pit. Three human skeletons lay among the embers.

The Corporal stopped by the pit and turned to Stan.

"Ground hard here, we think better burn dead."

"Easier, I guess," Stan said.

"Easier, yes, yes," Corporal Gil said, with a chuckle.

They pushed on for two miles through a leaf carpeted forest of white oak and alder. The sun was down when they reached the soldier's camp. It was in a small clearing with a stand of junipers on the western side. Four men sat by a blanket playing cards. A fifth was asleep in a lean-to.

Stan sat on his horse and watched the card players greet the Corporal and his men. A flask of white whiskey passed among the noisy group.

"We stay here tonight," Corporal Gil said, he handed the flask to Stan. "Tomorrow we go to village. You do what you do."

"How many are still alive?" Stan asked. Two of the men were building up the fire, and others carried in the hind quarter of a steer.

"They think twenty, and maybe onc more." Stan dismounted and took a swig from the flask. He shook his head. It was like straight alcohol.

"Have any of the Indians left the area?"

"No, but they track five who try go."

"Did they find them?"

"Yes, they shoot all them dead."

Stan, on hands and knees, followed the young soldier into the twenty-foot diameter dugout. Private Fabio, the junior member of the crew, carried a torch for Stan. The Private, in the past weeks, became experienced in dugout duty, dragging out the dead. The air in the village was bad, but the air under the dome-roof of the dugout was a syrupy fog. Stan gasped, the heavy gasses clutched his nose and throat. The moist air was a putrid blanket. For a moment, he almost panicked and backed out.

Stan's hands and knees encountered the slime of human waste pooled on the earth floor, he shuddered. He stood, and his head jammed into the packed roof. Stan again fought off a drowning panic to leave the dugout. From the flicker of the torch light, he saw the near naked bodies of three women and two men. Their bodies shriveled back to their bones.

Stan removed his vial and spatula from his shoulder pack and knelt by the first woman. He signaled Fabio to come closer with the torch. She was a young woman and alive. He saw her dark dilated eyes moving back and forth from him to the torch. With her fever and condition she wore only a loin cloth. It was odd she had no marks on her face, but the skin of her once full face lay on her skull in dark ripples like a bloodhound's.

While her face was spared of boils, her body was not. Pox boils covered her skin from her neck down. There were so many they broke and flowed into one another. Her breasts appeared like growths on a barrier reef. Stan gritted his teeth, and he started to collect the pustulate.

Stan moved from person to person, for he wanted a mix of pustulate. One of the women was dead; he passed her and went to the last man. He had been a large man before the infection, and he looked at Stan in rage. He had the strength to turn away when he saw the spatula. As he turned, his sleeping mat imbedded with toxic eruptions clung to his back. But slowly, in the jaundiced-yellow light, the mat and skin peeled away; it left the braves back a mass of tiny black and red rivers. Enough. Stan scrambled toward the dugout entrance and out into the blaze of the morning sun.

Corporal Gil and his men were waiting. Stan mounted and followed the Corporal across the river. He looked back once, and he saw the Private mount up and head for the burial area, dragging the dead woman behind him.

13

Corporal Gil raised his hand and squinted into the late afternoon sun. Stan reined up beside him. Five soldiers rode hard down a long grassy ridge toward them.

"Maybe trouble," Corporal Gil said, "look like Lieutenant."

Since leaving the Miwok village six hours before, they stopped twice, and then only to water their animals. Stan leaned on his saddle horn and watched the soldiers thunder in. The small troop must have ridden hard from Monterey, for a heavy lather streaked their horses. The grizzly Lieutenant rode right up to them, his dark eyes flashed. He spoke in a harsh Spanish to Corporal Gil.

The four soldiers fanned out twenty feet behind their Lieutenant. They sat with their rifles across their saddles. Dusty sombreros shaded their eyes, but they all stared at Stan.

"Lieutenant say," Corporal Gil said, he turned toward Stan with dark questioning eyes, "you under arrest. Must give me rifle."

"That's crazy," Stan said. "Arrested? What for?" He made no effort to hand over his Gibbons. The officer spoke to his men. They trained their weapons on Stan.

Stan slowly handed his rifle to the Corporal.

"He say," Corporal Gil said, "you friends raid Mission San Miguel. Steal many horses. Kill three men."

"Walker? Jed Walker is no horse thief."

"Me no know. They take you to Governor."

Two hours after sundown, they reached the dockside at Monterey. A fog shrouded the torch-lit buildings.

"You stay here," said Corporal Gil, "they take to Governor in morning." They arrived at what appeared to be the main barracks.

"Corporal," Stan said, "you've been a good friend. And thanks, but I want you to know my friends and I are not horse thieves and murders."

Corporal Gil shrugged. "I hope you right." He was not staying at the barracks, and none of the other men spoke English.

"Ask the Lieutenant if he would inform Captain Monroe and Sir Warren Kent where I am."

Corporal Gil and the Lieutenant spoke for a time with obvious disagreement. Stan dismounted and stood by his horse. The damp Pacific air chilled him.

"Senor Sir Kent," Corporal Gil said, he looked down at Stan, "has been arrested and is held in plaza jail. Lieutenant no time to look for Captain. I see if I find him."

"Thanks," Stan said, and Corporal Gil and his men rode off toward the plaza. Stan spent the night on a small cot surrounded by snoring soldiers.

A shrill bugle shook Stan from deep sleep. He bolted up. The dark room was a sea of shouting and running men. Within five minutes the room emptied. Stan sat on the edge of the cot. From the outside lights, he saw two guards posted at the barracks door. A third guard came with a warm plate of black-bean mash. Stan was eating when Captain Monroe entered. It was foggy, but dawn had arrived.

They shook hands and the Captain took a seat on a cot across from Stan.

"What's going on?" Stan asked.

"You may know as much as I do, but the night before last Echeandia got word the Mission at San Miguel was raided. San Miguel is about one hundred miles south of here. The Mexicans think it was Jed Walker and his men. I don't know. They'd been trapping near the Mission, and the raiders were gringo."

"That's ridiculous. I know Jed Walker."

"I hope you're right," said the Captain, "but in the meantime,

I'm trying to convince the Governor you and Sir Warren are not part of Walker's group."

Stan studied the Captain.

"Do you think Jed did this?" Stan asked. The Captain sat for a moment looking at Stan before he replied.

"I don't know. Trappers are like sailors. Both can be tough and unpredictable."

"Well, I don't have any doubts," Stan said. The Captain nodded his head.

"Still. . . for now it's better for you and Sir Warren to put distance between you and those trappers. . .how'd you make out with the Miwok?"

"What can I say? It's appalling. I doubt if a handful will survive. The strong ones try to escape and are shot." The Captain removed his cap and tossed it onto the cot.

"They put Sir Warren in the plaza jail yesterday," Captain Monroe said. "Then they sent men after you. The Governor thought you'd run off with Walker. We're to meet with him this morning, but I'm sure he wants to keep the smallpox effort going forward. Lynn and Diamond have done most of the work so far. Dr. Chavez is a lazy ass."

"Lynn," Stan said, "has a real love for medicine." He looked into the Captain's eyes.

"Yes," said the Captain, ". . . but after she and Eduardo start a family, I suspect it will become less important." Stan studied his own boots and said nothing. Her family was pushing Lynn. He couldn't believe that was what she wanted.

Two uniformed Captains stood behind Governor Echeandia's desk. A staff with the Mexican flag stood to one side. With arms folded, the Governor sat behind his desk. A guard ushered Stan, Sir Warren, and Captain Monroe to their seats. Stan had no chance to talk to Sir Warren. The Governor's face was pale and gaunt.

"Captain Monroe," said the Governor, "I'm sure in the future you will be more careful in your selection of which Americans to assist." The Governor forced a thin smile.

"Governor, I'm convinced these two gentleman had nothing to do with the raid at San Miguel. Mr. Kent is a Scottish sportsman who came to California to find his brother. Mr. Aldridge is his clerk. Walker and his men were hired to escort them here from Santa Fe. That is their only relationship."

"Perhaps you are right. However, I have ordered Captain Rodas to bring those trappers back to Los Angeles. Even if they are not guilty, they are to be held there. In these times, we can not have eight armed men roaming through the province."

Echeandia turned and spoke to his Captain on his left.

Echeandia placed both hands on his desk, and said, "Until we have further word from San Miguel, Senor Kent and Senor Aldridge will remain under house arrest. They will continue to help with the smallpox vaccinations. A guard will be assigned to each man. . . your daughter, Captain, I'm told has been most helpful. I have reported this to Captain Rodas." The Governor folded his hands and again forced a smile.

"Thank you, sir," Captain Monroe said, with a smile.

"Governor," Stan said, "I'm sure you will find Mr. Walker wasn't involved at San Miguel. In the meantime, it would be helpful, to me, if the person assigned to me spoke English. Corporal Gil proved very helpful at the Miwok village."

The Governor turned again and spoke to his Captain.

"Corporal Gil will be assigned to you. He has reported favorably on your trip to the valley."

Stan nodded his head, and Sir Warren got to his feet.

"Sir," Sir Warren said, "time is running out for my brother. I am already behind schedule. If the ship on which he is held sails for China, he is as good as dead. I must be allowed to contact the ship's captain in San Francisco Bay." Echeandia folded his arms and stared at Sir Warren.

"Captain Monroe," Echeandia said, " you sail for San Francisco Bay tomorrow. Could you send a man to ask if Senor Kent's brother is on this ship?"

"Yes."

The Governor, with a sly smile, looked back at Sir Warren.

"Governor," Sir Warren said, his neck reddened, "as a citizen of Great Britain I protest our treatment. I am sure this would not happen if I were in Mexico City."

The Governor stood, his face calm but gray. He turned and whispered at length with the Captain on his right. He then turned toward Sir Warren.

"Senor Kent, I remind you, you are in Monterey not Mexico City, and I am in command here. The Captain will return you to the jail. I am told your house woman has proven more useful than you at La Soledad." Echeandia turned and marched from the room, followed by the officer on his left.

"The bastard," Sir Warren said. His face was pasty white.

"Listen, Warren," said Captain Monroe, he put a hand on Sir Warren's arm, "don't bait him with Great Britain, America, or even Spain. Any inference Mexico is somehow second class sets him off."

"Can I bring you anything?" Stan asked.

"Thanks," Sir Warren said. He took a couple deep breaths. "But you will not have much time. You will be taken to the Mission soon I am sure."

"I'll stop and drop off a flask of whiskey before I go, and we'll talk about your brother," Captain Monroe said. "We'll find him."

"If they know you are here," Stan said, "they won't sail."

Stan and the Captain watched as Sir Warren was led from the room.

"Don't challenge this Governor," Captain Monroe said, he looked into Stan's eyes, "even in the slightest way." Everyone left the room except a guard at the door. Stan and the Captain sat down.

"The Corporal will take you to Mission La Soledad," said the Captain. "It's about thirty miles from here. Lynn and Diamond are there. The Governor didn't want the vaccination work done right here in Monterey. He's scared to hell of smallpox." The Captain placed his cap on a chair and mopped his face with a large white handkerchief.

"Elisa would be upset," Captain Monroe said, "if she knew Lynn was down there by herself."

"If Diamond is with her," said Stan, "she's well escorted."

"Yes indeed, she's some woman. But I've also passed the word Lynn and Captain Rodas plan to be married. That way, the military and mission people will treat her like a married woman."

"Has a wedding been set?" Stan asked. His voice sounded hallow to his ears. He hoped his face revealed nothing.

"Oh no, but it's a matter of time. Elisa has convinced me it would be best for Lynn. The Rodas family controls much of the import business into Mexico City. Lynn will have a good life. . . you'll head for the Mission soon. I understand they have thirty cattle ready for you to inoculate, and Lynn has vaccinated as many of her helpers as she can."

"I'm glad Lynn and Diamond are there to help. We should have it all completed in three weeks," Stan said. "But I feel bad about Sir Warren. He came all this way and is so close to getting Leon. He shouldn't be in jail."

"I'll do what I can," said the Captain. "You get the smallpox wound up and everyone safely back. . . and please keep an eye on Lynn for us."

"Yes, sir." He wished he could bring himself to tell Lynn how he felt. It was pride. There is a paradox in pride: it can make you ridiculous, but can also prevent you from becoming so. He would say nothing.

The sun was down for an hour when Stan and Corporal Gil reached the broad undecorated walls of Mission La Soledad. They passed through a guarded gate and dismounted.

"Where is everyone?" Stan asked. The two men led their horses into a dark stable.

"They sleep," said Corporal Gil, "sunset is bedtime here." Stan hoped to talk to Lynn. He'd have to wait for morning.

"Father Antonio seems cooperative enough," Stan said. He and Lynn had met with the Father and three of his priests. The two strolled down a long arcaded corridor leading from the mission offices to the guest quarters. The day was bright but chilly.

"He's a nice man," Lynn said, "but not much of a man for science like Father Carrillo. He's more of a philosopher." They passed two nuns, in long robes, who kept their eyes averted.

"I think you prefer the scientific," Stan said. The sun was rippling off her bouncing hair.

"Normally," Lynn said, her dark eyes flashing at Stan, "but not always."

"Oh?" Their eyes met and held for an instant.

"In this case, Mr. Aldridge," she said, with her chin up, "I was referring to Dr. Chavez." He had seen nothing of the man.

"Where is the good Doctor?" Stan asked.

"He's here, but we don't see much of him. He spends most of his time in his room with a favorite cleaning girl." They were now crossing the courtyard. They passed by a rotary mill crushing sugarcane into juice, and a copper-lined pan boiling it into cane syrup. There was a pleasant smell. It felt good to be with Lynn.

"Those things happen." They were nearing the women's quarters.

"I guess," Lynn said, she stopped and turned toward Stan, "but before you see Diamond, I have news for you. I have her speaking English, and she speaks almost as well as you or me."

"I always wondered about it," said Stan, "because she seems to understand everything." He looked at Lynn, and his eyes searched her face for a sign. There was none.

"It's odd," Lynn said, "it must have been the way she dealt with a strange culture, but she says she just thought she sounded funny. She has an English accent, like Sir Warren. . .she and I have grown quite close. She's a remarkable woman. A week ago, I told her it'd be a big help to me if she could speak English. So she did. For whatever reason she was reluctant to try around men, even Sir Warren. But just tell her how nice she sounds."

"I don't understand it," Lynn continued with a scowl, " but she thinks you can walk on water." Stan just smiled and shrugged. He saw Diamond coming out of the room waving at him.

The days passed rapidly. The inoculation of the cattle and the training and vaccination of Mission personnel consumed Stan's days and nights. On two occasions, he and Corporal Gil spent several days visiting Indian villages. Stan confirmed smallpox had infected both the Yokut and Kern River Indian tribes.

They gathered the last of the vaccine, and within a week they would return to Monterey to begin general vaccination. Stan and Lynn planned to send an Indian team to vaccinate the Yokut and other valley tribes. He enjoyed the days he worked with Lynn. They worked well together. At times he felt her watching him, but when he looked at her she would just smile and drop her eyes. Neither ever mentioned their time together in New York City, nor did they mention Captain Rodas, but Stan felt an unspoken spirit growing between them.

"Senor, Senor," whispered Corporal Gil. He shook Stan gently.

"Yes, yes," Stan said, setting up. The room was dark except for the Corporal's flickering candle.

"We go back Monterey."

"Why?" Now what?

"Senor Sir Kent has escaped from plaza jail. Governor want you return. Him very mad." Stan sat on the edge of his cot and rubbed his face. The room was freezing. Sir Warren's action didn't surprise him. They had no good reason to hold him, but the Governor would suspect his own shadow.

"I've got to talk to Senorita Monroe before I leave," Stan said, he pulled on his buckskin pants. "Could you get my horse?"

"Yep, but hurry. Lieutenant no happy."

Stan trotted across the courtyard toward the women's quarters. He passed the low stone wall of a small cemetery, and he saw far to the east the first profile of the Sierra Nevada Mountains. Diamond was heating coffee in front of the low adobe quarters that formed the eastern wall of the Mission. Stan wondered when Diamond ever slept.

"Would you wake Lynn?" Stan asked.

"Is something wrong, Master Stan?"

"Sir Warren has escaped from jail, and the Governor has ordered me back to Monterey."

"Lord, have mercy," Diamond said and hurried into the quarters.

Lynn came out wrapped in a green blanket. She looked small and pale in the firelight.

"Sorry," Stan said, "but I'm being taken to Monterey. Sir Warren has escaped from jail, and as far as the Corporal knows, they've never found Walker or his men."

"You could end up in jail," Lynn said. She hugged the blanket tight to her.

"With Echeandia, who knows. . . just stay with our plans. I'd get the Indian team into the valley before Chavez gets his nose into it. Hopefully, I'll see you in Monterey in two or three days. I'll tell the Governor that when you arrive, we're ready to start the vaccination. . . somehow I need to find a way to help Sir Warren."

"Be careful," Lynn said. She stood beside Diamond.

"Is there anything I can do?" Diamond asked. She put her arm around Lynn.

"No," Stan said. "But, keep an eye on Lynn. I promised her father we'd keep her safe for dear Captain Rodas." Stan looked into Lynn's dark eyes; he could see only the reflection of the fire.

Diamond put her hands on her hips and looked from Stan to Lynn.

"We wondered why you so cool to Missy Lynn. We both think you're a very special man," Diamond said, giving Lynn a big smile.

"No, Diamond. . . please," Lynn said, pulling on Diamond's arm.

They heard someone running across the courtyard toward them. It was Corporal Gil.

"Hurry, Senor," said the Corporal, breathing hard, "the Lieutenant madder than spit."

"Good luck," said Stan. Both women watched him with concern. Stan took a few steps with the Corporal then turned back and addressed Diamond. She had her arm back around Lynn.

"Ask Missy what she did with the letters I sent her from New York." Stan gave the women a slight smile before he and the Corporal hurried off across the dark courtyard. He hadn't planned to say that, but he felt relieved.

The men stopped twice during the day to water and feed the animals. It was dusk when they arrived at the plaza in Monterey. At the jail, the Lieutenant received new orders. Stan closed his eyes and leaned forward on the saddle horn while the officer jabbered with the jail keeper.

"What's going on?" Stan asked. Corporal Gil looked almost asleep in his saddle.

"Governor say you stay officers' quarters. Get officer food."

"Well I'll be damned."

"They catch men who raid Mission. They not your friends." The Corporal dismounted and handed Stan his rifle. He'd remain Stan's interpreter.

Stan and Corporal Gil ate a hearty soup of beef and vegetables and slept in a small barrack not far from the plaza. Stan understood he would meet with the Governor within the next two days.

It was near noon when Stan awoke. The barracks room was empty. It had been weeks since he slept in. In a small wash room Stan was able to shave and take a cold sponge bath. The Corporal arrived with a heavy blue woven cape, a pair of wool socks and a shirt.

"Captain of Ship want meet you at plaza," said the Corporal. The Corporal had trouble pronouncing Monroe. "Him here early this morning. You hurry, hear."

"These socks are a blessing," Stan said, "all that was left of my other pair is anklets." He put on the new clothes. "Thanks, partner, I'm ready." He slapped the Corporal on the back.

"You look, like big, important man," Corporal Gil said, flashing his broad toothless grin.

An hour later, Stan sat with Captain Monroe and the American consul, Ralph White, in a small coffee shop just off the plaza.

"It's odd," said Captain Monroe, sipping his espresso, "the difference a day can make. Three days ago I thought I might end up in jail, and I was sure Stan would."

"Catching the San Miguel thieves helped," Ralph White said. He was a frail man in his mid-fifties. "But, believe me, the big change in Echeandia came two days ago when he learned his duty here in the north would end in six months. His wife has wanted to go back to Mexico City since the day they arrived almost six years ago. She refers to the province as a 'wretched Indian outpost.' But don't get too comfortable, because here in Monterey, things change overnight."

"Does anyone know where Sir Warren is?" Stan asked. The consul signaled for more espresso.

"No, but we're sure he's headed for San Francisco Bay," said Captain Monroe. "But he won't find the *Helenka* there."

"She hasn't sailed for China has she?" Stan asked.

"No, no," said the Captain. "She's in Bodega Bay."

"Just where's that?" He watched as an old woman refilled the small rose colored porcelain cups.

"It's a Russian fort," White said, "about eighty miles north of Yerba Buena, which is the main village on San Francisco Bay. It's trouble for Echeandia, and frankly for us too. We don't need the Russians out here."

"Do we know," Stan asked, "if Sir Warren's brother is aboard?"

"Yes," said the Captain, "at least we think so. My first mate, Henry Stearns, took our small boat out to the *Helenka*. They wouldn't let him aboard, but Henry talked to Ivanov, who we believe is the first mate. Henry told him he had a message for Leon or the ship's Captain from Leon's brother. Ivanov went below for half an hour, then returned to say neither was available, but he asked why Sir Warren hadn't come himself. Henry told him Sir Warren was in Monterey, where he was detained by Mexican authorities. That's all we know. Henry didn't see either Leon or the Englishman."

The small, withered woman served a loaf of warm bread and a jar of honey. She again refilled their cups from a steamy pot.

"I need to help Sir Warren," Stan said, blowing on his small cup. "He's not just my employer. He's become a good friend. We've come a long way to free Leon, and I want to see it through. Do you think the Governor will be a problem?" Stan looked across the table at the American consul.

"Not if he is satisfied with the smallpox issue."

"I think it's in hand," Stan said, "except for the Indians already infected. We can't do much to help though, and the Mexicans don't seem too concerned about them." Through the window the men watched an Indian servant turn tortillas on a sheet of metal over a smoky, stone-rimmed fire.

"What about Jed Walker?" Stan asked.

"The last I heard, the Governor wanted them returned to Los Angeles," said Ralph White.

"Eduardo is hunting for him and his men," said Captain Monroe.

"If Walker doesn't want to come in," Stan said, "Eduardo won't find him."

"I wouldn't bet on it," said the Captain, folding his arms.

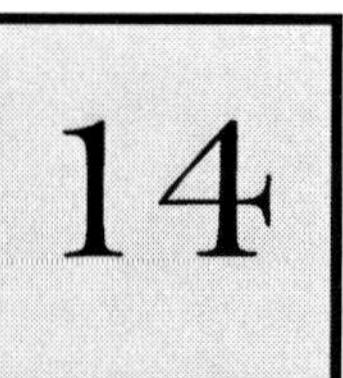

Despite the presence of eight active children, the wife of Corporal Hector Gil somehow managed a tidy home and garden. Earlier in the week, this meant little to Stan. Now, after visiting dozens of adobe homes and having vaccinated hundreds of men, women, and children, he knew it was unusual, and he wondered how she managed it.

The two youngest of the Gil brood, a boy and girl, clung to their mother's skirt and legs. Lynn knelt by the mother and whispered into the ear of the little boy. The Corporal's other family members milled in a sunny area in front of their adobe house. Slowly, the chubby boy released his grip on his mother's leg, and Lynn rolled up his sleeve to proceed with the vaccination. Stan smiled, for the boy held his free hand over his eyes.

This was the second day Stan had worked with Lynn; until now, it had been more efficient for them to work on separate teams. With the end in sight, they worked together. He watched Lynn quiet the second child; he'd struggled with children all week and wondered how she did it. She was good and they worked well together. Often he felt her eyes on him, but when he looked into her eyes she would smile for an instant and look away. Was he reading something that wasn't there? He knew how he felt, but he wasn't going to say anything, not again.

"Casta is last one," Corporal Gil said. "You and Miss Lynn

come in, have coffee with my woman and me. She make special for you." Stan walked to where Lynn was finishing with Casta.

"The Corporal wants us to have coffee with him and his wife. Do we have time?"

"There's only one more house on this road," Lynn said. She gave Casta a tap on the rump and the child skipped off toward her brothers and sisters. "We'll make time. I know you and the Corporal have become good friends."

Stan, Lynn, and the Corporal sat on floor mats around a low table. An adobe fireplace in one corner warmed the ochre-colored room. Years before, the Corporal told them, the surface of the tamped-clay floor had been hardened by soaking it with sheep's blood.

"Where you two go when finished with pox?" asked the Corporal. His wife, a round little women, served hot coffee flavored with cinnamon.

"I'm headed for Yerba Buena," Stan said, "to find Sir Warren." They looked across the table at Lynn.

"I'll be sailing home with my father," Lynn said. Mrs. Gil came and sat beside her.

"The coffee is delicious," Lynn said, she placed her hand on the woman's plump arm. "Thank you." She spoke to Mrs. Gil in Spanish.

Stan sipped his coffee, while the other three jabbered in Spanish. Poles suspended from roof beams held colorful blankets along the walls, and the small statue of a saint occupied an arched wall niche near the fireplace.

"Sorry, Master Stan," said Corporal Gil; the others were chuckling. Mrs. Gil held her hand over her mouth. "Pia think you husband of Miss Lynn. She tell us, she think, you two will have many babies together."

"Sounds interesting," Stan said. He smiled and looked into Lynn's eyes. She smiled at him, she was beautiful. "But Miss Lynn plans to marry another man." Lynn lowered her eyes.

"That's not," Lynn said, "quite-"

"Ah, too bad," the Corporal said, rapping his fist on the table. "Master Stan is best gringo I ever know." He put his arm around

Stan, and a huge grin lit his face. "Him treat me like brother gringo. Miss Lynn, me think Master Stan very special man. Pia right, him good for you." The Corporal and his wife gazed at Lynn. Lynn looked at Stan. Stan raised his eyebrows and shrugged.

"Oh yes," Lynn said, "others have told me what a fine man Mr. Aldridge is." She looked at Stan with a slight smirk on her face. "I've enjoyed working with him, but he has never. . . we're just good friends."

"Me think Pia right," Corporal Gil said, giving Stan a slap on the back. "Miss Lynn good woman for you. Master Stan, you go too slow, nice gringo man. Need step up, tell Miss Lynn you want marry her." Stan looked at Lynn, but her eyes focused on the table. For a moment Stan thought the Corporal might be right, maybe Lynn was just waiting for him to make a second try. He wondered if he was to proud to try, or was he afraid of rejection.

"Thank you," Stan said, "you're a good friend, and you and Pia have a wonderful family. But for now, I need you to tell me the best trail to Yerba Buena."

It was dark when they reached the corral. Lynn waited while Stan unsaddled their horses and turned them loose. Diamond would have dinner ready near their adjoining rooms in the officers' quarters.

When they went to pick up the medical bags, Lynn bumped into him. Without thought, he held her by the arms and drew her to him. Her face was close. They kissed for several minutes without a word spoken. Her lips were soft. He felt like he was floating. She held him tight and her lips seemed as eager as his. He now realized that this had been building up for weeks. After a time, she put her hands on his chest and pushed back.

"What's wrong?" he asked. He realized how much he wanted her, and now he knew she felt the same.

"This is. . . it's crazy."

"You don't mean that." He could see her face in the faint light.

"I'll admit," Lynn said "I've thought a lot about you since you returned, but it always comes out the same."

"How's that?" He took her by both arms. He studied the gleam of her eyes.

"It goes like this. You're a Yankee from back East. I'm a Mexican, my mother speaks of us as Spanish," she winked at Stan, "from the California. Besides, with us, the wishes of the family are very critical, and my mother has plans for me and Eduardo. It's all crazy: we're worlds apart. My mother would die if she knew I was doing this-"

"Didn't you read my letters?" Stan asked.

"I didn't get any letters." They started to kiss. He kissed various parts of her face. She closed her eyes, her resistance gone again. He determined to help her work through the problem with her mother.

"What did your letters say?" Her head was on his chest. He kissed the top of her head.

"I'd found another woman."

"Stanley Aldridge," she said, kicking at his shin.

"I suggested we get our degrees and start a practice together."

"And?"

They saw Diamond come out on the back porch swinging a lantern.

"Master Stan, is that you?"

"Yes, Diamond, we're coming." They picked up their bags and headed toward the barracks.

"Think about it," Stan said, he gave her a gentle bump with his elbow.

"It's still. . . insane."

"I love you," he said. She grabbed his arm and squeezed.

Iron Paso dismounted from Valor. He was showing his age. Stan trotted toward him. The two shook hands and shared a hug.

"Damn," Stan said, "it's good to see you."

"Good to see you, Stan. It seemed like a long ride up here this time. These cold winter days are rough on my old bones." He flashed his turned down grin.

"We didn't expect you," Stan said. They walked Valor toward the corral.

"Father Carrillo heard the Governor was givin' you men a hard time," Iron said. "He and Echeandia go way back to grade school, so Father wrote him a letter. I hadn't been north in a couple years, so I volunteered. I delivered the letter this morning."

"The Governor's been better," Stan said, "since they caught the San Miguel thieves, but the letter will help. . . I hope."

"I didn't see the Governor," said Iron, "but his aide said Echeandia was pleased with you and Miss Monroe's work with smallpox. He also mentioned the 'big black woman', but he didn't say a thing about the Scot."

"Sir Warren's okay," Stan said. "He just wants to free his brother."

"Reckon you're right," said Iron, giving Stan a wink. "Did you see who I brought?" Stan spotted his horse Midnight in the corral.

"Thanks, Iron." The horse came to the fence and Stan rubbed its ears.

"One more thing," said Iron. His eyes surveyed the area. "I know where Walker is."

"Good," said Stan. "Do you know they're still hunting him?"

"Sure I do, and Jed don't want anyone told but you— not the Scot, Diamond, Captain Monroe, his daughter. . . nobody."

"Alright," Stan said. "How's he doing?"

"He and his boys have had a good trap, 'cept Boatswain Brown shot himself in the foot. Jed said he wished you were there, but he and Cotton fixed Brown right fine. Cotton told me the Mex got pretty close once, but Walker's just too slippery. Walker wants to start back East before the first of April. He needs to be at the rendezvous."

Iron opened his pouch and added a pinch of tobacco to his chew.

"We'll have Leon and be ready well before then," Stan said. "I plan to head for San Francisco Bay the day after tomorrow. Can you come with me?"

"Yep. Walker ask me to help you keep the Scot out of trouble and find the kid. He's heard Rodas is getting more men. That just means trouble for Jed." Iron put one foot on the lower rail of the corral.

"They caught the San Miguel thieves. What's the problem with a few trappers?" Stan asked. He picked up Iron's pack; he could bunk in with him.

"I ask Father the same thing," Iron said. "He said Captain Rodas don't like Jed or you."

"Me?" They started to walk to the barracks.

"Yes, the Father thinks it's about the Captain's daughter." Iron looked at Stan out of the corners of his eyes. Stan had a sheepish grin on his face.

"So?" Stan asked. Stan had to smile, Iron had that grin on his face.

"Father Carrillo says the mother'd boil both you and her if she thought that." Stan's face was serious but calm. He took a deep breath, and he blew air out of his mouth.

"So be it," Stan said, shaking his head.

"Truth is," Iron said, "the Father thinks you and Miss Monroe would make a good match, with you both liking medicine and all. But the mother and Rodas are somethin' else. Those high Spanish types are a special breed. Miss Monroe is to do what they want, I'm sure."

It was late afternoon, and they were kissing. It was spontaneous. When they were alone, they were in each other's arms. Stan was leaving in the morning, and Captain Monroe was due back at any time.

"What are we going to do?" Lynn asked. Stan nibbled on her ear.

"We'll work it out." His hands rested on the upper part of her firm buttocks.

"But, how?" With her hands on the sides of his face she pulled his head down and kissed his face.

Diamond opened the door.

"I will come back," Diamond said, pulling back.

"No, please," said Lynn. She pulled away from Stan and stepped toward the door. Through the open door, they saw Captain Monroe and Iron talking by the corral.

"Come in," said Lynn, she took Diamond by the arm and closed the door.

"This is good," Diamond said. Her face was beaming. "I'm so happy."

"Thanks," said Stan, "but please keep it quiet. . . for a while."

"This is good, I am very happy."

"Diamond," Lynn said, her hands gripped the black woman's arms, and her eyes looked up into her face, "listen please, we must keep this quiet, like Stan said. We have to work things out with my mother, and dad too. I'll talk to you later."

"Alright, Missy Lynn." Diamond's eyes were wide and bright. Captain Monroe rapped at the door.

Diamond was outside brewing a second pot of coffee. Iron came in and sat at the table with Stan, Lynn and her father.

"You two," said Captain Monroe, studying Stan and Iron, "be sure and tell Warren the Governor is holding me responsible for both him and Stan. It's a game he likes to play."

"I hope we can find Sir Warren," Stan said.

"The Bay is huge," said the Captain, "but, except for a couple Missions and the main dock area at Yerba Buena, there's not much there. The governor promised to put out the word Sir Warren is no longer a fugitive. You should have a letter before you go."

"It's a good sign," Iron said, "maybe they're no longer hunting Walker and his men."

"No, no," the Captain said, "Eduardo has orders to bring him and his men back to Los Angeles. Echeandia don't want a group of armed Americans on the loose."

"I think it's an over reaction," Stan said.

"I'm not sure," the Captain said. Diamond came in and filled the coffee cups.

"Diamond," said the Captain, "Lynn tells me you're coming back to Los Angeles with us to help with the vaccinations. That's great."

"Thank you," said Diamond, "Missy Lynn is my good friend." Diamond stood behind Lynn and put her hand on Lynn's shoulder. Lynn reached up and squeezed Diamond's hand.

"Good, good," said the Captain, with a smile. "You can help chaperone Lynn and Eduardo for us. Since I've been up here I've gotten three letters from Elisa and all she writes about is Lynn and Eduardo. I think she has their whole life planned."

Lynn gave her father a thin smile and flashed a pleading look at

Stan. He saw a questioning look on Diamond's face. This was not the time to tell Captain Monroe; they'd wait. Stan looked at Iron, but the scout sat studying his own hands. Diamond went for more coffee. Paso broke a lengthy silence.

"Captain," Iron said, with his smile, "most women are the same as your wife, but, in the end, it's better if young people work out their own marriage plans. The match making days are numbered. Forcing a marriage can blow up on you." Iron then turned his eyes toward Stan. Stan gave him a slight nod. Iron Paso was good at reading more than trail signs.

"I know," said the Captain, smiling at Lynn, "Elisa and I wouldn't have been married in the old days. Believe me, at first, her family didn't think much of a gringo sailor. I don't want to push Lynn. . . but it does seem like a good match. . . " He raised both hands and gave a thin smile. Stan wondered if the Captain would understand what was best for Lynn. Would he be an ally?

They stood in the dark shadow at the side of the barracks. From there they watched the moon beams ripple out over Monterey Bay. It was cold, and Lynn shivered in his arms.

"I'm afraid," Lynn said. She pressed her head to his chest.

"Why?" He felt a shiver run through her.

"It's all so uncertain, and you'll be gone tomorrow."

"One thing is certain," he said. "I love you." He felt her arms tighten around him.

"Do you remember our strategy?" he asked. She pulled free and gave him a salute.

"Yes, Captain." He pulled her close and they kissed.

"On the trip home," she said, her head again nuzzled on his chest, "Diamond and I are 'very slowly' to work my father to our side. Then, all of us will 'very slowly' convince my mother what a brilliant man Stanley Aldridge is. . . when my prince returns from the north, everyone will welcome him with open arms."

"When you were growing up," he asked, "did anyone ever tell you that you were a smart mouth?" They held each other tight. "Anyway, you got it close enough. . . you'll see. . . it's easy."

"Sure." She jabbed her hand into his ribs.

Iron Paso led Stan northeast over the rolling Gabilan Range. Stan questioned why they didn't follow the coast north. Iron told him it was too rugged and wooded for easy travel. The first night they camped on Carnadero Creek. Iron made a fire while Stan picketed the five animals. In addition to Valor and Midnight, they brought mounts for Sir Warren and Leon, plus a well-loaded pack animal.

"Did you read the Governor's letter?" Stan asked, turning the steaks.

"No," Iron said, "but the Captain told me it says that the Scot is a free man. The Captain thinks the Governor regrets jailing him. Echeandia has calmed down and realizes it wasn't too smart to throw a big-shot European in jail."

"I hope he's alright." Stan said. "When he left Monterey, he didn't have a horse or rifle."

"He'll make it," Iron said, he placed two logs on the fire. "People with money always make out."

"There is no advantage to money," Stan said, "if you don't put it to proper use. And you have to admit, rescuing his brother is a good use. We hope." Iron looked at Stan and smiled.

The Mission San Clara was a prosperous enterprise and reminded Stan of the Mission at San Gabriel, with cattle, horses, grain, and rolling hills covered with a vineyard and fruit trees. But a cold rain moved in when he first saw San Francisco Bay. It was not the picturesque scene Lynn described for him. The tide was out, and off the Mission docks a marshy slate-gray water disappeared into the fog and rain.

"It's a good thirty-five miles from here to Yerba Buena," Iron said. "I wouldn't want to row it in this weather." He and Stan watched a group of Indians load two launches with hides and tallow.

"Can't they bring the ships in here?" Stan asked, he leaned forward to let the rain run off his hat.

"No, it's too shallow. When the tide is out, areas down here turn into salt flats. The ships stay up at Yerba Buena."

"Somewhere down there is Yerba Buena," Iron said, cracking a grin.

The rain stopped and it cleared to the east, but to the west, a white fog poured over the hills. From a hill to the east of the village, Stan looked down and saw nothing through the white blanket but the masts of four ships and a church steeple. To the east, the Bay stretched out a noble blue in all directions with green wooded islands and distant shores. At the eastern edge of the village, the rolling fog tore free like cotton and disappeared into the clear air farther east.

"Lynn told me this was a different place," Stan said. "It's beautiful. . . but strange."

"Let's go down and see if we can find a room at the Mission," Iron said. "They may know something about the Scot too."

Mission Dolores was not a massive ranch mission; it was a more compact harbor and village mission. But Iron knew the right people, and he and Stan were able to share a small, cold room.

"I think I have a lead," Iron said, coming into the room. Stan sat up on the edge of the cot. He had rested after caring for the animals.

"That was quick," Stan said, rubbing his eyes. He had fallen asleep.

"Yes," Iron said. "Two days ago a young priest visited a couple condemned men at the harbor jail. They'll be taken to Mexico City for hanging. In the next cell there was a man with a British accent, and he asked the Father if the *Norwood* was in the harbor. It has to be the Scot."

"Let's get the letter and go," Stan said, picking up his gray bollinger.

"Right," said Iron, "but first we'll stop by the kitchen and grab a loaf of bread and bottle of wine. Even with the letter the Mex may not move too fast, and jail grub at best is bad food."

"You know," said Stan, "I think you're beginning to feel for Sir Warren."

"I wouldn't go that far," Iron said, with a grin. "We'll walk down. It's only two miles, and there's no good stable there. Anyway, on the docks they'll steal your horse and your rabbit's foot too. Be careful down there."

It was dark and a fine mist was swirling through the cypress and scrub pine when they reached Yerba Buena. The town consisted of three muddy streets lined with crude plank buildings. The streets ran east-west and parallel to the docks.

"The jail is across from the east end docks," said Iron, "on the edge of town." They turned right off the mission road onto the broad street that ran along the wharf. Ahead they saw and heard a group of men milling about. Several carried torches. The fog shrouded docks were larger than Stan expected, several times larger than Monterey. They passed two ships and a brig. The vessels' topmasts disappeared into the dark and drizzle.

"What do you think's going on?" Stan asked.

"Likely a fight. Some of these sailors may not of had drink or seen a woman in a year." A wagon rolled through the mud toward them loaded with lumber.

"What's going on?" Stan asked of the driver, a young man his age.

"The town folk want to string up Frenchy and his partner." He stopped the wagon and looked back down the street

"Who's he?" Stan asked.

"Shit, you been in a deep hole? They're the two buggers who killed Art Daley, and raped and forced his Misses to do. . . shitty things."

"Have they been tried?" Iron asked.

"Shit yes, found guilty as sin and sentenced to hang. 'Cept the Mex guards have been ordered to take 'em to Mexico City. Ain't it the shits? Those greasers want all the fun." The young man turned back to his team and gave the lines a snap.

"Sorry boys," he said, "but I've gotta deliver this shit and get back in time for the hangin'." He drove off.

Stan and Iron made their way through a crowd of about thirty men who milled in front of the jail house. On a small wooden porch of the jail, two guards stood with rifles.

Three men blocked Stan and Iron as they neared the porch. The leader, in the center, was a man Stan's height with broad shoulders. He wore a black robe. A massive head of white hair topped his granite face. He carried a Bible.

"I'm the Reverend Dinman. Who are you gentlemen?" he asked. His voice was like a canyon echo.

"We are friends of Sir Warren Kent," Stan said, "and we have a letter from the Governor releasing him." A short man to the Reverend's right spoke up.

"Must be the dandy in the rear cell who talks like a English schoolmarm."

"Where's the letter?" asked the Reverend. Iron handed him the letter. The man on the Reverend's left held a torch and studied the letter with the pastor.

"It'd be just as well," said the torchbearer, "to get that fellow out of the way."

"All right," the Reverend said, "talk to the guards. But you'll likely have to wait for the Captain. If they let you in, only one of you go."

"What's in the bag?" asked the torchbearer. Stan showed him the wine, bread, and a hunk of roast beef.

Stan and Iron advanced to the porch where Iron talked to the guards at length in Spanish. The uniformed guards were young and nervous. One did the talking; the other youth's arms trembled as he clutched his rifle.

"Show them what's in the bag," Iron said. "They'll let you in, just go slow and easy, I'll be here near the porch. We have to wait for the Captain, too. Be careful, I don't like this."

The guard rapped on the door and spoke to someone inside. Stan heard a board slide back, and he stepped through the open door. To the left, a dusty lamp on a small table lit the room. Directly ahead was the larger of two cells. To the left, down a narrow hall-way, containing a barred outer window, was the smaller cell.

"Who are you, Mister?" asked a small young man clutching the bars of the first cell. He wore a dirty wool cap from which hung stringy blond hair. His face reminded Stan of a parrot. A huge man sat in the corner of the cell. He looked asleep.

Stan moved by the desk down the hallway to the second cell. The guard, an older man, secured the main door and watched Stan. He held his rifle ready.

"Stan, is that you?"

"Sir Warren?" Stan knew the voice, but hardly recognized the dirty, disheveled and bearded man who peered through the bars at him.

"Dear God," Sir Warren said, "this is the best day of my life, and I have had a gifted life, too." He reached through the bars and gripped Stan's hand with both of his. His grip was strong.

"How long have you been in here?" Stan asked.

"Almost a week."

"Hey Mister," said the young man, he was at the wall of bars separating the two cells, "my mother is the one you best hang, not me. The sorry little whore." Sir Warren motioned with his head and went to the end wall.

"That one is a loon," Sir Warren said, "but watch the big one. What a brut, and strong as an ox. It took six guards to get him in the cell. And last night, it was beyond belief. He sodomized the kid right here in front of the guard and me. Can you get me out?"

"Yes. Iron is out front. He has a letter from the Governor releasing you. We're waiting for the Captain."

"Good, but the Captain has more to worry about than me." Sir Warren looked past Stan and out the small hall window. Stan glanced out and saw the flicker of the torch lights.

"Did you find out any more about Leon?" Stan asked. He opened the bag and handed a piece of roast beef and a loaf of bread to Sir Warren.

"Dear God I am sick of beans. . . no, not really, other than the scow has gone up to the Russians at Fort Ross. She's to repair the foremast and pick up tallow. I was trying to get money for my pockets when they grabbed me. I should have known better." Sir Warren paused to take a swallow of wine. "The Mexicans have better communications and are smarter than I thought. . . I am glad Paso is here. We have to get to Fort Ross, and he always seems to knows where he is and where to go."

"Hey Brit," called the young man, "how about sharin' those vittles with Frenchy and me."

"His name is Sandy," Sir Warren said, "just ignore him. . . what is it like out front?"

"Not good. The Reverend looks like a tough man. We don't want to get caught in the middle of this thing. Do you know anything about it?"

"A little. One of the guards likes to talk. I know these two apes killed a man named Daley and raped his wife one night a week ago. Daley ran a dry goods store on Mission Road. The wife is alive but a basket case. She is also a niece of the Reverend Dinman."

Shouts and two shots came from the street. Frenchy got up and walked across to the front of the cell. He was six feet tall and weighed three hundred pounds. His greasy, black hair curled down over his massive shoulders. A dirty beard covered his broad face.

"You ready to have your neck stretched?" he asked Sandy.

"They won't hang me. I didn't kill nobody. My mother made me what I am. Have I told you she and my stepdad dropped my little brother in a tub of boilin' water? The bastard screamed for a time. She hit him with an ax handle. Kill him. Shit, why'd they want to hang me?"

"To hell with your mother shit. You sure liked that fellow's woman suckin' your pecker," Frenchy said. Sandy slapped his knee and laughed.

"Yea, it was fun. We sure had us a time."

There was a rap at the door, and the Captain of the guards entered. He was a small, trim man with silver hair. He gave rapid orders to his guard.

"He is telling the man," Sir Warren whispered, "to fire two shots into the floor, leave the keys under the table and report to the presidio."

Sir Warren spoke to the Captain in Spanish, but the man ignored him and left the room. The guard secured the door and fired a shot into the floor. The sound was deafening.

"Christ!" Sandy shouted. "What you doin' asshole?" The guard reloaded his rifle and fired a second shot. "What's he doin' Frenchy?"

"Shut up," Frenchy said, "let me think." The guard tossed the keys under the table and left the room. Stan reached for the keys. The door opened and the Reverend Dinman entered, followed by two men.

"I'll take those keys young man," said the Reverend. Stan looked up into the barrel of a rifle. He handed the keys to Reverend Dinman. A smoky torch lit up the room.

"Save me Reverend," Sandy said, "my mother forced me to evil ways."

"Indeed," said the Reverend, "'evil events from evil causes spring.' But fear not. You will soon have a chance to repay your sins my boy."

"Can we free my friend?" Stan asked. The Reverend nodded and handed the keys to the man with the rifle. Stan helped the man unlock Sir Warren's cell.

"I didn't kill nobody," said Sandy. His pale blue eyes moved from person to person.

"Shut up," Frenchy said, "I ain't afraid of their damn rope. Shit, I'll go first." Stan got the cell door open and the two friends walked out. Sir Warren carried the wine bottle.

"You tell 'em, Brit," Sandy yelled, "I didn't kill nobody."

Iron was on the porch, where he and Sir Warren shook hands.

"You need a shave, Warren," said Iron, with a grin.

"Thanks for coming," Sir Warren said. He lay his hand on Iron's shoulder as they came down the steps.

"Let's get back away," Iron said. "There's a lot of booze bein' passed around. No lynching's a picnic, but this one could get ugly."

"What happened to the guards?" Stan asked.

"They fired a couple shots into the air," Iron said, "and left with the Captain. The Reverend told the Captain he and his men would report the guards put up a noble struggle before giving up the prisoners."

"Is that true?" Stan asked, the three stood at the edge of the crowd, which had doubled in size and now contained a number of women and children.

"'Questioning is not the mode of conversation among gentlemen,'" quoted Sir Warren. Stan smiled and gave Sir Warren a slap on the back. "It's good to have you back."

The Reverend summoned several additional armed men into the jail. A half-hour passed. Men came and went, in and out of the jail. A vendor with a cart of wine came by, and Stan bought a jug. The mist stopped but the cold fog swirled about the dock area.

The jail door opened, and the Reverend came across the porch and into the street, flanked by two men with torches. He was followed by four men with Sandy and four with Frenchy. The crowd packed in and grew silent. Sandy and Frenchy had their hands tied in front of them and their ankles were tied together with short cords.

"It is hard to believe," Sir Warren said, "they have been able to tie up Frenchy without someone getting maimed or worse. The brute seems almost anxious to die."

"He wants to show the crowd he ain't afraid to die," Iron said.

The Reverend led the torch-carrying crowd back west along the wharf singing *Onward Christian Soldiers*.

They stopped where a rope hung over the long jib-boom of a ship. The boom extended thirty feet over the dock at a height of twenty feet. The rope had been tossed up over the boom. Below the boom, standing in the bed of a wagon, two men were completing a hangman's knot.

Two men helped the Reverend into the wagon, and he held his arms above his head to stop the singing.

"Let us pray," said the Reverend, his deep voice rolled through the fog and over the crowd. He led the crowd in the *Lord's Prayer.* The fog whirled through the crowd, and Stan felt a deep chill.

"Bring forth the young man," said the Reverend, at the conclusion of the prayer.

"Let me go first," yelled Frenchy. The crowd cheered.

"No! No!" said the Reverend. "That one needs more time to repent his sorrowful life." The crowd cheered, and the Reverend climbed down from the wagon.

Three men lifted Sandy onto the wagon bed. He had walked down the wharf in a trance. But on the wagon, seeing the knotted rope hanging from the boom, he fell to his knees. Stan figured Sandy was no more than twenty years old, if that.

"Oh, God, God!". . . he said. His bound hands came up to cover his face. . . his lips quivered, and his body shook. The loop was forced over his head and fitted around his neck.

"Do you have any final words?" asked the Reverend.

"Oh, God, dear God!. . .I can't think. . .give me my hat. . . it was my mother, she worked in a brothel. . . hang her." The crowd jeered, and two men yanked Sandy to his feet. They adjusted the rope and made it taut. One of the men picked up Sandy's hat and pulled it down near his ears.

"Let the Lord's work be done," said the Reverend, and the wagon inched forward.

Sandy fought to hold his feet to the wagon floor, but the wagon pulled off and he dropped two feet into space before swinging free. His kicking feet touched the ground. The two men in the wagon struggled with the free end of the rope. They yanked the twisting, choking man up four feet. A wild gurgle came from Sandy's throat as he struggled. A man from the crowd, finally, ran forward and grabbed Sandy's feet and gave them several hard jerks. But another minute passed before the death struggle ended.

"Dear Lord, what an awful death," said Sir Warren.

"He didn't fall far enough," Iron said. "They don't know how to hang."

"Yes," Stan said, "the neck needs to be snapped."

"Thank you, doctor," Sir Warren said, taking a large shallow of wine.

They pulled Sandy's limp body high up near the boom, and the men secured it for all to see. Near the wagon a group of men gathered with the Reverend.

"Reverend, Reverend!" yelled Frenchy, "I repent my evil life, but grant me the wish to leap from this life. Hang me high."

The crowd chanted, "Hang him high, hang him high."

Two men boosted the Reverend into the wagon, and he held up his hands to silence the crowd.

"Your wish shall be granted," said the Reverend, the crowd cheered, "you will be hung from the balcony of the new Bay Hotel." The crowd cheered, and the Reverend took a seat by the driver. The wagon rolled down the street. The torch-carrying crowd followed, again singing *Onward Christian Soldiers*. Four small boys remained and tossed stones at Sandy's body.

The Reverend led the crowd west, then south, through the fog, to where the three story hotel was still under construction; it would be the tallest structure in town.

"Did you ever wonder why we're here?" Stan asked. The three men stood and watched the two hangmen secure their rope to the rafters of the roof above the third story balcony. The balcony was still under construction and had no railing.

"It is strange," Sir Warren said, "like a country carnival." He took a swig from the wine jug, and they watched four men lead Frenchy up the outside steps to the balcony.

"'Sin,'" quoted Iron, "'shall not have dominion over you. For the wages of sin is death; but the gift of God is eternal life.'"

"Hear, hear," Sir Warren said. He handed Iron the jug. The two hangmen secured the rope around Frenchy's neck

The Reverend stood in the wagon below and called up to Frenchy.

"Have you any last words?"

"Yes, Reverend, I have" Frenchy said, stepping to the edge of the balcony, "I want all of you to know I have no fear. . . and I have no shame for the life I chose. I'm proud I took what I wanted in this life." Stan felt a chill pass through the crowd. The man's eyes picked up the red from the torches below. Frenchy ended, "And I spit on you." He hacked up phlegm and spit down toward the Reverend. "If my dick hung out I'd piss on you all. I'd shit on you."

"Hang the bastard," yelled someone. The crowd roared its approval, and two men stepped forward to shove Frenchy off the balcony, but somehow, he grabbed the coat of one of the hangmen with an iron-grip. Both men fell together.

The rope was too long. Frenchy's neck hit the end with an awesome force, but the rope held. Blood shot up from his nearly severed neck, raining on the Reverend and torchbearers below. For a brief moment Frenchy held the kicking hangman, then the man dropped free onto the team of horses below. The animals bolted forward spilling the Reverend and two men out into the street.

Ever so slowly, Frenchy's huge body stretched his shattered neck. The blood covered body finally broke free from the neck and head, and it crashed to the street near the Reverend. His massive, dripping head with its tail-like neck, entangled in the hangmen's knot, swung back and forth high above.

"Dear God in Heaven," Sir Warren said. The empty wine bottle dropped from his hand.

"The terrible wages of sin," said Iron.

15

Father Gallo told me," Iron said, "the commandant's wife is a royal princess of a sort. You should feel right at home." He handed Sir Warren a cup of steaming coffee. Stan saw a grin on Iron's face. His two friends had become closer during the week since Sir Warren's release. The three men camped for the night along the Russian River, one hundred miles north of San Francisco Bay.

"I doubt if you will believe this," Sir Warren said, "but the Russians are even more prone to royal titles than we are in Scotland, more than even the shameless English."

"I was told," Stan said, he watched the flames lick up around an added log, "the Californios trade a lot with the Fort."

"Fort Ross," said Iron, "is run by the Russian American Company. They're here for a profit, like the Hudson Bay Company, and just as tough. We may find as many people up here as we did in Yerba Buena. It's a big operation."

"I just pray the *Helenka* is there," said Sir Warren. A fine mist was drifting down through the pines. Stan tossed two logs on the fire.

"Can I ask something?" Stan asked.

"Sure," Sir Warren said.

"Have you got the ransom money?"

"No. All I can do is sign an authorized note," said Sir Warren.

"I have talked to Captain Monroe, Father Carrillo, and others, including the only banker in Yerba Buena. That is when the Mexicans picked me up. Out here it is still a barter economy, one good for another. Gold is used, but little Mexican money, or Yankee, or Russian either. I hope to have the Fort Commandant draft a note for my signature. It will be good when the pigs get to London or New York."

"But didn't they want gold or silver?"

"Yes," Sir Warren said, "but I could not raise five thousand pounds of gold or silver either in Santa Fe or here in California. It is the best I can do."

The three studied the fire. Stan heard the wind rustle the top of the pines. He wondered how Whitelaw would react to no gold or silver.

"I do not know what I would have done," Sir Warren said, "without you two and Jed Walker. Well one thing. . .I know. . . I would have never have made it this far." He took a handkerchief out and blew his nose.

"I'm going to turn in," said Iron, standing. "I'll be going to get Walker tomorrow."

"What?" Sir Warren asked.

"Yes," Iron said, "he's about a day's ride from here, where this fool river turns from the north. He wants to be near just in case there's trouble." Sir Warren stood, walked around the fire and gave Iron a hug. Iron smiled, pushed him off, and slapped him on the back.

"I hope there's no trouble," Stan said, standing, "but if there is, it'll be nice to have Jed in camp."

"Yes indeed," Sir Warren said. He came and shook Stan's hand. His eyes were moist.

The Russian Orthodox chapel at Fort Ross contained both a belfry and a dome. It was one of the prominent features of the sprawling Fort, and like many other buildings it was outside the original stockade.

"There isn't much security," Stan said, rubbing Midnight's neck. Since they left the Russian River, he and Sir Warren rode north along a sandy road that at times ran only two hundred yards from the ocean. Coming north, they passed two wagons with lumber and one with hides. They were approaching the Fort.

"It does look like any coastal town," Sir Warren said. It was clear, but a cold gusting wind blew off the ocean. Two ships rode at anchor in the small cove. They passed three barns and a slaughterhouse. Everyone was busy, and no one gave them more than a glance.

"Iron said there is a large trade-goods store here," Sir Warren said. "We will stop there for supplies and information."

The trading room was at one end of the main barracks. It was a large room piled high and cluttered with hundreds of items. There were few objects of wood, metal, or leather the occupants of Fort Ross could not make, and they were there, from ploughs and axes to combs and shoes. There were also items brought by Russian and American traders.

A clerk in a stovepipe hat was serving two Californios. Stan smiled as he saw Sir Warren head for the wine drums. A dumpy woman, with a towel rapped around her head and carrying a broom, trailed after Sir Warren. The woman spoke poor English and no Spanish.

"We need these jugs to welcome Jed," said Sir Warren, he filled four jugs and placed them on the floor. Soon the clerk with the stovepipe hat appeared. He wore a black coat and bow-tie.

"Can I help you gentlemen?" he asked. He had a Boston accent.

"We will take the wine, and a few items. Do you know if the *Helenka* is here?" Sir Warren asked. The man studied Sir Warren and Stan for a moment.

"Is this your first time at the Fort?" he asked.

"Yes," said Stan. "Are you from Boston?"

"Indeed. . . yes, good. . .actually from Quincy." He smiled at Stan.

"We're looking for the *Helenka*," said Stan.

"What do you want with her?"

"My friend's brother is aboard."

"I think she's in Bodega getting a new mast. She ain't a company ship you know."

"Do you know when she heads for China?" Sir Warren asked.

"No, but it's not been a good year for the sealers. In the past years they've killed most of the buggers off. Now they load up with tallow and hides."

"Do you know who owns the *Helenka*?" Sir Warren asked, rummaging through a stack of wool shirts.

"Some say the Commandant's uncle," said the clerk. "They say that's why the ship gets treated like a company ship. Who knows?"

"Have you ever seen her Captain?" asked Stan.

"Sure. Big fat limy, ain't too friendly though. He has supper with the Commandant now and then. They're two of a kind."

"How do I get to see the Commandant?" asked Sir Warren. The clerk studied Sir Warren. He adjusted his stovepipe hat with care.

"You'd have to arrange with a guard at the Rotchev House. You may see the Princess Elena out with her roses or in her greenhouse. Everyone here loves the Princess."

The clerk adjusted the sleeves of his coat. "By the way. . . I meant no disrespect to the Commandant."

"Is there anyplace we could stay a few days?" Sir Warren asked.

"The crop barns near the chapel may have room. Not many hands needed this time of year. Ask for an old man named Jurg."

They were able to share a dusty grain storage room with two Indian laborers. The stable was clean, and there was a fire day and night for cooking. They would meet with the Commandant in the morning.

"When I get a note for the five thousand pounds," said Sir Warren, "we will head for Bodega Bay." Stan slid a rusty iron rack into the edge of the fire pit and loaded it with beef ribs.

"Don't you think we should wait for Iron and Jed?" Stan asked. It was dark and they were alone at the fire.

"No. They could be a couple more days. I need to get a feel of the situation. The note should be acceptable. If I were King James, I could not find five thousand in gold coin out here. They must be intelligent enough to understand. It is elemental. They get a good note and I get Leon."

They did not meet with the Commandant at Rotchev House, but in an office in the officers' barracks. A uniformed guard took them to an unoccupied office that contained several chairs and three small desks. They waited alone in the room for half an hour.

The Commandant entered the room alone and shook hands. He was a large, uniformed man gone soft with years of rich food and drink. He sat in a chair and put his polished boots up on a desk. His breath carried a trace of alcohol.

"What brings you two to Fort Ross?" he asked. He spoke slowly with a heavy accent.

"We came to find my brother," Sir Warren said. "We believe he is on a ship at Bodega Bay."

"What ship?"

"The *Helenka*." The Commandant removed his feet from the desk and sat up in the chair. He set his cap on the table.

"She is not a company ship. We do repairs. . . but nothing else."

"I understand," Sir Warren said. "My request is that your office draft a note for me. The note would be payable from my accounts in either London or New York." The Commandant studied Sir Warren. He smoothed down his gray sideburns with large workman-like fingers.

"What name on the account?"

"Warren Johnson Kent, Scottish Lord of Grandtully."

"Ah. . .you have proof?" he asked. Sir Warren nodded his head.

"There will be a fee," said the Commandant. He stood and put his cap on. Stan and Sir Warren got to their feet.

"Stay here," he said. "I send James to do the papers."

"Sir," Stan asked, "do you know the *Helenka's* captain?" The man turned and looked at Stan as if seeing him for the first time.

"No," he said. He left, closing the door.

"Friendly chap," Sir Warren said, sitting back down.

"I don't think I'd ask him for any help," Stan said.

A hard rain whipped off the ocean when they reached Bodega Bay. The bay was larger than the cove at Fort Ross, but the community was much smaller. Its main purpose was ship repair and the construction of small launches and other boats used by the Russians and their Californio neighbors. Stan and Sir Warren rode through the stinging rain to the main dock. It was mid-afternoon. Not a person was in sight.

"That must be her," Stan said, shielding his eyes from the rain. Just visible two hundred yards off the dock, a small brig held firm to its forward anchor. The main mast was missing.

"Yes," Sir Warren said, he wiped the water from his face, "at last."

"It isn't what I expected," said Stan. The two men studied the vessel.

"No," said Sir Warren. "There is no mistaking her for the pride of the East India fleet. We had better find a campsite." He shouted through a heavy gust of wind and rain. "Nothing is going to get done today." The squall pounded the coast for another two days.

The morning of the third day dawned bright and clear. At first light, Stan and Sir Warren were moving west toward the bay.

"You were up during the night," Stan said. Their camp lay in the rolling forest east of Bodega.

"When the rain stopped," Sir Warren said, "and I knew it was clearing, I thought this could be the day I see Leon. Gracious, I hope someone on the dock can speak English."

"With a Captain named Whitelaw," Stan said, "the crew must know some." Near the dock ten men worked on a forty-foot launch. A young man with a red wool hat and shirt stepped out toward them and held up his hand. He spoke to them in Russian.

"Sorry," Sir Warren said, "we do not understand. Can you speak English?"

"Ah," he said, "me boss man, speak." He held up his hand with a small gap between his thumb and forefinger.

"What you want?"

"We want to talk to the Captain of the *Helenka*." Sir Warren pointed out toward the brig at anchor. He spoke slow and loud; several men hammered on the launch. The stocky man studied both Sir Warren and Stan.

"*Helenka*?" he asked, he pointed toward the brig. Both Sir Warren and Stan nodded. The man signaled them to follow him. He led them along the dock area about fifty yards to where four men were removing the bark from a long cedar pole. One of the men stopped work, and he and the young man talked in Russian. The man was middle-aged, tall and wiry, and dressed in grease covered leather clothes, including his cap.

"Me Ivanov," he said, "who you?"

"I am Sir Warren Kent." Sir Warren spoke slow and deliberate; he introduced Stan. "I am looking for my brother Leon Kent."

Ivanov's eyes were the bluest Stan had ever seen, but they were inert and cold as they studied him and Sir Warren. He turned his head but still eyed Stan and Sir Warren; he issued commands to his men.

"You stay," Ivanov said, pointing to the ground at Sir Warren's feet, "me go to Captain."

"Is Leon on your ship?"

"Dah, dah."

With that said, Ivanov and one of his men hustled down the dock and climbed over the side. Stan and Sir Warren watched the two men row out toward the *Helenka*.

"Have you ever seen eyes like those?" Stan asked. He and Sir Warren stood and watched the two remaining sailors work on the huge pole. They wore the same oily leather outfits.

"We have made it," Sir Warren said. He put his hand on Stan's shoulder. "Lord knows, there were times when I had my doubts."

"Doubt can be overcome," Stan said, "if the want is there." Stan now hoped that Leon would live up Sir Warren's expectations.

"Yes," said Sir Warren, peering out at the *Helenka*, "'Life is a progress from want to want, not from enjoyment to enjoyment.' And, I know we are not done, but think. . . Leon is right out there." They watched Ivanov and his mate tie up at the *Helenka* and climb aboard.

An hour dragged by; the wind died down. At last, at the *Helenka,* two men entered the small boat and started for shore. Stan and Sir Warren stood on the dock and watched them approach.

Sir Warren blew air out through his mouth. "I should be happy, but I feel. . . strange," he said.

"You've done all you could," Stan said. He placed his hand on his friend's shoulder. "Most trouble we anticipate never comes." Sir Warren gave him a thin smile, and they watched Ivanov climb hand over hand up the rope ladder. The second sailor remained in the boat.

"We take to Captain," Ivanov said, to Sir Warren. In the bright sun, the first mate's chiseled face revealed a scar from his ear to his chin. He walked back and gave orders to the remaining men. One returned with him.

"Bring no weapons to ship," Ivanov said.

Both Sir Warren and Stan handed their rifles to the sailor with Ivanov. Ivanov spoke to the man, and the sailor stepped forward and presented both rifles to Stan.

"I'm going," said Stan. He refused the rifles.

"No," Ivanov said, "him go," he nodded toward Sir Warren. "Not you."

"He is going with me," Sir Warren said.

"I say no," Ivanov said. He grabbed the rifles from his man and thrust them into Stan. The rifles fell to the dock.

"We will leave our weapons, but we both go," said Sir Warren. He handed the sailor his pistol.

"You go," Ivanov said. He walked to Stan. "Him stay," he poked Stan's chest with his finger. Stan looked into the cold sapphire eyes and suppressed a desire to smash the man's face.

"What do you want to do?" Stan asked.

"I will be fine," said Sir Warren. He looked into Stan's eyes. "It may be better this way. You can keep an eye on our things, and Iron and Jed might show up. The ship is not going anywhere without a mast."

"We go," Ivanov said. Stan stepped forward and shook Sir Warren's hand.

"Good luck," he said. Sir Warren's face was pale. His hand felt cold and stiff.

Stan sat on the edge of the dock and watched the small boat pull for the *Helenka*. Sir Warren looked back once and raised his hand. Stan watched until Sir Warren disappeared aboard the ship. An empty feeling flooded through him. He gathered the weapons and headed back to re-picket the animals.

A half-hour later, he was back sitting on the dock. There was no wind and the winter sun was warm. Soon he'd see Sir Warren and his brother being rowed ashore. His thoughts turned to Lynn, as they did each day. She'd be home by now. He pulled back from the edge of the dock and lay down. The sky was a deep blue, with gulls gliding about. By now, Captain Monroe would be convincing his wife that Stan was ideal for Lynn. Stan couldn't believe they'd want their daughter spending her life in Mexico City. He closed his eyes; he could feel her lips. . .her hand was on his shoulder.

He opened his eyes and saw the silhouette of a man with a head band and long hair. It was Iron Paso. Stan sat up, adjusting his hat.

"I must have fallen asleep." Stan got up and shook Iron's hand. The scout had a grin on his face.

"Your brother," Iron said, "could nap at anytime, but like him, you're ready when the action starts. Where's your Scottish brother?" Stan told Iron the events of the last days.

"Did you find Jed?" Stan asked.

"He, Cotton, and Labrosa are camped about four miles back in the hills. Jed doesn't think this is going to go as smooth as Warren does. He said, 'gettin' the beaver out of a trap ain't always pretty.'"

"Jed could be right," said Stan, "Ivanov is the kinda man you'd like to smash in the mouth." Both men took seats on the edge of the dock and watched the *Helenka*. "Besides, all of them look and smell like they've rolled in a trough of back-fat."

"Sealers are like that," Iron said. "They're boilin' blubber all day and night. If they can't get blubber they buy tallow from the rancher's or Indian's. Besides," Iron turned to Stan with a grin, "if they fall overboard, they don't get wet."

"Is Jed coming down?"

"No. He thinks it's better not to show our whole hand. Who knows? Could be everything will go like Warren thought- they take his note and give him Leon. Then you men can head East." It was mid-afternoon and white clouds were blowing in from the northwest. Stan felt Iron looking at him.

"What are you going to do about the Monroe girl?" Iron asked.

"Why?"

"I ain't blind," said Iron, "and I talked to Diamond. Besides, I've known Lynn through Father Carrillo for several years. She's a special lady." Stan looked at him with a smile and shook his head.

"Yes, I know. . . I'm not sure. She's close to her mother. . .and her mother has her practically married to Captain Rodas. . .We'd like to go back East and finish our education. . . "

"When the time is right," said Iron, "everyone must leave the nest." Out in the bay at the *Helenka,* they watched two men climb down into the small boat and start for the dock.

"I don't see Sir Warren," Stan said.

"Nor I."

16

The one in the front is Ivanov," Stan said. He and Iron watched the small boat tie up to the dock.

"Something's not right," Iron said, "or they'd be bringin' Warren and his brother."

"We'll soon know." They watched the skilled first mate come up the ladder and onto the dock. He stepped right up to Stan.

"You come ship," he said, "Captain want." His voice was harsh, piercing.

"Why didn't you bring Sir Warren and his brother?"

"Captain say, come ship, now."

"I'm going with you," Iron said.

Ivanov turned to Iron. "Who you?"

"A friend."

"Captain no like Indians. You go good-bye." Ivanov said, jerking his thumb toward the hills. He walked back and spoke to his men.

"You'd better stay," Stan said, "just in case. The ship isn't going anywhere. I'll be fine." He handed his Gibbons to Iron. "If we're not back by dark or when he picks up his men, get Walker."

"I don't like it," Iron said, "but you're right, that tub ain't goin' to sea. I reckon this is what the Scot came for. There's bound to be wheelin' and dealin' to go through, and they don't know about

Walker and his boys." Stan gripped Paso's hand and looked down into his friend's grin.

"I guess," Stan said, smiling. "They may be after what hard cash is available. Thanks. . . standby."

He followed Ivanov to the edge of the dock and down the ladder into the small twenty-foot boat. The sailor in the boat motioned Stan to the forward seat, but Ivanov moved him to the rear of the five-seat craft.

The two able Russians shot the launch forward with each pull of the oars. The bay turned choppy, and the water slapped at the boat's hull. A fine mist drifted back into Stan's face. He pulled his bollinger down firm on his head, and looked back at Paso. He gave his friend a final thumb up. Iron raised his hand.

On approach, the brig appeared darker and larger, its towering foremast silhouetted against a bright afternoon sky.

Long use had worn each plank of the small boat sliver-free. The wood felt as oiled as the outfits of its crew. From time to time, Ivanov turned back to position the boat and the brig; otherwise, his frosty blue eyes focused on Stan. The second oarsman was Stan's age and stocky with a round face and gray eyes. Stan gathered his name was Yasha; the younger man talked to Ivanov, but he seldom received more than a grunt in reply.

Yasha secured the boat to two ropes hung from the starboard side-boom. Ivanov grabbed a third knotted rope and, cat-like, went up the rope and across the boom to the main deck. Soon a rope ladder unrolled down the side into the small boat. Yasha motioned Stan to go up. Stan felt awkward, but he climbed up and over the rail.

On deck was a group of a dozen curious and brutish sailors. Most wore double-soled boots, coming up to their knees, and well greased. They wore a mix of dirty woolen pants, shirts, frocks, and caps. Stan's first impression of the *Helenka* and her crew was one of filth and grease. It contrasted starkly to conditions aboard Captain Monroe's *Norwood*.

"Come," Ivanov said. Stan followed the mate forward across the main deck. He stepped over lengths of large hawser cables snaking about. They came to a door locked from the inside. Ivanov yanked a heavy cord several times. Stan heard an inside bell ring.

"Hi, hi," said a voice from behind the door.

"Sing, Ivanov," said Ivanov. Stan heard a board slide back, and the door opened.

"You, go," Ivanov said.

Stan stepped through the door into one end of a long narrow passageway. Several oriental-style lanterns hanging on the walls lit the passageway. The polished floor, walls, and ceiling reflected the lanterns. The door closed and Stan faced a massive Chinese man. The man was Stan's height, but twice his weight. He wore a stone blue kimono arranged with black dragon motifs.

"Please remove your shoes," he said, he spoke with a slight accent, "and put on the slippers." Stan pulled off his moccasins. He slipped into a pair of clean white slippers with draw strings, and he placed his moccasins on a polished shoe tree. Stan followed the man down the hall past two closed doors on the right: the smell of incense was in the air. The man stopped once and removed a white cloth from his sleeve and dusted an area below a lamp. He adjusted the lamp's opaque globe and then moved on to the final door at the end of the hallway. He tapped on the door.

"Come in, Sing."

Sing opened the door and motioned Stan to enter. It was a large, dimly-lit room, with an odd sweet smell. Ahead was a circular black table with an ornate tea setting. Captain Whitelaw sat on the far side in a chair with gold arms. He wore a black Manchus kimono emblazoned with the twelve imperial symbols. A soft chill rippled down Stan's neck and arms.

"Have a seat young man," said the Captain, he pointed to a chair across the table.

"Can Sing serve you tea?"

"No thanks." The Captain was a large fat man with heavy lips and puffy slits for eyes. His graying hair was cut like a page boy's.

"I am the Captain of this foul scow, but you see I prefer to live much as I do in civilized Hong Kong. Ivanov handles all the ship's chores. The Russians are a stupid, greasy lot. Lee's brother tells me you went to Dartmouth."

"Yes. Where is Sir Warren?"

"Ah, 'Sir' Warren is it?. . . You will see him before you leave. He speaks highly of you, Mr. Aldridge." The Captain took a sip of tea and studied Stan. It was impossible to see the man's eyes, just two puffy slits.

"Lee, aren't you going to meet Mr. Aldridge?" At the far end of the room, a figure rose from a pillow-covered couch and sat on the edge.

"Why? He's most likely just another dumb Yankee," Lee said. He stood and walked to the table. He was of medium height and weight and wore a flowery yellow kimono. His entire head was shaved.

"Mr. Aldridge," Captain Whitelaw said, waving a hand toward Lee, "meet 'Sir' Warren's brother Lee, or, as he called him, Leon." Stan stood and extended his hand toward Leon, but the young man just looked at him with dull hazel eyes. Stan retook his seat. An angry feeling spread through him. He needed to get Sir Warren and get off this ship.

"Captain," Stan said, "I want to talk to Sir Warren."

"You will, you will," said the Captain, "but first you must understand the situation." He pulled his chair up to the table.

"Sing," Leon said, "get me a pipe."

"Your employer, 'Sir' Warren," Captain Whitelaw said, "was a fool to come here without the coins. . .bringing a God damned piece of Russian paper." His jowls quivered.

"He wasn't able to raise the gold or silver out here," Stan said.

The Captain slammed his hand on the table. The teaset rattled.

"I will not accept that for an answer." His face was livid.

Sing came and placed a clay pipe, a silver stylet, a miniature lamp and an ornate pillow on the table by Leon, and he stood by with a small open container.

"The bastard," Leon said, "travels the world with my money in his dirty pockets." He used the stylet to collect white powder from the container Sing held.

"Sir Warren," Stan said, "is the eldest son. It's English law the inheritance passes to him."

"Be damned the stupid code of primogeniture," Captain Whitelaw said, "this boy must have his money." Leon held the powder-laden stylet over the flame.

"It is Sir Warren's wish," Stan said, "to share the wealth with Leon."

"Hayden," said Leon, he placed the small ball of heated opium in the pipe, "do you hear this ass."

"Mr. Aldridge," said the Captain, "it seems you know your role well. You sound like brother Warren himself. Good. Lord knows, dear brother needs loyalty now as never before." Leon rested his head on the pillow; he held the pipe over the flame and inhaled.

"You see, good fellow," continued the Captain, "you are the sole human who can keep Warren Kent alive." Stan felt a knot grow in his stomach.

Leon blew the last of the smoke from his lungs, and he raised his head. Sing cleared away the materials. Stan felt light headed, nothing seemed real.

"Hay, sweet," Leon said, going into uncontrolled giggling, "have Sing break the bastard's arm. . . I want to hear it pop like Brother's." He put his arms on the table and lay his head on them laughing uncontrollably.

Stan got to his feet. "Where is Sir Warren?"

The Captain stood, pointing a finger at Stan.

"You'd better understand this," the Captain said, poking his finger across the table at Stan, "and well. You get five thousand, I repeat, five thousand pounds of gold or silver to me at Yerba Buena by the first of March." His voice screeched like chalk on a blackboard. "I repeat, by the first of March. Or your Baronet of Murthly is. . . " The Captain ran his hand across his throat.

"Hayden," Leon said, raising his head up, "you promised we'd keelhaul him, gold or no gold."

"Shut up, Lee. . . Do you understand, Mr. Aldridge?" Stan glared across the table, but the Captain's eyes remained dark slits.

"Yes. . . I understand," Stan said. "Where's Sir Warren?" Stan suppressed an urge to smash the man.

"Sing," the Captain said, "have Ivanov take Mr. Aldridge below to Leon's brother. Have him help with the arm. Mr. Aldridge is supposed to be a medical man. We wouldn't want the dear brother to die on us, would we?" The Captain's heavy lips cracked opened, revealing two rows of tiny yellow teeth.

"I'll get the money," said Stan, "but you'll never see it unless Sir Warren is in good health." Stan turned back toward the door, Sing at his side.

"He may," Leon said, his voice squeaked high, "look oily when you come. He can have all the tallow he wants to eat." Stan heard Leon's laughter as he followed Sing down the hallway. At the end of the hallway, Sing rang a bell and they waited for Ivanov. Stan put on his moccasins, trying to gather his thoughts.

Sing spoke, at length, through the door to Ivanov. He then opened the door and pushed Stan out.

"You come," Ivanov said, leading Stan back aft over the smutty deck. A launch was alongside, unloading sacks of tallow. Ivanov and Stan followed two of the sack-carrying crew below into the hold. There, with Ivanov carrying a lantern, Stan followed him forward past bins of tallow, hides and other goods and supplies. The overhead was low and Stan was unable to stand at full height, the air was damp, foul. They were approaching a forward bulkhead when Ivanov stopped and held up the lantern. Stan peered into a five foot square starboard bin. Curled under a dirty blanket was Sir Warren. Ivanov yanked off the blanket, and Sir Warren stared into the glare of the lantern.

"Sir Warren, it's me, Stan."

"Stan, dear God." Sir Warren struggled to stand with Stan's help. His left arm was in a sling. Stan gripped Sir Warren's right arm and they stood face to face. The Baronet's face had aged ten years since dawn.

"How's the arm?"

"Have you seen Leon and the Captain?" Sir Warren asked. His voice was hollow.

"Yes, I'm sorry."

"I think of Pepe, dear man," Sir Warren said, his eyes shut, "and Walker's arm and all. . . to what end?" With his eyes still closed Sir Warren took a deep breath and exhaled.

"We'll get you out of here." A length of chain bolted to the bulkhead secured one of Sir Warren's ankles.

"Stan," said Sir Warren, he opened his eyes and seized the front of Stan's shirt, "thank everyone for me, Jed, Iron, and every man who came with us, and make sure they are paid as agreed to-"

"Sir Warren, stop we'll-"

"You," Ivanov said, poking Stan in the back, "look at arm. Captain want."

"How is the arm?"

"I think it is set properly," Sir Warren said. Stan examined the arm. "This pig here brought the Chinaman down. I passed out, but I think he knew what he was doing. Watch out for Sing. I went for Leon and he snapped this arm like a twig. He is a martial arts man. . . like you."

"The arm is set fine," Stan said. He adjusted the sling.

"Help Diamond get back to England. She can look after my mother. It would be good if you could go there and explain all this to Mother. . .perhaps she could shelter some money. When they get rid of me, Leon will take everything."

"Sir Warren, I'll get the money."

"Listen," Sir Warren said, his voice hoarse, "even if you got the money, I am a dead man. They don't care. . . Leon will get ten times the money with me dead. Stan, they are playing a game. I walked right into their trap."

"We go," Ivanov said, grabbing Stan's arm.

"I'll be back," Stan said, yanking his arm away.

"You are," Sir Warren said, "the brother I hoped for." The lantern revealed a trace of moisture in Sir Warren's empty eyes. Ivanov pushed Stan down the passageway.

"Don't give up," Stan shouted back. "I'll get Jed, we'll be back." For the first time in his life he fought back an urge to kill a man. His knife was on his back. Ivanov wouldn't know what hit him.

Sir Warren seemed resigned, abandoned. Finding his brother like this devastated him. His friend had given up on life.

Jed Walker's face hardened as Stan told of his visit to the *Helenka*. Iron added a log to the fire, and the three men watched small red and yellow devil's tails whip around the new log.

"Cotton," Jed called. The veteran trapper was at a nearby fire. He came to Walker.

"How's about gettin' Sky Bear over here," Walker said. "The old goat said he wanted to help us. Just maybe he can."

"Should I tell him anything?" Cotton asked. Cotton stood behind Stan with his hands on Stan's shoulders. He, like all the men, was glad to have Stan and Iron back in camp.

"Tell him we may have a job for those canoes he's been braggin' about." Cotton saddled up and left camp.

"We've traded for good fur with the Pomos," Walker said. "They used to hunt seals before the Russians killed them off. Sky Bear and his boys don't think much of the Russkies."

"You reckon," Iron asked, "we can get Warren off that tub?"

"For once," Walker said, rolling a cigarette, "I agree with that dumb Scot. Far as his brother and Whitelaw are concerned, he's better dead than alive. They just head for London or Glasgow, dump Warren overboard on the way, and the dirty queen, Leon, takes the family money."

"You've been aboard. What do you think?" Iron asked, turning to Stan.

"Sir Warren is depressed," Stan said. "In his mind he rebuilt Leon into a loving brother, needing help. Then to be deceived and humiliated like this. . . it was all too much. . . he seems to have given up."

"But what are the chances of getting him off?" asked Iron.

"Ivanov must have a crew of fifteen or twenty. . .plus the three in the love nest."

"Do you know how many hatches lead off the main deck?" Walker asked.

"I think three: one forward, one aft, and the Captain's quarters. But there could be others." Stan tried to visualize the main deck. There might have been another passage below, near the eyes of the ship.

"Have you seen the boats?" Stan asked.

"No," said Walker, blowing smoke into the fire, "but the Chief thinks they can handle them better than anyone alive... .Were there any crew's quarters in the after-hold where they've chained Warren?"

"I didn't see any. It was mostly tallow and hides, with store goods. It's pitch black down there."

Isaac Labrosa came into camp with a large doe strapped behind his saddle. Stan got up and shook his hand. Labrosa gave him a big smile and a bone-crushing hug. Stan, smiling, returned to the small fire with Jed and Iron.

"You know," Walker said, "Isaac has turned into an almost likable man. It's strange."

"It was on the Green River, weeks before our fight, that Warren got Leon's letter," said Stan. "It all seems like years ago."

"You know," Walker said. He ran his hand over his shaggy chin, "if we sealed off the forward hatch and the Captain's cabin, we'd have to deal with only two or three men on watch."

"Damn," Iron said, rubbing his hands together, "I think we can do it. A lot depends on the Pomos and their boats."

"Shit, Iron," Walker said, "I think you might almost like the Scot."

"Well," Iron said, cracking a smile, "the fancy bugger does grow on you."

"It must be tough to have a brother like Leon," Stan said. "But, how are we going to cut his chain?" he asked. "It was good-sized."

"Cotton has a blacksmith's saw," Walker said, "It'll cut through most anything."

It was dark and they'd finished supper when Cotton arrived with Sky Bear. The Pomo Chief was a short, flat-faced man. He wore a dirty, woven, yellow headband. Most of his gray hair shot out from about the band. The Chief was a great talker and he and Iron engaged in a lengthy conversation.

"Cotton and I," Walker said, "have communicated with signs. I'm glad Iron can understand the bugger, but you can't shut him up."

"How far are we from the coast?" asked Stan.

"About five miles due west," Walker said. "We're about ten miles from Bodega. Sky Bear stays well south of the Bay and Fort Ross."

"Iron," Walker said, interrupting the conversation, "has he talked about the boats yet?" Iron shook his head. But Iron took over the conversation. While Iron spoke, the Chief's black eyes shifted to Walker and Stan. Ric came and sat by Walker.

"He claims," said Iron, listening to the Chief, "to have been aboard the *Helenka* twice. He says he and his men have boarded most ships who are here a while. Says the dumb Russians sleep like winter-bears. He and his men are just shadows in the night"

"How many boats has he got," Walker asked, "and how big are they?" This took Iron a while to sort out.

"Four eight-man and three two-man, I think."

It was two hours after sunrise; Sky Bear proudly uncovered the first of his seven dugout canoes. It was a heavy fifteen-foot craft carved from a giant red cedar.

"He says his father bought this one from a tribe of Coos far to the north," said Iron to Stan and Walker.

"It's been around a while," Stan said, running his hand on the worn surface of the animal head shaped bow. It turned out the Pomos hid this canoe and two larger ones. They also revealed three of the small two-man crafts.

"Let's sit down with Sky Bear and think this thing out," Walker said. "Those three larger canoes should do it. We'll get Warren."

"Good. When do you think would be best?" Stan asked.

"Tonight," said Walker.

17

Stan and Cotton waited in the high grass of the dunes. Delicate cirrus clouds raced past a brilliant quarter-moon. White breakers came and vanished on an endless stretch of sand. It was an hour past midnight, and Stan flexed his shoulders and took a deep breath. It was almost time.

"Don't get this shit in your mouth," Cotton said. He spit into the grass. He and Stan applied a black paste, provided by Sky Bear, to their faces.

"It must be bear grease and charcoal," Stan said. At the pow-wow, Sky Bear insisted everyone on the raid use the foul grease. Three canoes would go to the *Helenka* to rescue Sir Warren. In addition to Sky Bear, there were nine Pomo braves involved, three in each canoe.

"I hope those buggers can handle the canoes like Sky Bear claims," Cotton said. "I ain't much for swimmin' in this freezin' water"

"The two rowing us looked a tad old and fat," Stan said, "but Fish Eye is a man I wouldn't want to tangle with. And, he's been aboard the *Helenka* once before." Stan, Cotton, and young Fish Eye were in the same canoe. It was their job to go aft and free Sir Warren.

"When you smile," Cotton said, he gave Stan a jab, "those pearly whites make you look like a St. Louie stage nigger." Stan smiled, but he gazed down the beach to where Walker and Sky Bear waited. They were responsible for sealing off the Captain's quarters. Further down were Iron and Labrosa. They were part of the third boat crew. They would seal the forward crew's hatch.

"Here they come," Stan said. Like dark sea demons the three canoes maneuvered in toward the beach. Stan walked back a few feet and took a leak. All afternoon, Walker, with Iron his interpreter, reviewed the plan and the duties of each crew. It was a solid plan, and Sky Bear and his braves seemed to understand it.

"Do you have everything?" Stan asked. The canoes were almost to the breakers.

"Yep," Cotton said, "I'll get through that chain before Sir Warren knows what's goin' on." They saw Walker and Sky Bear move out over the sand. It was time to get aboard. In addition to his knife, Stan wore a pistol and carried a length of rawhide rope. He was ready.

Fish Eye and the rear oarsman were out of the canoe, holding it. Stan and Cotton clamored aboard. Stan moved forward and picked up an oar. He helped as they pushed out through the breakers. It was three miles north to Bodega and the *Helenka*. The dugout was wide enough in the center for two rowers to kneel side by side.

A damp breeze gusted out of the northwest, and Stan was glad Iron suggested they wear knitted woolen caps. Cotton carried his saw rapped in a woolen robe and cap for Sir Warren. Looking toward shore, Stan watched the other two boats pull north with them, dark and strange with their animal-head bows. He could make out Walker in the next canoe; he paddled well with one arm.

A solid layer of cirrostratus clouds screened the moon. It often meant a storm, but out beyond the breakers the water was as calm as Monterey Bay. His thoughts turned to Lynn. Surely by now she and Diamond had convinced Captain Monroe Stan was the logical match for his daughter. He worried about Lynn. She and her Mother were so close. He would have liked to avoid the family tensions that were sure to develop.

The Pomo oarsmen slowed their pace. Ahead loomed the dark outline of the *Helenka*. Stan and Cotton placed their paddles carefully in the dugout. From here, with silence essential, the braves would handle the canoes.

The bay lay flat and dark under the blanket of clouds. The three canoes glided in around the *Helenka's* small boat, still tied to the boom. Stan saw the brig's crew had not bothered to pull up the rope ladder.

A brave named Far Reach, from Iron's boat, would be the first man aboard. Far Reach, with a knife in his mouth, went and up and over the side. He would scout the main deck and locate the men on watch.

Stan's canoe tied up under the existing ladder, between the *Helenka* and its small boat. The two other canoes tied at the front and the rear of Stan's. Fish Eye and a third brave followed Far Reach up the ladder; both braves carried additional ropes. They would provide each dugout with an exit ladder.

Minutes dragged by. All blackened faces focused on the brig's gunwale.

Far Reach appeared, and all three rope ladders were soon in place. Stan, with a coil of rope over his shoulder, went up and over onto the main deck. Fish Eye waited with a short spear and an unlit torch. Stan helped Cotton over the gunwale, and led Cotton and Fish Eye across the shadowy deck toward the after hatch. The main deck was quietly alive with the shadowy movements of men on their missions.

At the hatch door Stan signaled Fish Eye to light his torch. One torch was already lit amidships. In the light, Stan saw a pool of blood to the right of the hatch. To the side, he saw the crumpled body of a Russian sailor, his throat cut. Far Reach slit him as he slept.

Stan went through the hatch and down the six steps to the greasy deck below. They moved forward, and Stan had Fish Eye light each bulkhead lantern. The damp sea air was heavy with the rancid smell of hides and tallow.

Sir Warren lay curled up and asleep, but when the light entered his cubicle, he started to moan.

"Oh, please no," he said, he curled tighter under the thin blanket, "no more, Leon, please."

"Sir Warren, it's Stan." Stan knelt by his friend. Fish Eye held the torch as high as the overhead allowed. Stan placed his hand on Sir Warren's shoulder; slowly, Sir Warren turned to face him. Stan felt the shaking of his friend's body. Sir Warren's stubbly face was yellow, his eyes dull gray saucers.

"It's me. . . Stan." Cotton was already working on the chain.

Sir Warren stared into Stan's eyes, and they soon cleared with recognition.

"Dear God," Sir Warren whispered, "it is you.. . it is you, Stan." He reached out to touch Stan's blackened face. A bloody rag covered his free hand. Tears ran down his face.

"What happened to your hand?" Stan asked.

"Cotton Crevier?"

"Yep, it's me, and we'll have this chain off in no time."

"What about your hand?"

"They cut a finger off?"

"Who?. . Why?"

"Leon and Sing. . . is who."

"But, why?"

"Leon enjoys it, he is going to cut a finger off each week. . . until he gets his money. Sing held me. Leon sang, laughed and sawed.. . I believe I passed out." There was a snap as Cotton's saw broke through the chain.

"That's it," Cotton said, standing up.

"Let's get out," said Stan, he helped Sir Warren to his feet.

"Stan," Sir Warren said "there is a way into Whitelaw's cabin from here. Sing and Leon always come from somewhere forward."

"Cotton, take him out," Stan said, "We'll block the forward door, now we won't be able to block the main hatch." They had removed the hinges when they opened the hatch.

"Watch the torch," Sir Warren said, "there is gunpowder stored in these next bins." Cotton and Sir Warren started aft. The iron ring was still on Sir Warren's ankle.

Stan signaled Fish Eye to follow him forward. They passed numerous bins of supplies. At the end of the passage were three steps up to a door. Stan went up the steps. He found the door ajar. He closed it and secured the bolt.

Stan turned back down the steps toward Fish Eye. He saw

movement behind the young Indian. It was the Chinaman, Sing.

"Watch-" Stan called, but it was too late. Sing's samurai sword flashed and decapitated Fish Eye and severed his torch-carrying arm in one vicious stroke. The Pomo's head slipped from his neck, and blood showered up, drenching the overhead. The arm crashed to the deck, the hand still clutched the torch, which sizzled out in a rain of blood.

Stan turned back up the stairwell and felt his way to the hatch door. He unbolted it and stepped through into what must have been Sing's room. Stan locked the heavy oak plank into place. Just in time; Sing's shoulder hit the door with an awesome force. The Chinaman pounded the door, shouting Russian.

Stan turned and faced Captain Whitelaw. The Captain wore black silk bloomers, and clutched a foot-long dueling pistol with both hands.

"I do hate to bloody up Sing's room," he said. The pistol quivered. "But I must kill you." He took a step toward Stan. The flab of his milk-white upper body trembled.

"I would think," Stan said "this is Sing's dirty work."

"True, Mr. Aldridge, true." Stan took his eyes off the Captain's slit-eyes and stared for an instant at the space behind the Captain.

"Leon?" asked the Captain, he turned his head a fraction of an inch.

Stan leaped forward, his right foot sent the pistol flying into the bulkhead. On impact, it discharged with a mind-splitting report. Whitelaw charged by Stan to open the door. The Captain had one hand on the plank when Stan delivered a blow to the side of his neck. Whitelaw collapsed in a heap at the base of the door. Sing stopped his pounding. The cabin was silent, with no sign of Leon.

Stan cut two short pieces of rawhide rope and tied the Captain's hands and ankles. Then, with his pistol in one hand and Sing's lamp in the other, he proceeded forward through the cabin area. The after cabin he had entered belonged to Sing; the next cabin contained the bath area. Doors connected each compartment as Stan moved forward. Forward of the bath was the Captain's cabin. The large cabin contained a canopied bed, a desk and two chairs. The port bulkhead contained a door and a wall of books. There were two portholes in the starboard bulkhead looking out on the bay. Heavy bolts secured both doors. That was likely why he hadn't seen Leon.

Stan eased the bolt from the port-side door. It led to the long passageway he'd used on his first visit to the *Helenka*. Every other wall lamp glimmered. There were just two doors forward to the end of the passageway. Leon's room must be the next room, forward of the Captain's. He'd be waiting.

Stan returned to Whitelaw's cabin and scratched on the inside door to Leon's cabin. He then returned to the passageway and proceeded forward to the end door. He'd surprise Leon from the rear.

From the passageway there was a porthole looking out onto the main deck. The deck, lit by a hazy quarter-moon, looked deserted. Where was Sing? Where were Walker and the rest of the men? Stan paused at the end door. This was the door to the cabin where he'd first met Captain Whitelaw and Leon. It was unlocked.

He placed his pistol in his belt and cracked open the door. The room was dark and deserted. If the door to Leon's room was unlocked, Stan had him. He set the lamp quietly on the table and turned to secure the passageway door.

Something was wrong. Stan drew his pistol.

It was too late; massive arms gripped him from the rear. Stan's arms were pinned to his body in a vice-like grip. It was Sing. The man's bear hug drove the air from Stan's lungs. Stan twisted his body hard right then left; Sing took short steps to the right then left. Stan felt he might wiggle loose.

Sing head butted the rear of Stan's head. A flash of white fanned out in all directions. The cabin turned milky, gauze-like, then gray; it collapsed into nothing.

It was gray. Stan's face felt cold and numb. He opened his eyes. Leon sat on his chest and slapped Stan's face back and forth with a wet towel.

"His eyes are open," Leon said.

Captain Whitelaw came and peered down at Stan. "Good," he said. "Sing, get him up." Sing grabbed Stan by the shoulders and yanked him to his feet. Stan's hands were tied behind him and his ankles were bound. On his feet, he felt weak and dizzy. The room was blurry.

"Put him in a chair," said Whitelaw. He took a seat near Stan.

"Where is Warren Kent?" Whitelaw asked.

Stan's mind struggled to clear. Leon stepped forward and slapped his face hard with the wet towel. His face smarted from the blows and the greasy charcoal.

"Answer him, you stupid Yank," said Leon. "Where is my brother?"

"He's ashore by now," Stan said.

"Shit," Leon said, again he whacked the side of Stan's head a stinging blow with the towel.

"Untie my hands and try that," Stan said. He took another blow.

"Enough!" Whitelaw said. "I've got to think."

"Sing, hold the shithead," Leon said. "I'll saw off the bastard's pinkie." A wicked smile creased Leon's face.

"No, damn it, not now, stupid," Whitelaw said. "I don't want this cabin bloodied up. Jesus, let me think. Sing, make a pot of tea." Leon went to a small couch in the corner and slouched down, sniffing from a handkerchief. Sing heated water on an oil burner.

Stan closed his eyes. The back of his head throbbed. He wondered what happened to the rest of his group. They had not discussed being captured. He opened his eyes. Whitelaw, wrapped in a heavy white robe, studied him through his dark crevices.

"You didn't see Ivanov?" Whitelaw asked.

"No," said Sing. "I'm sure he's locked in the crew's quarters."

"Damn!" Whitelaw said, he slammed his hand on the table. "How could this happen?"

"Are we prisoners on our own ship?" asked Leon.

"Shut up," said Whitelaw. Sing served him a small cup of tea.

Stan tested his wrists and ankles. Given time he'd squirm loose. Leon must have tied him. It was possible Stan's friends left, not realizing he was missing.

A banging, chopping sound came from the forward part of the ship. Whitelaw and Sing went out into the passageway. Leon got up, walked to Stan and kicked him in the shins.

"Warren thinks you're such a holy shit," Leon said, he gave Stan a second kick. Fortunately, Leon wore only white slippers.

"Enough," Whitelaw said, coming back into the cabin. "Pretty boy is our answer to getting 'Sir' Warren back."

"How do you figure?" Leon asked, he returned to the couch.

"Sing, get out there and open the hatch," Whitelaw said, "before Ivanov and his brutes tear this whole damn ship apart. There's no one out there. . . they've gone. But, dear Mr. Aldridge is all we need."

"He ain't so pretty, but how do you figure?" Leon asked. Sing headed back aft through Leon's room.

"You heard your brother," said Whitelaw, with a smile. "He said Mr. Aldridge was the brother he wished you had been."

"Warren's an ass," said Leon. He got up from the couch and walked to where Stan sat.

"Anyway, so what?" he asked. He held the white handkerchief to his nose.

"Think, Leon, think." Whitelaw said. "If your brother came all the way here to rescue the family's black-sheep, he's much too noble to leave Mr. Aldridge here for you and Sing to cut up."

"Noble. Shit," Leon said, giving Stan a kick in the calf.

"When Sing gets back," said Whitelaw, he rubbed his hands together, "you can take him below, but we need him alive and well. . .He's the ticket that will bring 'Sir' Warren back aboard."

There was noise coming from the cabin passageway. The axing of the forward hatch continued.

"Sing must have gotten our hatch open," Whitelaw said. He stepped to the passageway door and looked out.

"Shit. Come on, Leon," Whitelaw said. "Something's happened to Sing." Both men left the cabin and headed back down the passageway.

Alone, Stan struggled to free his hands. Out of the corner of his eye he saw movement from Leon's cabin. Through the door came Far Reach followed by Iron Paso.

Stan motioned his head toward the passageway door, and Far Reach looked down the long hallway. Paso cut Stan free. Far Reach signaled someone was coming. Stan stayed in his chair as if tied. Iron stepped back into Leon's room. Far Reach stood in back of the door.

"You Yankee bastard," shouted Leon, charging into the cabin,

"Sing is dead. I'm going to cut you to-". Leon never saw Far Reach; the Pomo's hatchet sliced into the top of his head and chopped down into his throat. Blood and brain matter erupted fountain-like into the cabin. A fine mist covered Stan.

Stan jumped to his feet and looked down the passageway. It was empty. He ran to the end and secured the hatch door. He could hear Whitelaw yell to Ivanov as he tried to free the hatch to the crew's quarters. Ivanov and his men would be free in minutes. Stan raced back to the cabin.

He leaped over Leon's body and slapped Far Reach on the shoulder. He shook Iron's hand.

"Ivanov's crew will be free in a few minutes. Are we the only three aboard?" Stan asked.

"No," Iron said, "Labrosa is down below with his guts hangin' out. He ain't goin'ta make it."

"Did you close the back hatch?" asked Stan.

"Yes, but it won't hold long."

"I'm going down to check Isaac," said Stan. "You two, knock out the porthole. We'll have to swim for it."

"We've taken care of all their small boats," Iron said. "They ain't going nowhere, and Walker has the canoes circling the ship."

Taking a lantern, Stan hurried through the cabins and down the ladder to the storage level. There, near where Sir Warren had been held, he found Isaac Labrosa. He was sitting up against sacks of rice. Both hands clutched his lower stomach. His eyes were closed.

"Isaac, it's Stan Aldridge," he said, kneeling near Labrosa.

"Ah. . . Stan, thanks," Labrosa whispered.

"I want to get you out of here."

"Hell, if I stood my guts would fall out. Damn Chinaman, but, I think I got him too."

"He's dead." Stan saw blood and viscera oozing between Isaac's fingers.

"Good. Aldridge, do me a favor."

"What?"

"Shoot me."

"I can't do that, Isaac." Labrosa closed his eyes, and Stan reached out and squeezed his arm..

"I'd like to go quick-like. . . you know."

"I understand. . . would you like to blow this whole damn ship sky high. . . take it with you when you go?" Labrosa opened his eyes. A pained smile broke on his hairy and blackened face.

"How can I do that?"

"There are two bins of gunpowder here."

The crew was free and Stan heard them axing the after hatch.

"Hurry, Stan, hurry." Labrosa closed his eyes and grit his teeth.

Stan hurried to the bins and broke open a barrel of powder. Using his hands he made a heavy trail of powder from the bins to Isaac. He broke open several barrels and tipped them over.

"Isaac," Stan said, he knelt by Labrosa, "you count to five hundred then use the lantern to light the powder." Stan placed his hands on both of Isaac's shoulders.

"God bless you," Stan said. Isaac nodded; tears ran down his face. Stan stood and ran forward toward the cabins. Ivanov's men were hacking at the passageway door and the after hatch.

Iron and Far Reach waited in Whitelaw's cabin by the porthole.

"Go," Stan said, helping Iron through the opening. He watched as Iron fell to the dark water below. Stan motioned Far Reach to go, but the Indian shoved him toward the porthole. Stan was too big at the shoulders to fit. He removed his jacket and worked his arms through first. For a moment, he didn't think he'd fit. He heard men running down the passageway. He squirmed. Far Reach gave him a push, and he fell.

Stan hit the water on his back. The cold pressed his breath from him, and he fought for the surface. On the surface he swam hard away from the *Helenka*. He saw nothing of the canoes.

Stan tread water and looked back at the brig. He couldn't see Far Reach, but he could see the open porthole. He started to swim again, and soon a canoe was alongside him. Walker and Sky Bear helped him aboard. Stan lay in the bottom of the boat a moment, cold and gasping for air.

"Did you get Iron?" Stan asked.

"The other boat has him."

"How about Far Reach?" Stan sat up, and Walker wrapped a blanket around him.

"Haven't seen him."

They sat looking toward the *Helenka*. The pounding and shouting of the Russian crew drifted out across the water.

The dark vessel, suddenly, became a fiery ball of splintering and flying timber. For a brief moment, the bay turned scarlet by the manmade volcano. A grip-like pressure squeezed Stan's body. The force rocked the canoe. Debris rained down in all directions, a mass of flickering candles.

Soon, all was black, but the tortured creaking and sucking sounds of the *Helenka's* last fight crept across the water. The battle was soon lost, and the brig slid into its black grave.

"Good Lord," Walker said, "we'd better look for survivors."

They found none.

18

Cotton, put two fingers here by the ear," Stan said, "and don't move." Stan stitched the torn scalp and ear of Boatswain Brown. Cotton and Brown had tracked a wounded deer into a thicket where a she bear jumped Brown.

"How you doin'?" Cotton asked.

"Shitty," Brown whispered. He lay in the shade of a group of scrub pine. It was a chilly valley afternoon.

"It won't be much longer," Stan said. After the incident, Walker made camp along the Sacramento River. The group left Sky Bear and the Pomo village three days before. They headed south through the central valley of California.

"That's it," Stan said, and Brown started to sit up, but he lay back down. The grizzly's claw racked Brown's head from above the eyebrow, up over the ear, and back down to the jaw. He returned to camp holding the side of his face up with a blood covered hand.

Iron brought a cup of whisky, and Cotton and Stan held Brown while he drank.

"Just rest," said Stan. Brown nodded, and Cotton put a blanket over him.

Stan walked over to where Sir Warren sat alone by the smaller of two fires. His friend seldom spoke since his rescue. Riding all day with a broken arm and injured hand had to be difficult.

"How's the arm?" Stan asked. He took a seat near Sir Warren

and added a log to the fire.

"Fine, I rode a bit today without the sling. How is Boatswain?"

"Hanging tough. The scar will be mostly under his hair. . . I hope. Let's have a look at the hand," Stan said. He got up and knelt by Sir Warren. The hand looked inflamed. "I'll heat a pan of salt water for you to soak it in. . .We don't want to fool with an infection."

"Yes, I would not want to spoil my future on the royal piano." Stan smiled at Sir Warren. Sir Warren returned a weak smile.

"It's good to have you joke again," Stan said. He placed a pan of water over the fire.

"'A jest breaks no bones,'" quoted Sir Warren.

The two friends stared at the flames.

"To me, it's like two years have passed since we came to California," Stan said. "But, you know, my mother claims you can't have a rainbow without clouds and a storm."

"Mothers are thought to be wise," Sir Warren said. "Perhaps she is right. In which case, I believe we are due for a rainbow." Sir Warren, awkwardly, reached out and squeezed Stan's shoulder. "Let us seek the rainbow, my friend. . . enough sorrow. . . 'sorrow is a kind of rust of the soul.'"

"Right," Stan said. "We'll find it. . . .it's out there." He slapped Sir Warren's knee.

"You two look in a good mood," said Walker, "and I haven't even shared this jug with you." Walker sat by the fire with his dog beside him. He carried a large jug of wine and a cup. Stan went to his pack and dug out two battered tin cups.

"We've decided to look for the rainbow of life," Sir Warren said.

"Shit," Walker said, pouring the wine, "the rainbows in my life have flat tails and eat bark."

"Are you going to do more trapping before we leave?" Stan asked.

"No," Walker said. "I'm ready to head East. The sooner we're over Cajon Pass, the better. I'd like to get out of here without fightin' the Mex." Walker rearranged the fire, sending a shower of sparks into the air.

"All I need to do is pick up Diamond," Sir Warren said, "and buy supplies at the Mission. Then, I am ready. . .believe me, I am as eager as you to see the last of this land of the Californios."

"I talked to Iron," Walker said. "He'll take you to the Mission. The boys and I will wait on the other side of the Pass. Anyway, we need four days to jerk the beef."

Walker refilled the wine cups and went to his bag to get a steer bone for Ric. The dog walked off a few feet.

"What's this Iron tells me about the Monroe girl?" Walker asked. He sat down and looked at Stan.

"I wanted to talk to you about it," Stan said. He felt a trace of heat run up the back of his neck. "I'd like to take her with us. With Diamond along, I don't think there'll be any problem." Walker's eyes showed nothing; then, he turned and studied the fire. Stan didn't know what more to say.

"Stan, I wish you had talked to me about this. When did all this happen?" asked Sir Warren.

"I was married once," Walker said. His eyes focused on the fire.

"I didn't know," Stan said, he enjoyed a momentary change of subject.

"No. Is that true?" Sir Warren asked.

"Yep. . . eleven years ago, I was trappin' up off the Sweetwater. Sublette and I had a good year goin', too. She was gone when I got back to St. Louis. She'd run off with a river boat pilot. Never saw her again. I'm told she lives in New Orleans."

"I'm sorry," said Stan. "Were you married long?"

"A tad over a year, but, ain't nothing to be sorry about," Walker said. "Although, I reckon it did shy me, some, off the women folk."

"Stan," Sir Warren asked, "are you serious about Lynn Monroe? Do I not recall her father told us she and Captain Rodas planned to marry?"

"No," said Stan, "Captain Monroe told us Rodas asked to court Lynn. That was all."

"I reckon the girl knows you're takin' her with us."

"Yes. . . we have it pretty well worked out," Stan said. "Diamond is helping. We hope to convince Lynn's mother this is best for Lynn."

"Oh Lord," Sir Warren said; he let out a low whistle. "'The triumph of hope over experience.' Let me sort this out. . . Madame Monroe is to send her only daughter with a man she and her husband hardly know, three thousand miles. . . Jed, you talk to our young friend." Sir Warren took a deep swallow of wine.

"Look," Stan said, "it might sound shaky to you, but Lynn and I have known each other for over two years. We both want to get through medical school and set up a practice, maybe even out here. I like it out here.

"Jed." Sir Warren said, closing his eyes.

"Stan does have an eye for Mexican gals," Walker said. "I don't know Missy Monroe well, but she's nice to look at."

"She's more American than Mexican," Stan said.

"You will have to help me understand that statement," said Sir Warren. "But, I maintain the real problem is Momma. I saw the Spanish fire in those eyes. . . I have a quart of fine Scottish whiskey that says Lynn Monroe. . .Stan, I am sorry to say this. . .will not be with us on our journey East."

"I'll take that, Warren," Walker said. Ric came and put his head on Walker's lap. "Stan is too handsome for her to pass up, Mom or no Mom."

"I recall Captain Rodas. He is impressive," Sir Warren said. He pronounced his words with care, "and I might even judge him a bit more dapper than Stan. Besides, and this is the big one, gentlemen, his pockets are not empty." Stan stood up shaking his head and smiling.

"I'm going to have Cotton cut us a steak," Stan said. He took two steps and turned back toward his friends. "When you two make your trip plans, plan on Lynn Monroe." Walker chuckled, and Sir Warren closed his eyes and shook his head.

Father Joaquin Carrillo sat at the head of the conference table. He listened to the story of Leon Kent and the *Helenka*. He looked at Iron, then Stan, and finally Sir Warren.

"I am sorry, Warren," he said. "Have faith, for 'God is our refuge and strength, a very present help in trouble. Therefore we will not fear, though the earth be removed, and though the mountains be carried into the midst of the sea.'"

"Thank you, Father," Sir Warren said. "I have good friends who helped all along the way." Sir Warren smiled at Iron and Stan.

"I understand," Father said. "Now you plan to head East?"

"Yes," Sir Warren said, "I will purchase supplies and pick up Diamond at the Monroe's. Then we will join Walker's party."

"Diamond is a remarkable woman," Father said. "She and Lynn have visited here several times. By the way, Stan, that was fine work you and Lynn did for the Governor, and I know he appreciated it."

"Thank you," Stan said.

"I would suggest, however," Father said, "you join Mr. Walker. For some reason, neither you nor Mr. Walker are favorites of Captain Rodas."

Sir Warren chuckled. "The problem between Stan and the Captain," he said, "is likely Lynn Monroe."

"Ah," the Father said, smiling. "I understand."

"Father, why are the troops here at the Mission?" Iron asked. Stan exhaled and looked at Sir Warren.

"Eduardo has stationed men here around the clock," Father said. "He thinks we're going to be raided by the gringos."

"How long has this been?"

"Three weeks ago, right after Captain Monroe headed for Boston. I understand he has men stationed at the Monroe's ranch also."

"Captain Monroe has gone?" Stan asked. A numbing seeped through him.

"Yes," Father said, "he won't be back for months. I understand Eduardo will look after things at the ranch until the Captain returns. He stays there overnight quite often I'm told." Stan, needing fresh air, gave a weak smile. His thoughts became confused, and he struggled to follow a discussion between the Father and Sir Warren about life in Scotland.

During the night, Iron woke Stan and asked him to come to Father Carrillo's office. He left Stan alone with the Father.

"Stan, please have a seat," Father Carrillo said, taking a seat behind his desk, "and I'm sorry to have to wake you like this. I hope and pray I am doing the right thing. But Lynn and Diamond can be very convincing, and I might add, Iron too." The Father put both hands on his desk and smiled. "I'm sure you know Lynn and I have become close over the years and share a love for medicine. Well, two weeks ago Lynn and Diamond came to me to discuss you, Elisa Monroe, and Captain Rodas." The father held up his hands, with a weak smile. "You get the picture."

"Yes sir, we'd hope not to cause trouble. We're in love. I gather Mrs. Monroe disapproves of Lynn and me."

"Disapproves yes," said the Father, with a soft chuckle. "She would not discuss the issue with me or her husband. I like Elisa, but I also believe the best thing for Lynn is to complete her schooling. Everyone tells me you are an honorable man. I put my trust in you." The Father looked into Stan's eyes.

"Thank you, sir," Stan said. "I will do my best for Lynn."

"Very good. I have worked with Lynn, Diamond, and Iron. . . I pray this is the last time I have to go through this adventure." The Father got up from his desk and folded his arms. Stan stood up.

"Tomorrow," the Father said, "when you go to the Monroe's you will be told Lynn and Diamond have chosen to remain in California. You must go along with this, show disappointment, but agree with their decision. We believe it is best if you say nothing of this caper, Lord save me, to Sir Warren." The Father moved around the desk and stood in front of Stan.

"Iron has worked with the two women for their departure. . . escape. If Elisa or Captain Rodas learn of this, Lynn would be placed under guard. God bless you, and take good care of Lynn." Stan looked into the Father's eyes, and they shook hands.

"She's in good hands, and thank you."

Stan followed Sir Warren. They rode past two wagons loaded with hides. The wagons rolled for Los Angeles. In an hour, he and Sir Warren would reach the Monroe ranch.

Sir Warren glanced at Stan as he and Midnight pulled alongside. They had talked little since leaving the Mission. Stan's mind was still a jumble of thoughts about Lynn.

"What will you do if she does not want to come?" Sir Warren asked.

Stan shrugged. "I don't know. It's hard for me to sort it all out this morning."

"I heard you up last night," said Sir Warren.

"I don't think I slept much," Stan said, with a slight smile. "At least I don't feel like I did." They rode on; Stan felt the morning sun on his back.

"I was a bit older than you," Sir Warren said, "when a girl I had my heart set on chose another man. Now, I believe it was best, but at the time I was devastated."

"I still think Lynn will come," Stan said, "but there will be a lot of pressure on her from her mother. . . it's not what I'd hoped for. . . and if Rodas is there. . . "

"I think we should talk about Rodas," Sir Warren said. "I have lost one brother out here; I do not want to lose you." The two men's legs touched; they rode side by side. "Rodas is no farm boy from down the road. A fellow you can punch in the nose and then sweep Lynn away to happiness in the East." Stan looked at Sir Warren and smiled, but the Baronet was serious. "Rodas is the law out here. Furthermore, he is a rich boy, like me, who is not used to being told 'hands off'."

"Warren, I can handle him."

"Listen, I know you can. . . I have seen you fight. . .listen please, even if Lynn wants to come with you, there is still one way the Captain can win."

"What's that?"

"He finds a cause to arrest you, then sends you to Mexico City. In a month he informs Lynn you were shot trying to escape."

"You have an evil mind," Stan said. He gave Sir Warren a quizzical look.

"My mind is not evil. What it is, is clear. Your mind is clouded by the thought of a lost love. . .'The way to love anything is to realize that it might be lost.'"

"So? What do I do? Steal her away?"

"You would not make it to the Mission road. The whole Mex army would be on your tail. The point is, you can do nothing. It is up to Lynn."

Stan 's eyes focused on the road ahead. He felt Sir Warren's eyes on him, but he looked straight ahead.

Stan pulled Midnight to a stop. Far ahead they saw the young oaks and the citrus of the Monroe ranch. For the past half hour the two rode in silence. Stan's thoughts cleared.

"Thanks, Warren. Do you mind if I drop the Sir?"

"If I had a good hand," said Sir Warren, "we would shake on it. I hoped we had reached this point. I never liked the employee-boss relationship. You have become a good friend. . . the best I have."

"Thanks," Stan said, "I've been thinking about your advice. It's what my brother would have told me. I'm not going to do anything dumb. I love Lynn, but if she doesn't want to come, I'll have to live with it. I'm lucky to have a friend like you. You've been a big help for me." Warren's eyes looked moist.

"'A man sir, should keep his friendship in a constant repair.'" Both men smiled.

"Good to have you back in style," Stan said. "Let's go meet the dragon."

Where the young oaks commenced lining the road to the ranch, Marco and two of his vaqueros waited on their mules.

"Hello, Gentlemen," Marco called. "We have been expecting you."

"Is everyone well?" Sir Warren asked.

"Si, Si. But you know Captain Monroe has sailed for Boston."

At the main entrance, a uniformed soldier sat smoking a cigarette. His rifle leaned on the wall. Stan and Warren tied their horses at a rail to one side of the patio entrance.

"Please wait here," Marco said. The two vaqueros stayed back in the garden near the fish pond. Marco entered the house.

"I see we have the military," Warren said, he took a seat on a stone bench, "plus Marco and his men. I believe the Monroe family is secure."

"Too secure," Stan said, taking a seat and rubbing his hands together. His mouth felt dry. "I don't know what to expect." They waited fifteen minutes. Stan got up and walked to Midnight. The soldier got to his feet and picked up his rifle. He sauntered to the edge of the patio and watched Stan.

The main door opened.

"Gentlemen," Marco said, "please come in."

They followed Marco across the marble-floored entrance way into a large sitting room. It was a pleasant room, which looked out on the irrigation pond. Stan noted the chairs formed an unusual pattern, as if for a meeting.

"Please sit here," said Marco, directing Stan and Warren to two side-by-side chairs. "Mrs. Monroe will be here in a moment." Marco stood at the room entrance while Stan and Warren took their seats. A semicircle of empty chairs faced the two men.

"It looks like a kangaroo court," whispered Warren.

Stan smiled but his lips were dry and stiff. He started to comment when Mrs. Monroe entered the room. Her dress was black with a small trim of gold. Her raven black hair was combed to a bun in the rear. Both men stood.

"It is nice of you to visit before your trip," she said, shaking hands. "Please take your seats." Mrs. Monroe took a seat in the center of the semicircle of chairs. Elisa Monroe seemed smaller and older than Stan recalled.

"Mr. Aldridge, we received a letter from the Governor-General," Mrs. Monroe said. She sat flat-footed; her arms rested on the arms of her chair. "He was most complementary of your work in Monterey."

"Thank you. I couldn't have done it without Lynn. Is she here?"

"She is out walking with Eduardo, but I'm sure she would like to see you before you leave." Mrs. Monroe turned toward Warren. "Mr. Kent, were you able to locate your brother?"

Warren did his best to give a short report on the events of the past weeks. Mrs. Monroe listened, but her demeanor was more business-like than neighborly. Twice Stan met her eyes, and once she gave him a thin smile.

"How did Diamond do during her rather lengthy visit?" Warren asked. He had completed his story of the *Helenka.*

"Oh my, she is a joy. She can do everything, and well too. Besides, she and Lynn are close. . . as you know."

"Yes, that worked out well," Sir Warren said. "We plan to leave the day after tomorrow, so I would like her to pack and come to the Mission tomorrow. Of course, if that is satisfactory with you."

"Well," Mrs. Monroe said, she moved forward in her chair and gripped the chair's seat, "we. . . this is an item we must discuss. . . It seems Diamond would like to remain here with us, and we have offered her a job."

Warren blew air out through his mouth, a puzzled look on his face.

"Are you sure? I was to set her up in business in northern Africa. We have discussed it numerous times. . .I cannot believe this." Sir Warren stood up and walked to the window.

"Marco, please bring Diamond in," called Mrs. Monroe. She sat back in her chair and sighed.

"I'm sorry, Mr. Kent," Mrs. Monroe said. "We just want to do whatever is best for Diamond."

"Yes. . . yes of course," Sir Warren said. He came back and slumped down in his chair.

"This is hard to believe," Stan said. Mrs. Monroe put her hand on her forehead and closed her eyes.

Diamond came striding into the room in a flowing, full yellow dress. She had gained weight and was enormous. All came to their feet, and she gave Warren and Stan crushing hugs. Mrs. Monroe waved her into a chair next to her own. They took their seats. Diamond's chair creaked under her weight.

"Diamond," said Mrs. Monroe, "I've told Mr. Kent you'd like to stay here in California with us." A tear ran down Diamond's face. She brushed it aside.

"Sir Warren," Diamond said, sitting straight up in the chair with her hands on her knees, "I have given this a great deal of thought in the past weeks, and I wish to remain here with the Monroe family." Stan looked at Sir Warren. It didn't sound like Diamond. It sounded like she'd memorized it. But, Sir Warren just looked at Diamond in disbelief. "I'm sorry, and I wish to thank you for all you have done for me." A stream of tears rolled down her cheeks. She looked at the floor, and dabbed her eyes with a handkerchief.

"Diamond, are you sure of this?" Warren asked. Diamond stood and walked to Warren. He stood and they hugged each other.

"Yes," she said, "I'm sorry." Stan stood and Diamond hugged him. "Good luck," she said. She turned and hurried from the room.

"When did all this happen?" Warren asked. His face was gray. He and Stan took their seats.

"I believe," Mrs. Monroe said, her voice low, "Lynn first mentioned it to me about the time Douglas left for Boston. In fact, he was still here because I discussed it with him. We were both surprised, but pleased in a way. She is devoted to Lynn, and we were having a difficult family discussion about Lynn's. . . education." Her eyes turned to meet Stan's. They were not unfriendly, but appeared questioning, wondering.

No one spoke for a long minute.

"I do wish," said Mrs. Monroe, "Douglas were here, for I have other engagements. However, can I have Marco serve you tea before you leave?"

"I'd like to talk to Lynn," Stan said. He glanced at Warren, but his friend sat staring out the window.

"Of course, of course. I'll see if she has returned." Mrs. Monroe got up and left the room. Marco remained at the door.

"I can't believe this," said Stan. He stood and walked to the window. Warren sat with his head in his hands looking at the floor. "That wasn't the Diamond we know."

"I am trying to think," Sir Warren said. "There is nothing I can do. She has found this is a much easier life than traveling the world with me, and she saw how Pepe ended up. I cannot blame her."

Stan heard voices from the entranceway; he returned to his chair by Warren. Lynn and her mother entered, followed by Captain Rodas. Lynn was in a white dress with a red sash. She looked thin. When she shook Stan's hand, he thought she gave an extra squeeze, but her eyes flashed into his for only a brief instant. The Captain shook hands without a smile. Mrs. Monroe took her seat with Lynn and the Captain on either side.

"Sir Warren," Lynn said, she crossed her legs and adjusted her skirt down near her red slippers, "Diamond and I have talked for hours during the past weeks, about her move. It has been difficult for her, and me, but we all feel it was in her best interest to stay in California."

"I confess," Warren said, "I am still in shock, but I will accept whatever Diamond has decided."

"When are you leaving?" Lynn asked. Since taking her seat, she had glanced only once at Stan.

"The day after tomorrow," Warren said, "Iron will take us over the Pass. We plan to catch up to Walker's party, they have left the province, for the trip East." Warren looked at the Captain, but his face showed nothing.

"Stan, will you be returning to Columbia?" Lynn asked. Her eyes turned to Stan, but they were glassy. She started to swing her right foot in and out.

"Yes. I hoped you'd join me there."

"We discussed that possibility," Mrs. Monroe said, she leaned forward in her chair, "before Captain Monroe left for Boston. In fact, we discussed Lynn going with him. But, in the end, we decided Lynn should complete her schooling in Mexico City."

"I wasn't aware there were medical schools, like Columbia, down there." Stan said.

"We have two, maybe three," the Captain said, "I'm sure, are as good as Columbia." Stan tried to catch Lynn's eyes, but she was looking out the window without expression. No one spoke for a time. Lynn placed both feet on the floor and looked at the ceiling. Sir Warren placed a hand over his eyebrows and studied the floor.

"As I mentioned," Mrs. Monroe said, "we have another engagement." She got to her feet. Everyone stood. "We wish both of you a safe trip."

"Lynn, may I talk to you a few minutes?" Stan asked. Everyone was shaking hands.

"Honey, we don't have time," Mrs. Monroe said. Captain Rodas took Lynn by the elbow.

"I'm sorry, Stan. We are rushed, but write me a letter when you get to New York. Good luck." Lynn, following her mother, left the room, with the Captain in the rear.

Warren slapped his hat on his leg and pulled it on; he put his hand on Stan's arm. "Let us get out of this place."

"You know, Warren, you're goin'ta have to change your livin' ways," Walker said. Stan and Warren were following him through the racks of drying beef. Jed grabbed a large piece and tore at it with his teeth.

"When will it be ready?" Stan asked. He chewed on one of the smaller dried pieces.

"All except the biggest pieces are ready. We'll be set by tomorrow night."

"What did you mean about changing my lifestyle?" Sir Warren asked.

"Stan and Cotton are good men," Jed said, "but they ain't no black Diamond. Who's goin' to fix those fancy vittles or shave and trim your hair?"

"We'll make it," Stan said, "but I was glad Warren talked Cotton into joining our group." Since their visit to the Monroe ranch, Stan's thoughts were jumbled. He'd thought of talking to the Father again, but what could he say? Would Iron and Lynn be able to pull it off?

It was the first of spring, a new beginning for he and Lynn, he hoped. They'd make their own rainbow.

The day before they left, Stan and Cotton repacked all their own and Warren's purchases and possessions. That way, they would have to unpack a minimum at each campsite. Warren knew he could not live in the same style he had when Diamond and Pepe were present. Stan bit his lip and said nothing.

The last supper was special, however, with plenty of steak and a half-keg of wine. There were several tins of rum cake. Stan joined in the singing; he drank two more cups of wine than normal.

"Whoa, whoa," Stan said. For an instant he was on Midnight. He opened his eyes. Someone was shaking him. Against a star-filled background he recognized Iron Paso. Stan sat up.

"Iron, I didn't expect you this soon. You make it?" He'd said goodbye to Iron at the Mission.

"I brought a couple folks into camp," Iron said, "I think you'd like to meet."

The fires were a dull glow. Stan struggled to his feet. He saw Walker near the fire pit used by Warren's group. His heart pounded. They'd made it.

"Where are they?" Stan asked. He and Iron hustled toward the fire. Back out of the firelight, Stan heard the rustle of animals being unloaded.

"You stay here," Iron said. Iron moved off toward the unloading. Walker added three logs to the fire.

"Have you seen them?" Stan asked.

"I've seen no one but Iron," Walker said, "He just showed up with a small group. He's damn frisky for 3:00 AM in the mornin', that's all I know." Stan started to walk out from the fire. He made out Iron and a small person wearing a large sombrero trotting toward him. His breath caught in his throat.

She started to run toward Stan, throwing off the sombrero. It was Lynn. Stan opened his arms and she flew into them. They held each other tight. She was crying; giant sobs shook her body.

"I didn't think we were going to make it," she said, still sobbing. "I'm sorry about at the ranch."

Stan relaxed his grip and held her back so he could see her. In the flickering light, her face was thin and tear-covered, but her eyes were shining bright. "There was no other way. Diamond and I started planning this a month ago. I'd have never made it without her and Iron."

Warren came to the fire, sleepy eyed, and hugged Lynn. Then Iron led Diamond to the fire and the huge woman put her arms around both Warren and Stan. Lynn became lost in the center of the dancing huddle of four.

Cotton came to the fire, and he, Walker, and Iron all smiled, watching the four jump with joy.

"You all better get to sleep," Walker said, "we start the march East in three hours. I don't want no trouble with the Mex."

"Father Carrillo said he'd convince Mother," Lynn said, "not to let Eduardo do anything crazy."

"Jed, I couldn't sleep," Warren said.

"Nor I," Stan said, still holding Lynn to his chest, "but, we'll be ready at dawn."

"I've got flapjack mix and a jug of syrup," Diamond said. "Master Stan, let Missy breathe now, and start the coffee. She's going to help me make us one fine marching-home breakfast. . .

come on, Missy."

"Fine," Walker said. "We eat and march."

"Gracious," Warren said, ". . . now I remember what I have been missing all this ugly winter. . . the true spirit of the trail." He and Walker watched Cotton and Iron build up the fire. Stan started the coffee.

"You know what, Warren?" Stan asked. He stood and with the other men watched the fire roar to life.

"What is it, my friend?"

"I see our rainbow."

"And by damn," Walker said, scratching Ric's head, "if I don't see a bottle of Scottish whiskey in it."